Stifling an impulse to put Caroline over his knee and shame her then and there before the astonished eyes of the prim virginal Miss Reeves, he turned on his heel, and without a shake of the hand or chaste kiss on his wife's brow, strode quickly past the footman to the front door and out down the steps to the drive.

Joanna touched Caroline's arm tentatively. 'It's all right, my dear. He's gone now. He can't hurt you in any way,' she said reasoningly. 'Not a nice man at all.'

Folly's End

MARY WILLIAMS

SPHERE BOOKS LIMITED

SPHERE BOOKS LTD

Penguin Books Ltd, 27 Wrights Lane, London W8 5TZ (Publishing and Editorial)
and Harmondsworth, Middlesex, England (Distribution and Warehouse)
Viking Penguin Inc., 40 West 23rd Street, New York, New York 10010, USA
Penguin Books Australia Ltd, Ringwood, Victoria, Australia
Penguin Books Canada Ltd, 2801 John Street, Markham, Ontario, Canada L3R 1B4
Penguin Books (NZ) Ltd, 182–190 Wairau Road, Auckland 10, New Zealand

First published in Great Britain by William Kimber & Co Ltd, 1985
Published by Sphere Books Ltd 1988

Made and printed in Great Britain by
Richard Clay Ltd, Bungay, Suffolk
Set in Baskerville

There's night and day, brother, both sweet things;
sun, moon, and stars, brother, all sweet things;
there's likewise a wind on the heath. Life is very
sweet, brother; who would wish to die?

Lavengro, George Borrow

1

Under a façade of charm and subtle flattery, he contemplated her shrewdly — assessingly perhaps was the better word. She was eager, avid for romance, young, and extremely good-looking in a pert way. Slim, delicate-featured, with an innocent manner of averting her eyes coyly which did not deceive him for one moment. A virgin? Undoubtedly that. But not half so naive as she pretended. And she liked him. The latter was an understatement. She was intrigued, and if he kept her dangling for a brief spell, he didn't doubt she'd capitulate when he offered his sprat to catch a mackerel. He needed a wife. She would do. Independent, yet secretly yearning — lusting perhaps — for connubial status. And she had money; no millionairess or heiress to a vast fortune, but rich enough through her mother, who had lately died, having sufficient in the bank to see him settled on his course.

Apart from that, he liked — even desired her. Otherwise he would never have considered the project. He found plain women boring and distasteful. Indeed she would undoubtedly prove titillating and rewarding. She might need a little education, if so, all the better. And he'd be good to her, in his fashion.

Yes. In his fashion. She couldn't expect more. She was astute enough to recognise that he must have known many women. He was thirty-four and since he was fifteen and a kitchen boy at the Regina, he'd studied, flattered, and learned to use them in his ascent gradually from menial work to houseboy and later assistant chef when his ambition had driven him to Paris. There he'd amassed such knowledge of the culinary and social arts that during the first ten years he'd had sufficient in his pocket to gain undermanagership of a smart select pension Le Chien D'or. From there his progress, although swift, had been steady; at this certain point of his career, his return to Britain held a new challenge on which his mind and determination were set.

The place? Cornwall, of course, which was becoming popular with visitors. The locality? Lionswykka, a headland stretching half a mile into the Atlantic with an island nearby which could be acquired at a reasonable sum from an impoverished old lord. Already the dream was clear. But the practical means needed imbursement, which this twenty-year-old girl could so easily provide. There was no doubt in his mind at all of the success of the prospect once it was established. The hotel itself would stand on the far point of the mainland — almost a peninsula — an attractive setting for those interested in sailing and wild life. A lucrative business could be set up running trips to the island which was well populated with seals, and birds of a wide variety. A caretaker would have to be established there, but no cheap shack or shop dealing in souvenirs. Anything to do with Lionswykka must have class, and sufficient imaginative character to tempt the rich as well as the middle-class public which in the eighteen-eighties was developing a taste for the dramatic and picturesque.

Caroline, on her part, would make an admirable chatelaine. Respectable, but sufficiently individual to cause an impression. Although not one of the New Women — so eager for equality with male contemporaries — she was well qualified in the arts, with a genuine gift as a water-colour artist. So painters, too, could be induced to spend periods at the establishment. Sunsets at Cormorant Island were magnificent. Turner himself, in his day, could not have wished for a grander vista. Oh, the possibilities were immense. The wildness of the surrounding country also appealed to him. Despite his acquired air of sophistry, Joel Blake's origins, a vagabond actress mother and errant father, the wild but illegitimate son of a noble family, still lingered in his blood, stirring him at odd moments to secret longings that temporarily had to be dispelled. Nothing must interfere with his ambition.

Nothing.

Caroline — his possession of her as a wife — would mean stability, giving fire to his pride. No prude, he decided, glancing at her over the glitter of wine glasses, but certainly sexually adaptable, able to be tamed, and to learn her place. She'd have to. Meanwhile, mustering all his charm, he said in his most casual yet subtly intimate way, 'Thought of getting married yet, Caroline?'

They were dining at a Plymouth restaurant to which he'd been invited by a business acquaintance, with a small number of select friends. Her cousin, Lawrence, had brought her, and had been thoughtful to hand her over while he sought other more titillating company.

She smiled, shrugged, then looked away with an attempt to hide her deepening colour.

'Occasionally. Most girls do, I suppose, in a vague kind of way. But, well, I've other interests.'

'Your painting?'

She looked surprised.

'I suppose Lawrence told you. He *would*. My family think it rather a joke.'

'How obtuse and unintelligent.'

'No.' He was surprised by the quick note of annoyance in her voice. 'Girls in my position are supposed to find an eligible suitor and marry him. *Then* they can have their hobbies.'

A hint of admiration lit his eyes. They were strange eyes — shrewd, greyish, flecked with darting sparks of gold, quite unlike her own which were vivid blue fringed by thick black lashes in contrast to her wealth of silky fair tresses. In other ways they were dissimilar too — he was tall, broad-shouldered, with a wide brow, from which the dark red hair sprang, thick and rebellious as a lion's mane.

So she could be pert as well as desirable, he thought appreciatively. A trifle old-fashioned in attire perhaps, but that could be remedied. Her coiffure for instance was too prim, parted in the middle allowing only a single curl to wander free above her finely arched brows. The subdued grey gown did nothing for her. The folds of silk drawn to the back in a bustle effect were too meagre. Her neckline was neither low nor high; her jewellery modest in the extreme. But such details would be rectified later when his course was firmly set. He would see then that she'd conform to fashion by displaying one of the popular enamel bracelets over long gloves, in the manner of Marie Louise, ex-Empress of France, and the Duchess of Parma. Her dresses would be violet or deep cornflower blue to enhance her fair colouring. Already he saw her seated at his table, chic and alluring as French women, and any London beauty. The picture in his mind was tantalising, taking priority for the moment over all others — the secret sly yearnings for adventure which told him that along with social ambition could be welded the darker, lucrative business of contraband.

Smuggling could still flourish under the guise of gentility. And he meant, outwardly, to be the personification of the latter — a gentleman.

'So you consider your undoubted gift with the brush a hobby?' he heard himself saying automatically.

'No. I was referring to my family.'

'Of course.'

'Not that I'm clever. I just like to be creative in some way.'

'So as you have no children and no husband, you take to art. Very worthy. I admire you. But your life might be more rewarding with all three. That's true, isn't it?'

She paused before asking, 'Why are you probing so closely into my life, Mr Blake?'

Without hesitation he answered bluntly, surprising himself by his own swift decision, 'Because I want to marry you, Miss Carnforth.'

The colour ebbed from her face quickly, astonishment widened her eyes, followed by a pucker between her brows.

'You're joking. You must be.'

He shook his head. 'I never joke over serious matters.'

'But—' she wavered before continuing, 'I hardly know you. It's so—'

'Oh to the devil with polite speech,' he interrupted sharply.

'For God's sake don't say, "It's so sudden". Trite phrases bore me. I'm asking you to be my wife.'

Her perfectly sculptured lips tightened.

'Why?'

'Because I think we'd get along. We're both free, with considerable potential for making a spectacular couple—'

'Spectacular?'

He smiled. His smile was a flash of white in his strongly carved face. Warm and flooded with charm. Then he leaned forward, one elbow on the table, staring into her face with such impelling determination she was transfixed, while her heart quickened, bumping against her ribs.

'Together we'd make an empire,' he said, 'in a small way of course. You suit me. I want you, Miss Carnforth.'

Noting he did not say 'love', she replied more coolly, 'Marriage should mean more than that.'

'I'm no sentimentalist, which you must be astute enough to realise,' he continued. 'I think you are. I don't go in for passionate speeches or pleading on my knees. If I did you'd turn me down. You see, I know women.'

'Do you? I wonder. It's all so unexpected and confusing. Ridiculous really—'

'Then think about it.' He took a gold watch from a fob at his waistband, glanced at it cursorily, and said, 'In an hour's time meet me on the terrace. By then you should have had sufficient fill of your prancing and dancing dandies to make a decision. Boredom, or excitement with me.'

He took her hand, raised it to his lips, got up and waited for her to rise, before putting the chair back into its place.

Then he escorted her to the door of the hall.

'I see your cousin Lawrence is already looking for you,' he remarked cryptically. 'No wonder, considering his dumpling of a partner.'

'She happens to be Lady Elizabeth Cheyne.' Her tones were stiff, formal.

'Then we'll have to see you a duchess one day, won't we?'

He was joking, but as he walked away she knew instinctively

that there was no situation in the world he couldn't handle, given the chance. And while recognising that she *did* attract him, the reasoning part of her mind told her that there was something else he also wanted of her. Money?

Well — most men expected a dowry to go along with a wife. There was nothing odd about that.

The only odd thing was that she should be considering the proposition at all.

*

An hour later Caroline Carnforth informed Joel Blake she would be his wife.

2

The marriage took place on a bright day in April 1880 at a village church on the outskirts of Plymouth. It was a quiet affair which pleased both Joel and William Carnforth, Caroline's father, who, after a show of opposition, had eventually agreed to the union with grudging condescension that was not entirely genuine. Most of his paternal interests were centred elsewhere, in the person of his elder daughter, Ariadne, Lady Perryn, who two years previously had given birth to a lusty boy, Jasper, his heir. William had wanted a son of his own; his second marriage to Caroline's mother had been prompted almost solely by this one compelling wish. But she had failed, and he had found it difficult to give much attention to this second daughter, who in every way appeared slightly inferior to the extremely beautiful, accomplished, and radiant young hostess presiding at the Perryn household in Devon and London. Ariadne's colourful reputation amused and titillated him. The hints of gossip-mongers in society circles and newspaper columns gave him, her father, a certain notoriety that used properly could be helpful in more than one way.

His estate, including one failing copper-mine, was gradually declining, due to lack of funds. But mention of the Perryn name could work wonders. Above all, Ariadne had produced a grandson to inherit who would one day become Sir Jasper.

Caroline was hardly likely to make such a brilliant match. Therefore, he'd argued with himself, after due consideration of all the circumstances, it was better surely to have her married off to a man willing and able to support her, without delving too deeply into his background. He didn't wish for a spinster daughter to be left on his hands. He had a perfectly satisfactory mistress installed in his home as 'social hostess', who was always willing to share his bedroom when he wanted, without imbuing him with any boring and restricting sense of responsibility.

That second marriage of his had been a tedious business. He was determined there should be no third wife. Agnes Poldew, the widow concerned in his domestic menage, agreed with him, although she was careful to exude an air of concern on Caroline's behalf.

'Of course,' she said, carefully and reflectively, bringing her brows together over her shrewd bird-like eyes, 'your dear daughter's happiness should be of primary importance. This man has a doubtful background and in my opinion may not be quite — suitable or good enough for her. On the other hand, I do believe she's in love with him, and he appears to be fond of her. Has anyone the moral right to interfere?'

Her sigh, the troubled manner of her query, the anxiety of her pink plump cheeks, and shake of the head, gave him the opportunity he needed, removing any shadow of doubt from his mind.

She was quite right, he thought, with a rush of relief.

Caroline needed a husband. Well, he'd be generous and give the couple his blessing in a guarded grudging way, ensuring at the same time his own future with the placid, well-corseted but somewhat bovine-looking creature confronting him.

He was not the slightest bit in love with her of course, but she knew her place, she was a good manager in the daytime, and a warm bedfellow at night. This was all he needed for the time being. When he required a change he could always take off to the city and a taste of club life. There would be no awkwardness from Agnes Poldew. She was well off in his house and knew it. In a few years as her amiable social graces and pretensions to comfortable good looks were fading, he would either relegate her to the position of an ordinary housekeeper, or, if funds allowed it, pension her off. There would always be some ambitious middle-aged or elder member of the farming community on the lookout for a wife with a dowry — however small — to nurture his later years.

So, with the problem of Caroline's marriage settled, the modest arrangements were completed, and on the appointed day, when his daughter made her way up the aisle of the church on his arm, everyone present admitted that she made a charming bride. She wore her late mother's white wedding gown, which had been cunningly modernised by Mrs Poldew, and had a wreath of orange blossom on her carefully dressed hair.

As for the bridegroom — the general opinion of villagers was that he appeared quite spectacular. He wore a dark grey velvet jacket, grey trousers, lemon waistcoat over a cream silk spotted shirt with a wide gold satin tie at his neck. His thick red-brown hair flowed luxuriously back behind his ears.

'Magnificent!' one guest whispered to another.

'A fine figure of a man,' came the reply. 'I'd have thought he'd have chosen someone more — vivid — than Caroline Carnforth.'

'These prim looking young women can be more alluring deep down than you'd imagine. And I've heard she has quite a temper when it's roused.'

A sigh. 'Ah well — one can never tell.'

One could not indeed.

Following the ceremony, when after a long coach drive the couple reached the vicinity of Lionswykka stretching its rugged arm into the sea, Caroline's first show of temper revealed itself.

Not because of the wild countryside and coast. She was Cornish bred, with something in her blood responsive to the Atlantic winds blowing inland over the grey rocks and moors – to the massed clouds rolling as gaunt galleons against the horizon – the high screaming of gulls as they rose and dipped again where heather and gorse crouched among boulders and dark pools of bog. She'd expected all that. But not the house. Had she realised Joel could have chosen such a desolate-looking place for their first home together she'd have refused, and insisted on somewhere brighter and better. She knew from a quick first glance at the granite square-faced building huddled in a tangle of bent bushes, thorn, elder and sloe, that she'd been stupid in not allowing him to show it to her first. But their wooing had been so quick, and she so bemused and ardent, so carried away by his impetuosity, she'd believed him when he'd said, 'Leave everything to me. The house is old; lots of character though, and when more improvements are made you'll like it. I want to surprise you. Women can be so damned tedious when they set their minds on changing this and that. And it's us who count, not bits of furniture.'

Well, she was certainly surprised. Obviously the building at some time or other had been converted from an old mine or stamp house. Its granite exterior had too few windows, and what light there was, was shrouded by twisted branches and bramble. There was no other building in view except a small farm some distance away in a fold of the moors. The peninsula itself stretched for a mile, sloping downwards from a thread of lane winding above the coast between land and sea.

Desolate. Frightening somehow.

A patch of ground had been cleared in a path to the front door of the house. As the driver of the vehicle accompanied Joel, carrying a bag in each hand, she stood quite still, watching. Her new husband turned his head sharply.

'Come along,' he said. 'What's the matter?'

'The *matter*? If you think I'm going to live *here*—' She broke off with her small face set challengingly. He strode back the few yards and took her arm.

'There's no thinking, darling,' he said, in a quiet voice but with his eyes glinting dangerously. 'This is Treescarne, our home.'

Only when the man had gone and the echo of horses' hooves and carriage wheels had died did she give full vent to her feelings.

She stood in the hall staring round at the gloomy brown wallpaper, the old-fashioned umbrella stand and clothes pegs above – the tiled floor which had cracks in it where damp had seeped through. Several doors on either side opened into a parlour, study, and presumably extra sitting or drawing room, eventually leading down to a shadowed area of kitchens. The portrait of a portly gentleman in a heavy oak frame with a sea-faring air about him hung halfway up the stairs on the darkened yellow papered walls. The carpeting was faded red, worn almost threadbare in parts. It was so depressing she shuddered.

Then when Joel said in quieter tones, 'Follow me, Caroline, and don't look so desperate. The bedroom's all right – we'll be able to do a bit of brightening up later on—' Again that touch on her arm.

She shook herself free.

'You said that had been done,' she remarked tartly. '*Why?* It's – it's terrible. Gloomy. How *could* you?' Her heart was pounding as she continued after a brief pause, 'What *was* this place? Whoever lived here before? Something to do with a mine, was it? Or – or what?'

'Once,' he admitted. 'Then a farmer converted it. He died last year. The house was left as it was for a caretaker to look after. She was a kind of dependent. You'll be able to rely on Mrs Magor—'

'A *caretaker?*'

Joel's chin took a stubborn thrust. 'She's provided for – up to a point. But I've arranged with her to be employed as a kind of cook/housekeeper—'

'Cook *housekeeper?* But shouldn't I have been consulted?'

'I told you there'd be servants.'

'A strange rough woman, I suppose, with – with—'

'The help of a youth. Peter Dory, her nephew.'

Caroline's form stiffened.

'I won't live here, Joel. I *can't*. Really. Please understand—'

'You'll live here and like it,' he told her. 'Now, up with you. Or do you want me to carry you?'

His voice was harsher than he'd intended, but he hadn't expected such opposition.

She obeyed mutely. And when they reached the bedroom her spirits lifted slightly. The walls had been papered in white patterned in gold stripes between tiny pink rosebuds. The bed, a canopied four poster, had a flounced pink eiderdown, the furniture though of solid mahogany, was not too heavy, the carpet echoed the general floral effect and was thick to tread on, although the pile was slightly worn by the dressing table.

'This came from a good place,' Joel said, glancing down at the luxurious pile. 'Got it for a song at a sale. You wouldn't have liked what was here. Tawdry. There's nothing tawdry about this room.'

Caroline glanced at him tentatively.

'Do you go to many sales, Joel?'

'When I need something good,' he told her frankly. 'I've a future to make, Caroline — for both of us. A little thought and economy's necessary at first to get a good beginning. Later on we'll be able to be extravagant.' He paused, then added, 'If it means so much to you.'

'Yes, I suppose so.'

She spoke without enthusiasm. Sensing her reluctant mood, he took her hand and pulled her to the window.

'Look at that — fine view, eh? Makes your blood stir.'

Before her eyes the stretch of moor rose dark against the fading light, streaked with splashes of gold where gorse flamed momentarily in the last rays of dying sunlight. A broken circle of standing stones was outlined sentinel-like, against the highest rim of hills. She had the impression of ancient bygone ghosts risen to challenge human intrusion. To the far east the rugged arm of the peninsula, Lionswykka, thrust far out into the Atlantic. Involuntarily she shivered.

Joel glanced at her shrewdly.

'What's the matter?'

'It will be so cut off here,' she said.

'Cut off? Nonsense.'

'But you said the house was near. Quite near the headland where the hotel's going to be.'

He laughed.

'Near enough. You won't want to be bothered with guests and visitors all the time—'

'How do you know?'

'Well—' he drew her more closely to him and she could feel her heart quicken '—sometimes we'll want to be private – just Mr and Mrs Joel Blake. We'll have our own rooms at the hall of course – we can always spend what time we like there.'

'The hall?'

'That's what it will be called. "Lionswykka Hall", or maybe just "Lionswykka". Anyway, we can decide on that later.'

'If you say so.' She was suddenly tired, and faintly apprehensive of his exuberance. After all – it was through *her* money he'd been able to even plan the enterprise. She pulled herself from him firmly, turned, walked to the bed and sat down, removing her fancy bonnet so a few tendrils of silky hair broke free, brushing a cheek. In two nimble strides he was beside her, loosening the cape at her neck, one hand fondling a breast possessively. She attempted to free herself, but after a soft laugh, his lips were warm against her throat, travelling to a rounded shoulder. Then downwards as he expertly unfastened the buttons of her bodice. Against her will she found herself responding to the male need and heat of him. There was no sound any more but the solitary squawking of a gull from outside and the impassioned rhythmic echo of their own breathing. No word of love, no real tenderness, only at the last, a moan of relief and fulfilment. Then he released her, and she fell back.

Her body was at peace, but her mind felt empty, drained. Nothing had been as she'd expected. In some curious way she was disappointed, while accepting that the next time she would respond in just the same fashion.

She'd hoped that Joel would be prepared to spend the following day with her. After all they were having no conventional honeymoon, but the first weeks of marriage should surely be romantic, with a new husband's interest concentrated in ensuring his wife was happy. She was not only disappointed, but deeply hurt when he left shortly after breakfast, saying he must take a look at the site where the future hotel was to be.

'I may be away for the day,' he said, 'but the housekeeper will see you're all right, and I expect that like most women you'll be all agog to get domestic arrangements properly settled.'

'What domestic arrangements, Joel? I thought you said Mrs Magor was completely in charge? You implied it.' There was a touch of rebellion in her manner. She did not care for the old woman who at their first meeting had shown veiled hostility to the intrusion of a young bride.

His eyes narrowed slightly. 'Just my way. You're my wife. In the end you'll take charge — naturally. But be careful not to upset the old bird.'

'I see.' She set her jaw and turned away. He laughed, pulled her to him, and kissed her on the lips, saying, 'Don't be a stupid, darling. What I do is for *us* — remember? Our future, and any kids we have. Oh — and now I think of it — I've an appointment at the bank tomorrow in Truro. There'll be things for us both to sign. So that'll be an outing for you. Yes?'

'If you've already arranged it,' she replied stiffly.

'*Can't* you show a bit of enthusiasm, Caroline?'

His voice held such disappointment, even pleading, she softened with a rush of contrition; telling herself that in spite of arrogance and 'lord-of-all-I-survey' attitude, he really did depend on her in a certain way.

'Of course,' she agreed, 'that will be lovely.'

'There's a little restaurant there where we can eat,' he told her. 'We'll maybe crack a bottle of champagne to celebrate,' adding warily, 'just for once.'

Champagne, she thought ironically, was that to mean his ultimate and most significant tribute to her? For a second, behind his manly façade, she sensed the boy, youth, and relentless young man who'd striven so relentlessly to achieve ambition to reach the point where they now both stood. Naturally, of course, she could have no idea of the hot steamy kitchens he'd first worked in, the sharp voices and abuse, the confined quarters where he'd slept, the aching limbs and controlled determination stiffening him where he'd learned to hold his tongue and not answer back. At times, as he longed for the fresh air, it had been hell, until gradually he'd found escape in a woman's arms. She'd been a cook, almost twice his age, stout, with broad pink cheeks, a large bosom, hearty laugh, and black greasy hair. She'd taught him many sides of sex: how to satisfy a woman's needs without personal involvement; how to recognise the different cravings of different types.

'It's the rich ones you have to be canny of—' she'd told him. 'Watch their eyes when they think you're not, and the way they move too. There's a swagger of the hips and behind that'll tell you whether they're the faithful kind or out for a bit of secret lust. Most of them are, those with husbands who're so concerned with the money bags they forget what women want. Oh, they're all the same at heart. And you've got what it takes, boy. Use it. I won't be jealous.'

She'd roared with laughter, thrust her big breasts at him, breasts as rich and ripe as melons, and in a few moments they were rolling on the floor, twisting and turning, until she pushed him from her saying, 'Now get up with you. On with your work. An' see you put in a bit of extra.'

She was the first. He'd never forgotten her. The rest had been quite different. There'd been a French girl Louise, black haired, saucy, lissom as a cat, who'd scratched and bitten him when he'd broken with her. He'd missed her for a time. But the widow of a wealthy businessman had come for a stay to the pension, and cunningly he'd enveigled himself into her favour. She was fifteen years his senior, slightly haggard, but beautiful in her faded way, lean and yellow-haired, displaying her furs and jewellery with the arrogant savoir-faire that he sensed immediately was little more than a trap to ensnare some desirable male for her needs.

He proved himself to be exactly that. But beneath the façade she was mean. The moment had arrived when tired of being her slave, and with something in his pocket, he ruthlessly put himself from her life, and turned his attention to matters and women more rewarding. The process had become first a game, then more habitual.

He wasn't proud of his achievements. He saw them for what they were — cheap, but of temporary necessity.

Now all was different.

In his conquest of Caroline he came nearer to loving than he'd ever thought possible. Still, she was a woman like the rest. In the end she'd recognise her place and accept the fact that however satisfactory their life in the bedroom might prove to be — and damn it, he'd take her, within reason, whenever he wanted — business remained his priority. Business — and adventure. Both fired his spirits. He'd made good contacts in Brittany that might be useful — very useful.

The prospect so excited him, that he forgot briefly his financial obligations to Caroline when they set off for Truro the following day.

'All you'll have to do is just sign your name,' he said complacently, 'of course, everything could go ahead without, but being as we are makes it easier.'

'What do you mean?'

'My dear love, you're my wife now. I don't have to ask your permission about certain matters, financially speaking.'

'I know that.'

The short sentence silenced him for a moment, then he said, 'Oh. So you do, do you?'

'Of course. What I have is now yours, Joel, and I don't mind at all. In fact I'm glad, so long as you don't forget it — I mean don't try and push me out of things.'

'Quite a business woman, in fact.'

'Naturally. Just commonsensical.'

'What words you use.' His hand enclosed hers warmly. She could feel his charm spreading around and through her. He sat back in the carriage abruptly.

'As I said before,' he remarked, 'we'll make quite a remarkable couple.'

'Perhaps.'

He glanced at her curiously, feeling an odd sense of admiration stir him.

Indeed, he thought, with a touch of irony, dealing with a woman of Caroline's calibre might be very different from what he'd previously imagined.

Different and also titillating.

He'd see, however, that her astuteness was put to good account on his behalf, and in the end she'd be thankful to be rid of tiresome business probing. When their first child came along she'd have other things to think about, and enjoy it.

In this respect all women were alike.

It never occurred to him that he could be wrong.

3

By early spring of 1881 the building of Lionswykka Hotel was progressing at a speed gratifying to Joel. From the first he had kept a keen and wary eye on the workers, but he was as well generous when necessary, and gradually the men — many of whom had been unemployed through the failure of a nearby coppermine — grudgingly began to trust him, and even foster a secret admiration for the 'furriner' who had brought regular payment providing food for hungry bellies with a little over to spend at the Silver Goat on a Saturday night.

The kiddleywink, which was popular with natives, stood in a fold of the moors, a mile to the west of Lionswykka. Its reputation was dubious, its clientele colourful. Many devious and unsavoury deeds had been hatched there. It was a meeting place for fishermen, seamen, pedlars and adventurers of a higher order who made it their business to pursue any likely plot calculated to further their own ends. Certain members of the Preventive occasionally called at the premises, presumably on duty, but quite prepared to turn a blind eye to any suspicious act should it prove advantageous and worth the risk.

Whiskey from Ireland, lace and brandy from France had been secreted cunningly underground near the building. From a nearby cove a tunnel used half a century earlier from a derelict mine now led inland beneath the moor to various dumping places – one, the cellars of the rectory at the village of Zaren. The vicar, a jovial individual with a benign air, and assiduous attention to his duties as father of his flock, was not above accepting little gifts to warm the cockles of his heart, providing he could repay on his own terms. This meant a hidey-hole on his own land which opened through a pigsty to a position on the moors, close to the high lane, from where any valuable goods could be transported to Redruth without official questioning. As well as parson, the reverend gentleman was, after all, a property owner in a small way, renting out two small farms in the vicinity. Favours between owner and workers provided a basis for a comfortable existence. Most of the natives thereabouts knew what was going on, but all kept their mouths shut. So the trade continued.

Joel, learning of certain exploits during the few occasions he took his pint with the dubious crowd, began to envisage once again working a similar line on a larger and far more lucrative basis.

Once he had his own small fleet of pleasure boats, big business could accrue. Diversion of contraband to his own particular coastline was possible provided it was contrived carefully under the façade of hotel business. His quick mind was gratified at the thought of outwitting the law.

Looking at things from every angle, life, at that point, became for him a stimulating affair, his marriage both advantageous and sensually rewarding. It never occurred to him that Caroline, in spite of their passionate interludes, was left frequently lonely, because once physically satisfied he could so swiftly turn his mind to more practical matters. He was faithful to her, and gave her no cause to doubt it, but she was chilled by a certain look in his eyes — wary yet excited, and remote from her, proving he had some secret wild dream in which she could have no share.

One day in early March when she was wandering about the moors above the house she met a man cutting along a narrow track from the direction of the kiddleywink. He was short, sturdy, ginger-haired, with a jagged scar cutting from temple to jaw by one cheek. He had a seafaring look about him; his eyes, small and steely grey, had a cunning avaricious gleam.

He smiled, touched a straggling forelock, and said in thin high tones, 'That theer your home missus?' jerking a thumb ahead.

Involuntarily shivering, Caroline drew her cape more tightly over her bodice, and answered curtly, 'Yes. I'm Caroline Blake. Mrs Joel Blake. Have you business with my husband? Or a message for one of the servants?'

He shook his head, still staring at her assessingly, seeming to peer through the blue wool of her gown savouring every line of her rounded lissom figure. The thin wind blew against her, outlining the curved upturned young breasts, full column of her throat above its band of ribbon, wafting strands of silken hair against her bonnet brim. 'Luscious enough young wench,' the man thought avariciously, a real peach, ripe for the picking, but he wouldn't touch her, not even with a barge-pole when the business he had in hand with her rich husband was likely to prove so rewarding for his pocket.

'No servant, ma'am,' he said obsequiously, 'that's not my line. Jus' tell your fine man Marty called, an' that the work's on. That's all. It'll save me the journey.'

'Marty?'

'Marty Werne. An' you c'n give en this.' He handed her a scrap of thick paper with a crudely drawn sign on it that meant nothing to her. She took it, staring. 'All right. I'll see he has it.'

'An' no servant, mind.' Again the unpleasant grin. He touched his head, winked and before turning remarked,

'Between him and me it is, the master an' Marty. An' you ma'am, o' course, being his good wumman.'

Before she could reply he was speeding back the way he'd come, head thrust forward from his shoulders, like some cunning animal evading pursuit. She watched his nimble figure cutting round boulders, through clumps of flaming gorse and bent blown heather, until shadows cast by dying sunlight eventually claimed and obscured him. A thin soughing of the wind shivered through the bushes. Overhead a seagull screamed; in the distance the Atlantic glittered briefly against the bleak thrust of granite cliffs.

With a sense of foreboding, Caroline once more adjusted her cape against the chilling air and made her way back to the house.

Whatever business Marty Werne might have with Joel, she thought distastefully, it could not be good. Events later proved that she was right.

4

The kiddleywink was crowded late that evening, when a huge bearded man walked up to the shifty-eyed landlord who was serving ale to a couple of swarthy-faced seamen. They were accompanied by a yellow-haired woman exposing a plump breast invitingly. She was Sal, a well-known prostitute, who was generous with her body for a minimum of payment from sex-hungry sailors back from months at sea.

The light at the inn was meagre, consisting of two swinging oil lamps, and the dim glow of a fire.

In one corner of the small interior a pedlar was furtively delivering parcels from his pack to customers who secreted them with greedy hands. What the packets contained was dubious.

Those present were careful not to enquire in case a member of the Preventive might appear unexpectedly. Most of those present, however, were well aware of concealed drugs and maybe a smuggled diamond or two. Occasionally a fight ensued. But all that night there was comparative quiet, broken only by intermittent bursts of raucous laughter and whispered conversation dealing with hints and information concerning underhand business.

Whenever a strange or suspecting face appeared the sly atmosphere deepened into complete silence. Not all were in the know, but everyone kept sealed lips. The vagabond code between them assured, for the most part, strict loyalty. So there was a cessation of movement or talk of any kind when Joel, wearing high boots and a greatcoat, strode across the floor to the bar. The false wig and black beard were convincing enough in the cloyed atmosphere of smoke and thickened air to arouse instant suspicion. Any less befuddled by strong wines and spirits than the rest, *might* have guessed his identity. Only two *knew*; the bar-tender, and Marty who ambled up casually asking for another tot of whisky while the stranger who called himself Black Dirke demanded a word in private. The three of them went through to a stuffy parlour at the back.

'Won't be nuthen on tomorrer, mister,' Marty said on the first opportunity. 'You tell those Frenchie friends to bide a bit o' time. Cap'n Reeves 'bout — an' you knows what that means.'

'Reeves is a fool,' Joel said abruptly. 'I'll see he's taken care of — have him at the house at the time you're seeing things through. My wife will entertain him.'

Marty shook his head slowly.

'No, surr. Ted'n safe. Reeves is sharp beneath his fancy ways.' There was a pause before he added, 'A mos' *knowable* man. Duty — he lives by that. We've had trouble with him before. You watch out in case he doan' have a gun at y'r back — or mebbe haul 'ee up afore the Bench. Doan' risk it, surr. There's none of us'll back 'ee up this time. Next week. Well — mebbe. If Reeves is away well an' good. If not—' He shrugged. 'The time'll come. You mark my words—'

'I can't go on waiting for ever. That blocked passage from the cove leads straight to a spot near the old mine. Two-thirds of the way up it cuts in two directions, one to that greedy vicar's hide-away, the other to the cellars of Treescarne — that's my own house. I've cleared part of the rubble away already — and got through. It'll be possible in the future even to outwit the Rever-end Gentleman a little on occasions—' Joel's eyes gleamed with mischief. 'Not *entirely*, of course, I'm a fair man. But a little of the cream for you and me, eh? On top of our other gains which should be considerable.'

'Mebbe. But the timing's important. That's why the Frenchies must be warned—'

'Don't you mean *diverted* — to the other side of the creek? That can be arranged, with a perfectly legitimate cargo.'

Marty shook his head. '*No*. Keep 'em off. *Altogether*. I've been in contraband long enough to know what's safe and what's not. Have Cap'n Reeves to y'r house by all means, Mr Blake, but—'

'I'm Black Dirke now — you just remember that,' Joel inter-rupted fiercely. 'Keep your mouth shut or there'll be trouble for you.'

'That's right,' the landlord endorsed. 'On *my* premises any-way.'

'On *any* premises.'

Following a few more cursory and disagreeable comments, Joel eventually agreed for his first practical adventure in smug-gling to be postponed.

Caroline, who had been sleeping fitfully for the last few hours, woke abruptly when he entered the bedroom. She brushed the hair from her eyes, eased herself up, and said, with a slight frown puckering her forehead, 'How late you are. What happened? Where have you been, Joel?'

He gave her a brief glance, smiled, and kissed her more from habit than desire.

'Sorry. Business matters. Nothing to do with you, love.'

She sighed.

'No, of course not. They never are.'

The petulance in her voice irritated him.

'Go to sleep, and don't nag.'

'Nag?'

'Well, aren't you? A man's work's his own. I'm damn tired.'

She felt suddenly irrationally depressed. What he said was absolutely true, up to a point. But the two worlds could surely have some slight access to each other. She and Joel had been married only a short time, yet he was already holding half of himself away from her, and had become even ambiguous over the hotel project — the project she'd made a practical possibility. The fact appeared to have been conveniently forgotten. It was no longer what *we* can do, but what he would achieve.

She bit her lip, doing her best to keep silent. But when at last he lay beside her, frustration overcame wisdom.

'Joel,' she said sharply, 'we must talk.'

He glanced at her sharply. 'What about? And why now? In another few hours I've to be at the site.'

'Oh bother the site.'

'What do you mean, for God's sake?'

'Haven't you any feelings? Ever since we made that visit to the bank you've changed. It's as though I don't matter any more—' she broke off, edged a little closer to him, and said pleadingly, 'Don't you see, I *love* you, Joel, yet — yet — we can't *share* anything—'

He sighed.

'I haven't an earthly notion what you're talking about. We sleep and eat together, don't we? Anything you need for the home — in reason — you've only to ask for it and you get it. What more could a woman want?'

'I'm not just a woman. I'm your *wife*. You've had everything I have to give, from me. It hasn't mattered. I *wanted* it that way. But—'

'You're referring to the money, I suppose. Is that it?'

'Not only. But it's counted, hasn't it?'

'You're damn right it has, darling. Without it I'd have been in no position to lead Miss Caroline Carnforth to the altar. And that would've disappointed you, wouldn't it?'

'How *can* you speak so — so brutally? It's beastly of you, Joel. I *thought* you loved me.'

'So I do. But don't go thinking you bought me, Caroline.' His eyes glinted dangerously. 'And don't ever threaten me, my love. No more of your barbed insults, understand? There are some things I take from no woman alive, even you.'

'I didn't mean to insult you. I—'

'Shut up.'

She sprang up and was out of bed before he could stop her.

'I won't shut up, and I won't just be your — your little yes woman.' She was breathing quickly, the glow of a lamp caught the lines of cheeks and breasts lighting them to rosy gold. As she reached for her wrap hanging over a chair, anger, stirring with desire, filled him. He sprang after her, and caught her wrist. The sharp glance made her wince.

'What do you think you're doing?'

She faced him defiantly.

'I'm going to sleep in the spare room. Let me go—'

'I certainly won't. And you'll do nothing of the sort.' He pulled her to him and gave her a light playful slap, saying, 'Now do as you're told, and no more nonsense. If you act like a child you'll be treated as one in future. Get that into your head once and for all, Madam Caroline Carnforth Blake.'

Briefly hating him, with her mouth set into a hard line, she obeyed. Once in bed again, when tempers had eased, she waited for him to make some gesture of apology or affection.

None came.

Seconds later he was breathing heavily and was asleep.

Caroline had no such respite. She lay awake until morning, and when he, too, opened his eyes, it was as though nothing had happened between them. He was in a cheerful mood, and after getting up smiled winningly before kissing her.

'I shall have to hurry,' he said, 'but there's no need for you to. Have a lie in.'

How matter-of-fact, how chilling those few words sounded. She turned her head away. 'Perhaps I will.'

'I'll tell Mrs What's-her-name to send up breakfast.'

'No. It doesn't matter. I've changed my mind. In half an hour I'll be down.'

'Just as you like.' He paused, and then, briefly noting her beauty, and recognising his rather sharp mood during the night, said half-apologetically, 'I love you, Caro.'

'Thank you.'

He laughed. 'See you remember it, darling. One day I'll prove how much.'

One day, she thought, yes, perhaps, when he'd made some fabulous fortune or name to startle the world. But 'one day' wasn't what mattered. It was the present that counted, and the present seemed just then to grow more empty with every hour that passed.

*

During the next few days, when Joel thought matters over, in a calmer mood, he realised that Marty's intervention concerning the smuggling project was probably propitious and well-timed. He had more than sufficient work on his hands at the moment involving hotel business, which meant any deviation of interest could be disrupting. In the meantime, when the time was ripe for more adventurous pursuit, friendship between them would prove advantageous.

With this in mind Joel informed Caroline one afternoon that he had invited a Captain Reeves to dinner sometime in the near future, and that he hoped she would arrange a good menu with Mrs Magor, and be as charming as possible to their guest.

Caroline looked puzzled for a moment.

'You've mentioned his name before,' she said. 'A revenue officer, isn't he?'

'That's right.'

'I didn't know you were friendly.'

Joel gave her his infectious smile.

'We're not exactly that. Not yet. Just acquaintances you could say. But he's likeable enough in his fashion and accepted socially, and could be useful in many ways when the hotel's on its feet. I have to be in with the right people, Caroline, and I'm sure you do. You've obviously been bored lately. Well, here's a chance to use your very considerable charms for our mutual benefit. Do you understand?'

'Not entirely,' she answered truthfully. 'But if this Captain Reeves is so important to you I'll welcome him and do my best — naturally. What day were you thinking of?'

'Next week perhaps,' he answered, 'if that's convenient to you. Tuesday perhaps?'

She shrugged.

'Very well. That gives me nearly a week to think out arrangements.'

'I'll get in touch with him,' Joel told her, 'if not Tuesday maybe Wednesday or Thursday. I'll let you know in good time.'

He glanced at her appreciatively, noting briefly how well the violet coloured gown she wore suited her, outlining exquisitely the tiny waist and gently swelling lines of hips and bust, how proudly set on its slim neck was her small head under the piled up silky fine hair. A single flower, the same shade as her gown had been placed there, and at her neck was a cameo brooch. From the waist draperies were taken back, accentuated by a bustle.

As it was daytime there was no train, but Joel had noticed a gown in her wardrobe that had one. He'd criticised her mildly at the time she'd bought it, thinking it ridiculously extravagant. But he'd no doubt now that she'd use it to good effect for the forthcoming occasion. So he said flatteringly, 'That rose-coloured thing you got — remember? I thought it a bit expensive.' His eyes glowed briefly between slightly narrowed lids. She certainly had style. A lovely creature, and all his. If he'd had time that moment he'd have got her to the bedroom immediately. But he hadn't. 'Well — maybe I was wrong,' he conceded. 'You dress yourself up a bit and wear it on the night, my love. He'll be bowled over.'

Dress up? Bowled over? — what a cheap rather common expression, she thought, with a spasm of distaste. Why couldn't he be a little more subtle? Flatter her more romantically — make her feel she was appreciated not only as a possession to be shown off in company and to other men, but in private as the woman he loved? Love! did Joel know the true meaning of the word? She doubted it, and the knowledge pained her. But then she told herself wisely, men were so different from women in their approach to life; devious, with the art of going to all means within their power to get what they wanted, and then, when they had it, accepting it casually as their right.

Even her father was mildly selfish in this respect. He'd wished vaguely for her happiness and hoped she'd make a good marriage, but when the right husband hadn't appeared had been secretly and placidly gratified by her betrothal to Joel who at least promised an affluent future for his younger daughter. And she had wanted to be married. Being an old maid would have been humiliating in the extreme. So it was obviously better to ignore Joel's shortcomings rather than brood on them and try to change him. In any case did she really want him any different?

The self-question was disconcerting, because she could visualise him being other than what he was — domineering, vibrantly alive, and egocentric, yet with the capacity to so weaken all her resistance when he chose, that she responded with the foolish abandon of a woman desperately in love.

Yes.

That was the answer. For good or ill, she loved him.

Wednesday of the following week was settled upon for Captain Reeves' visit. Caroline was busy in the morning conferring with Mrs Magor about the menu, seeing that the new girl recently employed to help her was aware of her duties, and that the youth, Peter Davy, had a clean uniform and could be relied upon to show Captain Reeves in, politely, and take his coat, if necessary, to the side hall. Of course, it could take far longer than a week to train an uncouth serving lad with the semblance of a proper footman, but he appreciated the clothes that Joel had allowed to be sent from Truro just for the one special occasion, and he'd been quicker than Caroline had dared hope, in learning his manners.

'You're a damn good chatelaine and manager,' Joel told his wife, as he noted her arrangements: the extra candles and lamps glinting on the dining room table, with silver and glasses sparkling and newly polished, the fine lawn napkins elegantly folded, and a bowl of early pink roses providing an extra centre piece.

Caroline herself, had the exquisite appearance and quality of some fragile blossom newly opened from bud. Her pale hair had been curled, and from a centre parting piled to the top of her small head and pinned with a single flower. The voluminous pink panniers of her gown enfolded her like immense petals.

Placing both hands round her waist, Joel kissed her.

'You look — ravishing,' he muttered, in the appreciative manner he'd learned, from his past, no woman could resist.

Caroline blushed faintly.

'I'm glad you approve, Joel.'

'*Approve?* My dear girl, if it wasn't for Reeves' appearing at any moment I'd show you approval's not the right word at all. You're a maddening little coquette, darling. Wait till this naval fellow's gone and I'll teach you something. Something you've never had before. You don't know the half of me yet.'

She laughed, slightly embarrassed.

'Don't be silly. And don't crush my bodice. I've dressed care-fully, for the captain's benefit. Because you asked me to. That's right, isn't it?'

'Sure,' he loosened his grip. 'But don't go *too* far, my love, just far enough.' He grinned disarmingly, then turned away. 'Oh you'll work the trick all right. He'll fall for you good and hard.'

Fall for her? And Joel didn't mind? But he *would* mind — if it really happened and she responded. She'd learned in rare moments that beneath his casual façade was a strong vein of jealousy which might prove dangerous should doubt of her integrity enter his mind. It wouldn't of course — simply because no man but Joel counted to her, and he knew it. This was one of the troubles between them — he was too confident, took her too much for granted. 'Admire my wife as much as you like — within reason.' Such was his attitude. He had everything so neatly pigeon-holed; nothing short of an earthquake or some other unlikely event of magnitude would deter him from his set course. Even on the rare occasions when they went riding together over the moors above Treescarne, he'd appeared more concerned about the exact areas and boundaries of his territory than the wanton wild beauty of the landscape.

Once, when he'd found a company of gipsies camping by a copse just beneath the high ridge, he'd made a show of authority by making them move fifty yards to the right.

'You've my permission to camp there for a few nights,' he'd said with an air of generosity, 'provided it's not for long, and you don't take it as a right. If you catch a rabbit or two, that won't worry me either. But no birds, understand? No guns in the air, or I'll haul you in the dock and there'll be no mercy shown.'

A lean, dark-faced man, wearing a single ear-ring, and a scarlet shirt with a bright spotted tie round his neck, had nodded grudgingly, 'What you say, Mus,' he'd affirmed. 'Tomorrow — the next day, or mebbe the one after, we move over hill. Good kitchemir there. Space for Vardo, an' Lovel for a bit of work done.'

'Hm.'

Joel had regarded the group speculatively for a moment, feeling briefly a sudden swift bond of understanding. They'd travelled like he had, met and known all kinds of people, while retaining their own individuality. One thing was lacking however, ambition and purpose. Theirs was a day-to-day life, sleeping, living, and eating when and where they could, without worldly desire. Yet the eyes of an ancient crone smoking a clay pipe outside a tent had been bright as burning coals filled with a mysterious wisdom of earth, sky, rivers, clouds and the wanton winds blowing through furze, bent undergrowth and the great boulders strewing the moors. It was as though for a few seconds Joel had been caught into an earlier more primitive civilization — a civilization in which he could have been a king indeed.

He'd pulled himself to the present abruptly, lifted a hand automatically, turned, and kicked his black mount to a sharp canter in the opposite direction, and presently, with Caroline beside him, was at a gallop towards Treescarne.

Caroline's cheeks had glowed when they reached the stables.

'I enjoyed that,' she'd said. 'We ought to ride more, Joel.'

'We will, one day,' he'd promised, 'when the work's finished – the hotel, and—'

'Yes?'

He'd laughed, kissed her cheek lightly and answered, 'Never you mind. I've got plans for the future, as you well know.'

'But I *don't*. That's just it—'

'As much as is good for you. And what you've got to concentrate on now is Reeves' visit.'

Slightly nettled, she'd replied, 'I'm well aware of that. I only hope this Captain Reeves of yours is worth the trouble.'

'Oh, he will be, mark my words.'

She discovered later that Joel's assertion was true. The Captain, who arrived in evening dress for the occasion, was a handsome quiet-voiced man, slightly under six feet, with deeply set blue eyes under a wide brow from which thick curling brown hair swept back, leaving carefully trimmed side burns. His manner was restrained and courteous. A first glimpse of Caroline caused instant rapport and admiration between them. She sensed immediately that beneath the controlled exterior was a strong will, less fierce than Joel's, but just as formidable. Although lacking the quality of setting her heart alight and bounding as a touch and glance from Joel could, he possessed something she'd missed for a long time – which she had never had from a man – the promise of friendship. He was also a man of honour, and for a moment the thought of having deliberately to set out and captivate him as her husband directed was offensive to her. Why had she to flatter openly and divert matters into personal channels just for Joel's benefit? What devious game was he playing at? That it was a game was quite clear to her. Did Captain Reeves guess? Probably not – simply because when the first formal greetings were over, and by the time they were seated round the glittering dining table and afterwards, Caroline was not acting at all. There was no need. Conversation flowed easily between courses; without in any way making her feel ignorant, the Captain related incidents of historical sea-faring life, interspersed with recollections of times abroad and periods in London that genuinely held her interest, and caused Joel, eventually, to become bored.

'We're not city lovers,' he said abruptly at one point. 'My wife and I prefer country air. Never been used to anything else.'

'But surely during your successful career, Mr Blake, you must have travelled extensively?'

'True enough, and I've met some damned good characters on the way. That's life, isn't it? Knowing people and assessing situations?' He paused before adding, 'Your own duties must've taught you that.'

'Certainly.' The tempo of Reeves' voice did not change. His gaze was frank, his manner unruffled. 'And it hasn't always been easy. But in time the art becomes habitual — if you can call it an art.' A faint smile touched his lips.

'Oh, I'm sure it must be,' Caroline said quietly and unexpectedly.

Joel stared at her, puzzled. Then he laughed with a show of real amusement.

'Women like to think they're in the know about men's affairs,' he said condescendingly. 'You know how it is, Captain? Or perhaps you're not married.'

'I'm not. As yet it hasn't been my luck to find anyone quite to my taste—' His eyes rested upon Caroline briefly. 'Even if I did the uncertainty of my duties would make me rather an unsatisfactory husband, I'm afraid.'

'Duties? Yes,' Joel agreed. 'Especially when you're on to some clever smuggling operation, I guess.'

He waited for a reply to the unspoken question. There was a short pause before it came.

'Smuggling is merely a part of my occupation, Mr Blake.'

'Naturally. And I don't suppose there's much going on these days.'

'Now and again it happens,' the Captain shrugged. 'But with the vigilance of the Preventive Service very few large cargoes get by.'

'And I suppose you get local help?' Joel asked casually.

'Oh yes. Sometimes.'

'Count me in then, if there's anything I can do,' Joel said with a grin. 'I have a liking for a little adventure, especially if it's in a good cause.'

The Captain's stare became enigmatic.

'I certainly will, Mr Blake. We're always in need of reliable allies.'

Reliable? Caroline thought uncomfortably, but *could* Joel be relied upon in all circumstances?

She took a shrewd look at her husband. His pleasant expression betrayed nothing of the devious thoughts flashing like quick silver beneath the self-contained skilful façade. It was as though secret opponents were playing a clever game of chess each taking the other's measure before reaching a move. Of the two, Joel was obviously the more ruthless; but she doubted that he'd succeed completely in his intention to win the other man's confidence. Reeves was too knowledgeable in matters of law and assessing character. He must guess, surely, that Joel, the adventurer, was cultivating him for more than straightforward friendship?

Still, whatever she might think, and whatever Joel was up to, the evening passed pleasantly enough, and her vanity was titillated at moments when the Captain's eyes slid to hers briefly, with something glowing in them a little more than mere admiration. Occasionally, they conversed on subjects alien to Joel's experience — art, the study of modern painting in comparison with the great masters, books and wild-life in Britain and abroad. When Joel indicated irritation, talk was diverted into other channels. So everything outwardly was amiable and kept on a level key.

After Reeves' departure, Joel — who was cheerfully fortified by whisky and a good cigar — remarked to Caroline in self-satisfied tones, 'Well, I think we've got him all right. He liked us. You especially.'

Caroline shrugged. 'That's what you wanted. I did my best.'

The faintest of frowns puckered his forehead.

'In a way of speaking, yes. Next time, though, you could hold your horses a bit.'

She laughed.

'Whatever do you mean?'

'Keep the flirting out of it, love.'

'Flirting? Don't be absurd. There was nothing like that at all between us.'

'There could be though. I saw him looking at you. And all that stuff about *poetry* and *art*!'

'As you're contemplating artists visiting the hotel when it's built, it's good to know more about painting than I do,' Caroline replied spiritedly. 'So don't be jealous.'

'*Jealous?* I?' Joel looked truly amazed.

'Well — aren't you?'

'I could be — if you gave me cause.'

She shook her head. 'Not seriously. You're too sensible, too sure of yourself to bother about things that will never happen. Oh yes, I liked the Captain. But—' she broke off, uncertain, 'I didn't compare him — with *you* — I—'

'I should damn well think not,' he took her by the shoulders, stared into her eyes and said with his voice thickening. 'If I thought you were ever picturing yourself in another man's arms, my love, I'd put you over my knee and give you the hiding of your life. Do you understand?'

Feeling her heart quickening at the close contact of her body with his she replied, 'You're such a brute, Joel.'

'I can be, when it's necessary.' There was a pause between them. Then he lifted her from the ground, pressing her tightly against his chest; all memories of the Captain were obliterated as Joel mounted the stairs still carrying her, defenceless and compliant in his arms. The finale to the evening was a passionate one dispelling for the time being all doubts in Caroline's heart.

During the weeks that followed Joel's business energies were almost solely concentrated on dealing with hotel matters. He hoped and planned for the new building to be opened in the autumn, so the winter months could be a testing period for organisation of staff and practical running of the place. One or two guests would probably visit Lionswykka, and in the spring of 1882, following an advertising campaign, he'd no doubt the experiment would prove itself an expanding and remunerative concern. Meanwhile he got a wealthy shipowner from Plymouth to invest in taking up certain shares, also an Irish American with a taste and 'nose' for making money in any devious rewarding way. Both men had 'taken stock' of Joel's potentialities and considered there was little risk in either the hotel project or its proposed more dubious sideline. The man might be a bounder, the shipping magnate conceded to himself, but he was also a winner. Together the three of them could make a fortune. Joel naturally was in hearty agreement over this. But he was skilful in allowing only a percentage of shares to be taken up. Whatever money was invested must only be up to a certain amount. In all matters concerning Lionswykka, he was determined always to hold the trump card with the major assets of the company under his sole control.

His predictions concerning autumn and spring guests to the hotel had proved correct. By the New Year of 1882 the minimum number had swelled from a dozen to fifty. All were well-to-do people, mostly of the expanding wealthy middle class genre who took flattering accounts back to their homes concerning the situation, comfort and service of Lionswykka. Joel had been astute in employing a head cook knowledgeable in menus of a rare and appetising kind, while providing also for the more stolid tastes of rich Northerners.

The head waiter was French, possessing the expertise to control and instruct his staff into decorous and swift attention of guests' needs. Although secretly niggled by the expenditure of installing every comfort possible for visitors, Joel, recognising the necessity, had faced the fact squarely, and spared nothing.

The beds and furnishing of all rooms were of the best, the decor and carpets rich and lavish. Stepping into the great front hall was like entering another world — a castle from some bygone legend modernised and brought to life again.

The outside of the building, though designed to no particular period had a look of the Gothic about it, with turrets and towers rising from cliffs to the sky as though carved from the granite itself. In spite of this, the effect had been skilfully contrived to avoid any suggestion of ornate vulgarity. There was no ostentatious intrusion of the wild Cornish landscape. Imposing — yes, but always subservient to the character of the elements — of wind and rain, storm-swept moors gold with gorse and sunlight on calm spring and summer days — at other times brooding and overcast with mists creeping over the landscape like ghostly legions reborn from the past. The great boulders, then, assumed the watchful shapes of giant beasts conceived in mysterious primeval days when the earth was new.

It was this ancient primeval quality that gradually drew visitors to the rugged Lionswykka coast, which, combined with the carefully contrived luxury of the hotel provided a unique sense of experiencing two worlds at once. The climate also was a great attraction, and once the first pleasure boat set off for the island, nature lovers were delighted by the scene when they got there. Sleek-bodied shimmering seals watched curiously from behind rocks, unafraid, but cautious, their almost human faces raised, before waddling off on their flippers and slipping into the water again.

Joel was delighted by the successful beginning to the venture. In early May he and Caroline moved from Treescarne to the hotel for a period, partly because he knew that word of her expertise at painting would get around up country, and artists would probably arrive to give added colour to the enterprise, and partly because after its initial delay he was planning his first exercise in contraband — nothing too ambitious — 'feeling his way' as he put it. It was a cargo of spirits, shipped from Ireland, to be landed on the island at a late hour by small fishing smacks and stored in two pleasure boats before being disposed of in the tunnel leading from Lionswykka land to Treescarne cellars. At an amicable meeting with the vicar over vintage brandy and cigars, Joel had agreed for a minor portion of the liquor to be diverted to the reverend gentleman's property as payment for his silence.

'We both know too much about each other to take risks,' Joel had pointed out in reasoning tones, 'sharing as we do part of the main route. In other words, sir — you turn a blind eye to any little adventure I may get up to, and your pocket will benefit. This will enable you to assist any deserving poverty-stricken member of your parish when you wish. An admirable situation which you, as a man of God and strong conscience, must appreciate.' He had stared unblinkingly into the other man's bland face. The round rubicund countenance had deepened in colour slightly, but the primped lips smiled after a short pause. The jowls and heavy chin nodded slowly over the black collar and stout chest.

'As you say, sir, as you say,' came the reply presently. 'Where the welfare of the poor is concerned, one must not bother unduly about the petty restrictions of the law. Eh? A deep chuckle of laughter rumbled from his throat. Presently the two confederates had shaken hands after concluding the deal.

Hypocrite, Joel had thought, as he reviewed the conversation on his ride back to the hotel. That slimy bounder, his fat-bellied god! — what a farce! Well, the main problem had been solved anyway. He was assured that in the future there'd be no danger of the Reverend Carson putting an interfering finger into what could be a very profitable little business concern. He, Joel Blake, held all the winning cards, and the greedy parson knew it. Like the Lionswykka company he had both firmly under control.

This first venture was planned for early June, when, with daily trips to the island by the pleasure boats arranged, a little extra activity on the sea round the vicinity would hardly attract notice from the Preventive.

For some days before the plan was put into action, Caroline was aware of an added restlessness in Joel that told her something new was afoot in his devious mind. She questioned him once or twice, but he told her nothing.

'What's bothering you, Joel?' she asked the first time.

'Bothering me?' His eyebrows shot up in apparent surprise. 'Nothing. Why should it? Everything's going better even than I expected, as you well know. Hotel practically booked up until the next autumn, our little pleasure boat enterprise flourishing, and you as my loving wife — what more could any man wish for?'

Staring at him frankly she replied, 'You might perhaps. You're not just any man, Joel.'

He laughed.

'Damn well I'm not. And I've more to handle than most. But that doesn't mean I'm bothered. So stop fixing your attention on *me* all the time, and follow your own line.'

'What's that?'

'You know. Painting — amusing the visitors — entrancing 'em with your beauty if you like — anything but puzzling over me.'

'I see.' Her voice was cold.

'What's up now?'

'Nothing.'

She moved away from him, her chin firmly lifted, and after a moment retorted, 'So that's what I'm supposed to be — a mere diversion while you get entangled with something else.'

In a second he had caught her and turned her round to face him.

'D'you mind repeating that?' His voice was dangerously calm.

'There's no need is there? You heard what I said. It doesn't matter. Your business really *is* your own, I see that. But when we got married I didn't expect to be so completely pushed out of it. I *know* you're not only concerned with the hotel; maybe it's a sort of — of sixth sense in me, but I can *feel* it. And all this business with being pleasant to Captain Reeves and so many visits to the Vicarage!' She broke off for a second shaking her head. 'You're not a religious man, Joel — you're — you're involved in some sort of adventure, and I'd like to share it. Don't you understand?'

'Damned if I do. You're an odd sort of wife and no mistake. Clever too,' a tinge of admiration lit his eyes. 'But—' his voice changed, 'I don't want you poking your pretty little nose into my affairs. So you just remember, my love. Your place is elsewhere.'

'In the bedroom, of course. Naturally.'

'Yes. In the bedroom. And don't you go forgetting it. Maybe if you concentrated a little more on your wifely charms and obligations you'd succeed in giving me a son. Isn't that the aim of most women?'

Stiffly she replied, 'It's not a year yet. These things — starting a family, having children — don't always start so soon. I'm sorry you're disappointed.'

'I'm not. Just stating facts. Your aristocratic sister, I believe, was in the family way after the first month of marriage.'

'Ariadne's different to me, and she's my *half* sister.'

'Hm.'

'Joel — *please* not let's argue about nothing.'

'I'm not arguing, love, just irritated because I've a good deal to do.'

She sighed. 'Oh, very well.'

The subject ended temporarily, with relief and some disgruntlement on Joel's part. He hadn't expected such stubbornness from his otherwise satisfactory and gratifying wife. He knew very well she'd object to the contraband enterprise, considering he was endangering his 'reputation', and might even fail, which would mean the helpful nest-egg she'd brought him would be sacrificed on a lost cause. Oh hell! — why did some men have to get themselves so insidiously tied up? — simply because of a need for cash? Not that he wouldn't have married her without it, she was a lovely woman. Possessing her in itself was an exciting experience. But a man had to have other things too, and at the moment he didn't want or need emotional involvement.

The night for the smuggling enterprise arrived. It was a clear evening except for a few clouds blurring the fitful moonlit sky. Eight miles out at sea the Irish smack *Mary Lise* was anchored, while a number of smaller fishing boats laden with the cargo, set off to deliver the kegs at a narrow gully cutting into the southern side of the island. Marty had seen that the Revenue were tipped off on a false scent concerning another possible operation near the coast off Penjust, so there was every chance that the tiny smuggling vessels would be unnoticed. Once at the island the main part of contraband was to be stored in the cave leading from the gully, until a propitious time arrived for it to be taken in the innocent-looking pleasure boats to the tunnel cutting from Lionswykka coastline towards the cellars of Treescarne.

Part of the lighter stuff was to be delivered direct to the cove on the mainland.

The dangerous idea had occurred to Joel to invite Reeves to dinner at Lionswykka on that night. Having him under his eye while the operation was carried out would be reassuring. But the excitement of being on the scene himself changed his mind. It was essential, anyway, he decided, that he was available in case of any trouble arising. Reeves might or might not be in the vicinity. Probably the latter, due to Marty's devious planning. However, if the clever captain hadn't been fooled or was the slightest bit suspicious, the risk still had to be taken.

So at the appointed hour, Joel informed Caroline he had a business acquaintance to see at Penzance and might be back late.

'Can't say when,' he said casually, 'the whole thing's un-expected.'

It was already nine o'clock; the light was beginning to fade, and Caroline was standing adjusting her hair through the mirror of her dressing table before going downstairs again to join the guests at a social evening in the large lounge.

'Going *out*?' she echoed. 'At this hour? But why, Joel? Surely the meeting — whatever it is — could have been arranged for the daytime?'

'Not this one,' he answered abruptly.

She shook her head, realising that what she'd suggested was true. Joel's restlessness had been obvious. He was involved in something secret and dangerous which he had no intention of revealing to her.

'Very well,' she said coldly. 'If you have to. But I wish you'd tell me about this sort of thing earlier. I mean you *must* have expected it. If only you could confide in me. What *are* you up to?'

He bent down, placed a finger against a satin smooth cheek, then kissed her lightly on the forehead.

'My darling, that's my affair. Try and enjoy the charade or whatever it is — that's going on downstairs. If you don't, go to bed with a book. I'll see you in the morning, anyway.'

'The *morning?*'

'Yes. And don't look like that. Men *do* occasionally have a night out, you know.'

She could get nothing more out of him. A little later she watched, from an upper window, his dark clad figure riding towards the moors astride his black stallion. In a few moments horse and rider were lost in the shadows of the deepening light. Clouds were thickening from the west, taking the rising moon into fitful oblivion. At moments the sky cleared, sending shadows streaking down the wild hillside. There was no sign any more of Joel or his mount — only the great lumps of rock rising from heather and gorse, and the winged shape of a bird soaring upwards from the undergrowth.

Joel, meanwhile, had arrived at Treescarne, and was inspecting the cellars below the house. Mrs Magor, as usual, had retired at nine o'clock, to bed. The youth Peter Dory, who'd been bribed into silence over the forthcoming event, had already moved the large piece of rock blocking the entrance to the vault-like dank space at the end of the tunnel. From there a heavy iron studden door half rotted by the years had been partly heaved open, revealing the damp cellar below a few granite steps, and trap door. The remains of two broken barrels lay on the muddied flagged floor, with a coil of rope and an iron bar. It was quite clear that the unpleasant interior had been unused by any tenant of Treescarne for a very long time.

Joel had decided to remain at the receiving end of the operation so the kegs and other goods could be safely installed without interruption at the quickest possible speed when they arrived.

Marty and his men would be in charge at the other far end of the passage on the seaward side by the cove, and signalling by lights in case of danger was effectively under control. From there he would also be available to give help in case any unforeseen obstacle arose concerning the island operation.

So it was a matter of waiting, for Joel, until word was brought by a forerunner of the first small boat that the contraband had safely reached the coast.

Time passed slowly. At intervals Joel made his way through the trap door and kitchen to the house and took a brief glance from a top window to the sea. Through a blur of rising mist, an occasional light twinkling over the dark sea could be glimpsed. It could have been a star over the horizon or that of a small craft. As the moon streaked momentarily through a break in the clouds a dark shape jutting from behind a rock, swayed for a second and was then lost again. This was followed by another.

They were coming.

On light feet Joel made his way down again to the cellars, sensing it would be safer at that point to remain below. There was no telling when the old besom Mrs Magor might wake and want a finger in the pie. Ancient as she was, she was a stubborn character, and he wouldn't trust her an inch with any secret unless she was to gain by it considerably.

Eventually, leaving Peter Dory at the receiving end, Joel, with head thrust forward, left the cellars for the tunnel, forcing himself forward between dank and dripping walls down the incline leading towards the sea. Just before reaching the spot where the passage divided, cutting upwards again towards the vicarage land, he saw the glimmer of a light bobbing eerily in the darkness.

Marty Werne.

'Theym cummen', surr,' the harsh Cornish voice muttered on a low key. 'Cargoes arrived. No trouble at all. No one 'bout — them Revenue men's fallen for the bait — good luck to 'em.'

He laughed.

Triumph rose in Joel. Easy as that was it? By God! he'd go in for a richer deal the next time.

A little later the kegs and bundles were joisted and forced tortuously by Marty's men up the steep ascent to Treescarne. Joel delivered payment immediately. 'Next time,' he said, chuckling, 'the whole load could be of gold itself — providing you've the guts and strength to carry it.'

There was muffled acquiescence, with one voice proclaiming above the rest, 'Hell, master! Wi' gold in the bags an' beef in the muscle there edn' nuthen can't be tackled wi' a tot o' rum in the belly.'

The actual operation of getting the goods from the boats to the cellars took no more than an hour. When the men at last made their furtive exit from house to shore again, hurrying with heads and shoulders bent like haunted animals evading capture, the moon still blurred by thickening mist was a mere vague glimmer.

Joel was standing at the door of the house on the sea side when he saw briefly, a caped shape half scrambling up the moorland path on his left which led in the straightest course from Lionswykka. He stood perfectly still, eyes screwed up, puzzled. The captain? Or Marty? No, all had gone. When the sky momentarily cleared there was no mistaking a woman's shape. A figure he knew surely.

Caroline.

What the hell was she doing there? he thought savagely. Spying? Creeping up on him?

Without more ado he cut down abruptly to meet her.

Her hair had fallen and was loose and dripping round her face. She had one hand clasped at her throat, and was breathing quickly.

Joel grasped her forearm.

'What are *you* doing here? What the devil do you want?

'Oh, Joel, I was so worried. I thought there was something wrong. I saw you earlier riding to Treescarne. At least—' She broke off for a second, sensing how very angry he was. 'Don't you *understand*? I was worried – for you. That talk about business – it wasn't really true, was it? You   you—'

'Yes?' The word was deadly.

'I suppose I shouldn't have come. But I couldn't sleep. I tried and tried, then – it was no good. I just had to know what was going on.'

'And what've you learned? Anything? No. But *I* have – just how devious and interfering you can be when you've a bee in your bonnet. Well, this is the last time, understand? I won't have my life muddled up by any nosey woman wanting to pry into my affairs, even if she happens to be my wife. Another thing, madam, don't you dare traipse the moors at night half dressed beneath that cape thing. Next time you'll smart for it or my name's not Joel Blake.'

'But—'

'And there are no buts about it. I mean what I say. So get back down there as fast as you can.' He paused before adding, 'On second thoughts I'll accompany you before you get up to any more tricks.'

'But, Joel, I—'

'Shut up.'

He'd a sudden desire to fling her down in the heather, then slap and take her into submission. But he stifled the swift sexual impulse, took her firmly by the shoulders, and forced her ahead. When he reached Lionswykka he saw her inside, then turned.

'Joel — where are you going? Aren't you—?'

'I'm going back,' he answered shortly. 'And don't argue. Just keep your pretty mouth shut and stop making a fool of yourself or I'll have to deal with you in the morning. And if that's the way you want it, darling, you'll know better in the future.'

He turned on his heel, slammed the door, and walked sharply away. Miserably, Caroline made her way upstairs to the bedroom.

'Why did I have to fall in love with Joel?' she thought. 'Why couldn't it have been someone gentler and more honourable like Captain Reeves?'

She did not know it then, but the Captain had asked himself the same question, more than once.

5

The summer months passed without undue excitement at Lionswykka. As Joel had predicted, the number of visitors to the hotel had steadily increased. Successful artists and photographers willing and able to pay the price came to portray the unique views and revel in the pristine clear skies and translucent shades of the Atlantic sweeping the Cornish coastline. The rich upper and middle classes frequently prolonged their stay and at available points even ventured to paddle in some quiet nearby cove that was well sheltered from the winds. The trips to the Island were a great attraction; women wearing sealskin coats of their own had been overheard to remark they would never buy another, the seals themselves were such 'darling sweet creatures.'

To all this Joel nodded in agreement without any serious thought of his own on the matter except from a business point of view. The fate of seals in far-off climes was no affair of his, but on his own property, being such a draw, with their obvious capacity to increase Lionswykka's money making value, they were protected from fishermen and exploiters of the more adventurous kind. To hunt or harm a seal was an offence. A coat-of-arms was devised for the hotel and its surrounding acres, including both a seal and a mermaid entwined in fanciful letters depicting a large L and A.

'Lionswykka Arms,' Joel exclaimed when he settled on the design. 'That's it — old world and legendary in one. Quite a bright idea, don't you think, Caro?'

'I'm sure it will be popular,' Caroline agreed. 'But don't you have to have a permit from the College of Heraldry for such a thing?'

'For a *hotel*? – an inn?' Joel answered scornfully. 'Really, Caroline! I'm not passing myself off as a *lord* or anything—' he grinned. 'This is just a *name* – to head notepaper and all that – like you have in most decent public houses.'

'Yes, I suppose so.'

'Think it a bit ostentatious?' he queried. 'Maybe it is. I happen to be a somewhat ostentatious fellow myself. Or hadn't you noticed it?'

She laughed. 'No one could help it.'

'Thank you.'

'But I quite like it. You, I mean.'

'Which is as well, my love. Right now I mean to show you that goes for me too.'

And without further ado, he did.

After their love-making Caroline as usual was left feeling exhausted, and exhilarated at the same time, still throbbing with passion and love for this unpredictable man she had married. Nothing, she believed then, could come between herself and Joel. Whatever strange business he became involved in – however much he bewildered and hurt her in colder moments, he was hers completely. Their relationship was secure.

Then, at the beginning of September, she had a letter from her half-sister Ariadne, Lady Perryn, who wished to visit Lionswykka.

Dear Caro,

I hope all is still well with you in your new marriage. I heard – in a roundabout way – that your husband, Joel Blake, is quite a colourful character – 'rather out of our class, my dear' – as one of my friends put it, 'but likely to put his stamp on the world'. How absolutely titillating and exciting! I should like to meet him, and you, of course. Life is good in London at the moment, Willie still adores me, poor lamb, although I know I lead him a hell of a dance sometimes. All the same there *are* moments when I feel you can have too much of a good thing. You know what I mean? Boredom. Yes, I do sometimes get a bit sick of the eternal social round, the entertaining and operas, and high-life small talk. The Prince of Wales has a new mistress I understand. There are so many it's hard to keep up with them. The usual gossip goes on, of course, about marriage scandals, and wars — wars! — wars! — especially over Egypt, and the eternal Irish problem. Parnell must be quite outrageous, but he *does* have the courage of his convinctions, and was decent enough to condemn those awful Phoenix Park murders.

People say the Queen and Gladstone don't get on at all! Poor woman! I'm sure she had a terribly *feminine* penchant for Dizzy, and Gladstone with his prim talk doesn't fit the bill at all.

Oh dear! how stuffy this letter is. What I want to say, really, is that can your smart hotel book me a room for the end of the month? I'm dying to have a good old 'gossip' with you, and of course meet Joel. You don't mind my calling him that, do you? Although we've never met, I *am* his sister-in-law, so it's a duty for me to arrange things. Families *should* be in some sort of contact. I promise you I won't force my charms or try to lure him away — to be quite frank I'm rather sick of male adulation. You mayn't believe it, being the faithful type, and me so outrageous, but it's true.

Let me know what date is convenient. A whiff of Cornish air will be marvellous after the tiring summer we've had.

Yours ever,
Ariadne.

P.S. Willie sends his regards and best wishes. Being such a pet, he really means it. Poor Willie!

Yes indeed, Caroline thought, pushing the letter aside with a mild feeling of apprehension, poor Willie. He was outstanding in no way, except for being a lord, which she supposed counted for something. Caroline had met him only once, at the wedding. He was a thin man of medium height with pale eyes and a fair moustache. A little aloof, which might have been assumed, but apparently lacking the male qualities to keep a character of Ariadne's type in order.

Joel was gratified by the idea, although he did not show it openly. After all any connection with the aristocracy could be advantageous.

'By all means tell her she's welcome to come along at any time,' he told his wife, adding recklessly, 'as our guest, naturally.'

'She'll want to pay, I'm sure. Ariadne has all the money in the world to throw about.'

'In that case we mustn't hurt her pride,' Joel agreed, with relief. The thought of giving money away, even in such circumstances didn't appeal to him, and if the wild Lady Perryn wished to squander a little on Lionswykka's behalf, then let her. He needed all the backing possible to cover the sum he'd spent in outlay on the estate.

Eventually the beginning of October was fixed for Ariadne's visit.

She arrived on a calm autumn day when the moors were washed gold from the afternoon sun, with a thin haze lying over the hills where gorse still flamed between granite rocks and clumps of purple heather. The sea was at ebb tide below the cliffs throwing glittering crests of spray on the pale sands where the waves broke.

Ariadne, attired in an elegant silk gown and embroidered jacket under a pale lilac-coloured velvet cloak, and a fashionable forward-tilted hat with veiling falling back over her shoulders looked, as she had been described in a fashion magazine 'truly delightful', elegantly beautiful as a creature from a dream.

Her silver-gold pale hair had been swept back in ringlets from her face to be held in place by a fine net. Her pale skin and exquisite features, though fragile, glowed with health. Her wardrobe had been specially planned for her by the successful Charles Frederick Worth who through his association with Princess Metternich — known as 'Madam Chiffon' — was put in touch with Empress Eugénie, and had achieved instant and lasting fame.

'Oh, darling,' Ariadne gushed as she threw her arms wide to embrace Caroline, 'how perfectly lovely to see you again.'

They were standing in the great main hall of Lionswykka, as luggage and boxes were taken upstairs by servants to a principal guest room overlooking the sea. Behind the two women Joel looked on with faintly sardonic amusement. He was well aware that Ariadne was conscious of his presence, and guessed that the loving little scene had mostly been contrived for his benefit; when at last, after the first introduction, he was able to take her hand, the strength of her slim palm and fingers under his was a surprise. He took a quick searching look at her face. The blue eyes under the velvety dark brown lashes were so vivid and alert with life, interest in her turned to quick admiration. This, he thought with a momentary stab of male excitement, was no cool-as-a-cucumber fashion-plate young woman, but one with exceedingly passionate potential, and not much of a conscience either. He would have to be careful — *very* careful indeed. The Perryns would be useful. He must in no way annoy that ineffectual husband of hers. On the other hand — to have her dangling on a string, and willing to co-operate in some way with his business objectives, might prove useful. Also amusing.

Watching them converse on trivialities under a veneer of politeness, Caroline was annoyed and mildly resentful. It was always the same, she thought irritably, wherever she was, Ariadne managed to be the centre of attraction. Devious, she always had been. Her air of innocence was simply a guise to her vanity. Yet there was nothing to complain of in her impeccable behaviour, though Caroline didn't believe Joel would be fooled by the elegant façade. They were two of a kind in some subtle way; already a bond of instinctive understanding had been created between them which roused her suspicions to fleeting jealousy.

That night, as she brushed her hair before the dressing table mirror, Caroline glanced back at her husband who had just entered from the dressing room ready for bed.

'You admired Ariadne, didn't you, Joel?' she asked in calm tones. 'You thought her beautiful.'

Joel shrugged and with a casual air replied, 'She's nice enough to look at. But not a patch on you.'

A warm rush of relief surged through her, causing her skin and whole body to glow. Her translucent eyes were bright, when she said, 'Now you know that's not true. She's quite lovely. In a magazine they said—'

'Oh damn the magazines!' his voice was husky, a touch on her shoulder changed into a caress. 'It's you I want. Only you.'

'*Only*, Joel?'

'As a woman,' he answered.

He lifted her up, and with hands gently but firmly about her breasts and buttocks, carried her to the bed. Response deepened in her, while he took her presently to a leaping climax of forgetfulness and ultimate peace.

When she went down to dinner next day any apprehension or faint jealousy of Ariadne had completely disappeared. She felt secure in Joel's love; there was no longer a trace of envy in her heart for any woman — even for her half sister, who looked ravishingly beautiful in palest silver grey that deepened into shadowed folds of mauve and elusive sea-green with every movement. A single white flower starred the silver-gold hair. Round the column of the slender throat above the gently swelling breasts, a necklace of diamonds glittered. A fragile lacy shawl was draped round her shoulders which she unobtrusively removed before sitting down to the meal.

How beautiful she was, Caroline could not help thinking. No wonder Sir William Perryn had desired and still wanted her sufficiently to shut his ears and eyes to the conflicting and scandalous tales concerning her affairs with other men.

Were they true? Once or twice as she glanced at her half sister, Caroline caught Joel's eyes also on her speculatively. Was he thinking the same? she wondered. Would Ariadne try her ardour on him? That evening, as on the previous night, there was no sign of it; Ariadne behaved with decorous dignity suggesting even an air of modesty hardly applicable to her colourful reputation.

'Well?' Caroline asked her husband later in the bedroom, 'what do you *really* think of my sister? She *is* lovely isn't she?'

Joel shrugged, assuming an indifference he didn't entirely

feel. 'She's all right, in her way, I suppose. A charmer who knows it. Most of her behaviour tonight was an act.'

'What do you mean?'

'My dear love, your sister's no innocent. I know the type. I've met them before. Qualified coquettes who want one thing — apart from money which your sister certainly doesn't need — power over men. Sensuous power. Understand?'

'You may be right.'

'Damn sure I am.'

'And she didn't — she didn't affect you in that way?'

Joel laughed.

'Don't you know me yet? I know the side my bread's buttered. No rich nobleman's wife's going to upset my apple cart.'

This was not the answer she'd expected.

'Because of gossip you mean? It wouldn't suit you to get involved?'

'What do *you* think? And why the devil such a load of questions? You're my wife, aren't you? Isn't that enough? Do I have to go on my knees every time I meet a pretty woman, and swear faithfulness to you?'

'Oh, Joel. What a stupid thing to say.'

'Yes, and you're stupid. Men get bored by clinging wives asking the same question time after time — "do you *really* love me? If you'd met her first would you still have married me?"'

'I didn't *say* that.'

'As good as. Now let's drop the subject of Ariadne. I've things to deal with tomorrow — a bit of business that could be tricky. I want a good night's sleep.'

Knowing that after a number of whiskies — and Joel had certainly indulged that night — he could be irritable, Caroline let the subject drop. But before she went to sleep her mind darted this way and that, trying to come to a satisfactory conclusion concerning Joel's recently acquired new business projects. Ever since the occasion when she'd made the nightly traipse over the moors towards Treescarne and been caught by Joel, she'd known, secretly, that he was involved in contraband or something equally dangerous and against the law. She'd even made a point of going up to the house when Joel was away for the day, and making tactful enquiries of the sly-looking Mrs Magor, and her nephew Peter Dory. Mrs Magor had been sullen, resentful, saying there was 'nuthen' to know. Nobody was up to 'anythen', and she slept well at nights after her glass of 'tonic'. As for Peter — he remained obtuse, surly, and stubbornly disinclined to talk at all except to say, 'Everythin's all right at Treescarne Missis, ef et wasn't master'll know. I'll tell en what you did say, an' ask 'en.'

'Oh no,' Caroline answered quickly, 'there's no need. I accept your word. I shouldn't like to think — *he* wouldn't either, the master — that I was prying into his affairs and business worries.'

Peter's wary expression changed to one of triumph. 'I think y'r right, missis. Keep quiet. Both of us. That's the way.'

So Caroline held her tongue, doing her best to shut her ears and eyes to any unsavoury mysteries in Joel's life, also to the fact that as the days passed both he and Ariadne displayed a certain deepening awareness of each other's presence. Caroline had thought her sister's stay was to be of short duration — a week, or fortnight at the most. But when, by the middle of October she showed no signs of leaving, Caroline asked bluntly, 'How long are you staying, Ariadne? Isn't Willie wanting you back in London? I'd have thought so, for the winter season.'

Ariadne's beautiful eyes widened in apparently innocent astonishment.

'*Winter*, darling? But it's still like summer here,' she sighed. 'And Cornwall's so beautiful — so dramatic. Joel really has achieved something with this hotel. You're lucky to have such a husband.'

Caroline's lips tightened perceptibly. 'I know. So are you. It's nice to know you appreciate Lionswykka. But—'

'Oh I do, I *do*. And you mustn't worry about Willie,' she smiled, sweetly. 'He's a club-man, you know. And his friends on the Stock Exchange — they're not really quite *me*, darling.' She paused before continuing, 'Do you *want* to get rid of me, Caro? I mean, am I in the way?'

Yes, Caroline thought in a wave of resentment, Ariadne *was* in the way. She didn't trust her an inch, simply because this beautiful half-sister of hers seemed to have no aim in life except to entrance men. Collecting male scalps was an art with her, and to add Joel to her collection would be a very agreeable achievement. But Joel had admitted he wanted no trouble with the Perryns; surely he wouldn't allow himself to be ensnared by such an obvious flirt and coquette?

The effort of conjecturing and resentment gradually became a strain; Caroline showed little bursts of temper that before had been alien to her. Ariadne, recognising the signs of jealousy, was secretly triumphant. She had no conscience whatever about her sister. After all, she argued to herself, Caroline should have learned to behave more subtly. Also she should have been more observant and sufficiently reckless to invade Joel's other life — the adventurous wild moments he was away from her.

After the first week at Lionswykka, Ariadne, through devious means, had learned something of the truth. Joel was an opportunist and a scamp. He was also brilliantly dedicated and would spare nothing to gain his ends. She was more than titillated by his insolence and strength, he was a challenge, an enigma she meant to fathom before returning to poor old Willie, who though devoted to her in his stuck-up way, and rich enough to indulge her most extravagant whims, was nevertheless dull, and completely unrewarding, either sexually or emotionally.

October was a flaming month of rich colours and varied weather, with calm dazzling days of misted hues alternating with tossed wild periods when high seas lashed the gaunt coast-line, and winds roared round the ancient stones and menhirs of the purple and russet moors.

Ariadne still showed no sign of departure. Once Caroline said to Joel tentatively, 'Don't you think *you* could suggest my sister leaves, Joel?'

His manner was cool and preoccupied when he asked 'Why?'

'*Why?*' Exasperation seized her. 'Because I think — surely it's time we were alone together.' She waited, and when no answer came, continued bluntly. 'We didn't marry to be a threesome. At least, I didn't imagine so.'

Joel, shaken briefly by her tartness to amusement, laughed.
'I thought maybe it would be a foursome by now.'
Her cheeks reddened.
'You mean children. That's always on your mind, isn't it? You make it so obvious.'
'It *is* important. I want sons.'
Her temper flared.
'And do you think Ariadne would have served you better?'
He regarded her quizzically, thinking, 'She's jealous. I've got her right where I want her. The stupid little madam – as though all I had to think about was *women*.' In fact, during the very period of her questioning he'd been planning a challenging smuggling operation which would make them rich for the winter months when remuneration from the hotel venture was at its lowest ebb.

He took Caroline's pert chin in one hand, lifted it to meet his eyes and said, 'You silly chit. Ariadne's nothing to me, and you know it. So stop behaving like some naive Miss Nobody, and be the sophisticated wife I need. *Comprenez-vous?*' At odd moments Joel could not help reverting to a French phrase or word that he'd learned so aptly in his early days as master chef in a Parisian restaurant. Women liked it, and it usually diverted any awkward line of questioning into one of titillating admiration.

Caroline's response, though not amused, was typical.
She sighed, once more captivated by the charm, arrogance and amazing good looks of the man she'd married.
'I suppose so,' she said, automatically.
His lips sought hers.
'I love you. Don't forget it,' he said.
The statement was true, but he also loved the excitement of the double life opening up for him. And he knew Caroline's jealousy in one way had a cause where Ariadne was concerned. She wanted him as a lover – had implied it in many subtle ways without committing herself. The game between them was daily becoming more dangerous, because she stirred his senses profoundly, and was astute enough to realise his illegal involvements.

How she'd got on to the truth heaven alone knew; the vicar no doubt had helped. After a first chance meeting with the reverend gentleman on the moors, Ariadne had called on the vicarage with some veiled excuse both had appreciated was mere opportunism. At first, when he'd guessed what was going on, Joel had been irritated and annoyed. Then he'd realised, shrewdly, that the relationship might prove advantageous. Where women were concerned the lecherous old cleric was, in Joel's terms, an ass. Through Ariadne any private little plan hatched concerning contraband could be utilised to Joel's advantage.

By the end of the month when the few remaining leaves on bushes and trees were driven on wanton rising winds from the sea, Joel was roused at Treescarne one afternoon by the arrival of Ariadne, who'd ridden there in borrowed breeches and riding boots under a black cape. She had tethered a grey mare from Lionswykka stables to a twisted elm below the garden, found a side door of the house open, and unobserved had gone through. Joel was in the dark hall just leaving his study.

He stopped abruptly when he saw her, startled by her beauty which was emphasised by a fitful ray of light washing the pale hair to silvery radiance. The cloak fell back from her shoulders giving her the legendary quality of a huntress — some dreamlike Diana searching for — what?

'This is a surprise,' he managed to say in ordinary tones.

'A pleasant one, I hope.'

'It could hardly be otherwise, although I'm busy.'

'I know.'

'How do you know?'

She smiled and drew closer.

'Because I'm quite astute, Joel, in spite of my looks.'

Mildly irritated because she was so sure of her appeal and that he'd fall into the sensual trap most men of her own circle must have done, he retorted abruptly.

'You're talking in riddles. I haven't time for games. Just tell me what you want, and then I must be—'

'Going about your business,' she interrupted. 'I realise that also. I'd like to be in with you. Not necessarily financially; a sort of helpmate — partner.'

'*Partner?*' He was more than astonished, quite aghast, 'I don't know what the devil you're talking about.'

She lifted a slim gloved hand to his shoulder.

'Don't try and fool me, darling. You know very well, and so do I. You live dangerously, like me. We're very similar in some ways and I *have* been dreadfully bored these last months with Willie—' she sighed, lifting her eyes and lips beseechingly to Joel's. 'Kiss me, Joel.'

He stood staring at her for a few moments, rigid and unyielding, then told her coldly, 'I'm not one of your pet popinjays, Ariadne. What you hope to gain by this seduction act I've no idea. But for once you're the loser.'

Her colour deepened.

'Oh *no*. I'm no loser Joel. I want you. Yes, and you want me. We can have fun together, quite a lot if we're careful. And we have to be, don't we? I mean it would be such a pity for your honourable high minded friend Captain Reeves to have a clue about your *real* activities wouldn't it? The spirit and the lace? The other stuff—' Her lovely eyes narrowed perceptively.

'You're talking nonsense.'

She shook her head.

'No. I've proof.'

'Proof? *How?* What the devil've you been up to? That devious vicar I suppose. He's been talking. *Now* I understand. Those "charity" jaunts up to his house — the suggestion for helping the poor — your simpering sweet smile! What a hypocrite you are. Was he an easy conquest, Ariadne? Did you appreciate his sickening fat belly against you?'

She brought a hand stingingly against his face.

'How *dare* you, Joel Blake? Don't you *ever* touch me again or I'll—'

'Deliver me to the gallows? To be hanged, drawn and quartered? That's what they did in the old days, I believe. Well — if *I* go to hell, sweet sister-in-law I'll see you go with me. So don't you forget it. And in case you're under any illusion let me remind you I know women, and how to use a horse-whip. So no more threats. Understand?'

She smiled enigmatically. 'I think so.'

Wondering what the next move was to be, and with his senses already aroused by her innate sensuality, he asked, 'Would you like a drink?'

Her face brightened with childlike excitement. 'Oh yes. I'd love it.'

'What?'

'Whisky, I think. Neat.'

He brought out glasses and a decanter from a nearby cabinet, and poured two to the brim.

'Your good health, Lady Perryn.'

There was the chink of glass. Then, after the first liberal taste he threw discretion to the winds, and kissed her suddenly hard and searchingly on her lovely ripe lips.

Afterwards he said casually, 'Don't take that as a gesture of affection. You're a temptress and a trollop, a breed I've become accustomed to through the years. If I need anything of you, I'll have it in future. But if you breathe a word of it to my wife I'll see you smart so you'll not ride any horse in months. And that's a promise. Understand?'

She smiled demurely.

'I think we both do, Joel. So now — shall we talk?'

They did so. The outcome was that Ariadne, Lady Perryn, became the accomplice of Joel Blake, adventurer and man of many parts.

6

At the end of the month Caroline told Joel that she was returning to Treescarne.

'I'm not needed at Lionswykka now as a show-piece painting,' she said bluntly. 'There are only a few guests left, and I'm tired of the atmosphere.' She almost added, 'and Ariadne', but refrained.

'No,' Joel was very definite. 'You've every comfort here. Treescarne's too exposed for the winter. When Christmas is over and with spring coming maybe we'll make the move. Not until then.'

Her chin took a sudden thrust. 'I don't understand. At first you said our private life was to be at the house. Now you hardly allow me up there. Why? I know you're hiding something. And Ariadne—'

'Yes? What about Ariadne?'

'She's forever walking about the moors, near the house. Do you meet her there, Joel?'

'Occasionally, just by chance.'

'And you invite her in.' The short statement held dull acceptance of the situation.

'I do nothing of the sort. As your sister I can hardly send her away with a flea in her ear. But I can assure you—' his lips took a wry wary twist, '—there's nothing going on between us.'

'I didn't suggest it,' she replied coldly.

'No? Well you gave a very good imitation of the jealous wife.'

She turned away. He caught her swiftly and turned her round to face him.

'Don't be a fool,' he said softly. 'I love you, Mrs Blake.' He kissed her, and she softened, went limp against him, thinking, 'and I love *you* Joel. So very much. I wish I didn't.'

The suggestion of course was a lie. In spite of its difficulties, loving Joel was to her the very essence of being alive. When they were not together and she was forced to ride or walk alone, the world seemed desolate, empty; the wild wide expanse of sea and rugged coastline — the brown moors under grey and stormy skies — the boulders and standing stones, relics of a former civilization — held to her heightened fancy menace that was almost a physical threat.

One evening when Joel, later than usual, still had not arrived at Lionswykka by nine o'clock, she saw Ariadne, riding wildly down the moor from the direction of Treescarne, looking like a risen creature of the elements through a fleeting streak of moonlight — cape and pale hair blown back in the wind, head lifted to face the night sky as she gave free rein to her mount.

Caroline, unable to suppress a stab of jealousy, rushed downstairs, and was in the hall waiting, when Ariadne entered the house from the stables.

'Where on earth have you been? Riding at this time?' she asked. 'You look—'

'Yes?'

Caroline shrugged and looked away. Something triumphant and chillingly cynical about her sister's smile, disconcerted her. 'I don't know. I suppose it's not my affair. It's just that I'm not free to gallivant about like you. There are the guests to think about. Joel expects me to be at hand if they want anything, or to amuse them. Sometimes it gets lonely and boring.'

'Then why do it, Caro? Believe me, men may *like* to get chains on a woman, but when they do they often don't want them so much — you should be more independent.'

'What are you suggesting?'

'Nothing, darling. And I don't want your man, your successful ex-chef and restaurant keeper, either. Oh, he's a remarkably splendid physical specimen no doubt. But hardly of my world. I have Willie; remember?'

She patted Caroline's cheek lightly, and walked away, hips and buttocks swaying challengingly. At the foot of the stairs she turned, adding, 'Don't worry. I had a letter from him yesterday.

And I'll be leaving soon. There's nothing like a little absence to fan a man's lust — provided it's not *too* long. And diversion, of course. Your feelings are too obvious, Caro. Why don't you work your charm on that nice Captain Reeves for a bit? He dotes on you. It's quite obvious. Cultivate him, darling, and you'll have Joel eating out of your hand — well *almost* in no time.'

Caroline temporarily ignored her sister's sly comment but later the words returned with added meaning. Perhaps Ariadne was right. Perhaps she *had* been too easily available at any time Joel wanted her. The possibility put her on the defensive, and the next time her husband sought for intercourse, she refused, saying, 'Oh Joel! *please* don't. I'm tired tonight.'

Puzzled, he gave in to her.

The next time it happened, he ravished her with unusual force and ardour, and despite the pain and exhaustion, Caroline was gratified.

At the beginning of November Captain Reeves accepted an invitation to dine at Lionswykka.

The following week Will Perryn was to collect Ariadne and take her back to London, so she dressed extra exotically, but with smart sophistication, determined, despite her apparently sisterly advice to Caroline to have Reeves at her feet for an hour or two, since Joel was hardly likely completely to capitulate to her charms in the short time left to her at Lionswykka.

Caroline also made the most of her fawn-like grace and allure by wearing subtly fitting satin pink.

The evening was unseasonally calm and warm when the Captain arrived. From the dark velvet sky stars glimmered candle-like over the moors as he walked smartly up the terrace steps to the front door. His mount had already been led away by a groom to the stables. From a front window of the drawing room the two women watched curiously, both admiring the slimness and grace of his uniformed figure.

'I thought he'd be in evening dress,' Ariadne said. 'perhaps he should be on duty or something. Or perhaps he just wants to impress you.'

'*Me?* Why should he?'

'Oh, he admires you,' Ariadne replied with a swift sly glance at her sister, 'which you know very well. You could make Joel terrifically jealous.'

'I've no reason or wish to make Joel jealous.'

'You're so sure of him, aren't you?' Ariadne shrugged. 'Maybe not. I suppose I'll have to "take Reeves under my wing" then. What a ridiculous expression! He's certainly out to make an impression. It would be a shame to disappoint the poor darling.'

'I'm sure there's no chance of that with you around,' Caroline retorted quickly.

'That's true, I suppose,' Ariadne agreed. She sighed theatrically. 'I must admit I've a weakness for games — *romantic* games. And men usually respond. It doesn't mean anything though. I've already told you heaps of times I wouldn't hurt Willie for the world. But I'm not like you — I *must* have a bit of excitement in life. There's no harm in it. It's just me.'

The evening however did not entirely go to Ariadne's advantage. From the very beginning, even before the meal, Captain Reeves' attention was diverted time after time from her lively chatter to Caroline, who in contrast appeared exquisitely demure, allowing only occasional stray glances in his direction. Ariadne did her best to appear nonchalant, but at moments her voice had a tart edge to it. Under her lovely smiling exterior Joel sensed chagrin, and was amused.

'Aren't you enjoying yourself?' he asked his sister-in-law once. 'Isn't the party entirely to your liking?'

They were standing near the conservatory, with wine glasses in their hands.

'The party's quite titillating, Joel,' Ariadne answered oversweetly, but with her beautiful eyes fierce as a tiger's between narrowed lids, 'as you should know.' She gave a shrug of her creamy shoulders, 'But to be quite honest I find Caro's intellectual discussions rather boring.' She paused before adding, 'Quite clearly the Captain doesn't. He seems to be obsessed with her.'

Joel's face darkened. 'Rubbish. Reeves has more on his mind than women. So have I.'

'*You*, Joel?'

'And don't play the innocent. You know what I mean. Next week, two days before you leave, there's a very exciting business operation brewing.'

'Business? What business?'

'Something you may enjoy, if it interests you,' Joel replied ambiguously.

'Tell me about it.'

'Later,' Joel said shortly. 'In the meantime be patient; try not to show your feline jealousy too obviously, and smile for God's sake. You've every reason to. You look quite — ravishing.'

Under his admiration Ariadne thawed. Joel's confidence in her — his assumption that she was to be included personally in another — and presumably more important 'adventure' than he'd been involved in previously, titillated her vanity. She didn't press further for information that night, and when the guest had departed was charmingly courteous to her cousin.

'You enslaved the captain completely,' she told Caroline, 'and Joel noticed it. I could see he was jealous.'

'Oh, nonsense,' Caroline retorted, as her delicate pale complexion turned to deepening rose. 'There was nothing to be jealous about, anyway. Captain Reeves and I were just talking. Joel wanted me to be nice to him, and I tried.'

'Such an effort on your part,' Ariadne commented drily. 'But don't try and fool me, darling? You were enjoying yourself.'

'Yes.'

'You see? I told you. What puzzles me is how you two found so much in common so quickly.'

'He's travelled. Not only that — he knows a lot about art, painting and sculpture. He's been even to South Africa and visited the gold fields. You can read about such places of course, but hearing about the circumstances and the way people live, firsthand, is somehow so much more stimulating—'

'Naturally. And why did the gallant Captain bother about gold when he was in the services of his Queen and Country?' There was underlying irony in Ariadne's so-sweet voice. 'Was he leading a double life, darling? If so, beware.' She laughed with a tinkle of real amustment.

'Don't be ridiculous.'

'Oh, but I'm not. He happens to possess a very dignified and quiet exterior, but obviously there's more to it than that. A lot of it's façade, and beneath his courtly manner I suspect — not exactly a wolf in sheep's clothing — but a very iron will. He may even be *using* you, Caro.'

'*Using* me? Don't be stupid. In what way?'

'Don't ask me.' Ariadne turned away, shrugged, and as she left the room added, 'To gain your confidence perhaps, just as Joel is using you to get Reeves.'

'Joel *isn't* using me.'

'No? Of course not. I didn't mean it. Sorry. I was only teasing.'

The door slammed.

Feeling curiously deflated, Caroline went upstairs to bed.

Joel did not retire immediately, but spent sometime in his study before joining his wife. He found her awake, lying staring reflectively at the ceiling. She was looking particularly desirable in a flimsy pink nightgown, and Joel's heart quickened.

'What are you pondering over, love?' he asked when they lay at last side by side in the great bed.

'Just something Ariadne said, about the Captain.'

'Really! And was it complimentary or otherwise? The latter, I expect. You really put her nose out of joint tonight.' A hand enclosed one of her breasts possessively.

Caroline did not respond to the caress, but answered coolly, 'No, she said nothing *against* him. It was merely what he'd done — where he'd been, and when I told her Australia, and Nova Scotia, and to the gold fields, she seemed to think it odd.'

In the darkness Joel's face hardened.

'*Did* she indeed? Why?'

'I don't know. That's the point. Naturally he'd have travelled wouldn't he? Being in the navy.'

'Naturally.' There was a pause between them until Joel continued, 'Forget it. Ariadne can't help being dramatic and very devious. Anyway—' his grasp round her body tightened '—what the hell have gold, Reeves, or Ariadne to do with us?'

With his warmth close against her, a surge of passion rose in her to meet his. In a moment or two the brief conversation with her cousin was forgotten. Only one thing registered — her love for this man who had inexplicably become the one reality of her life.

*

The next day Joel confided his plans to Ariadne. They met at a certain spot some considerable distance from both Lionswykka and Treescarne behind an ancient menhir standing on the far side of the ridge. Joel had been away for the day presumably 'on business' which had been his excuse to Caroline. Ariadne had ridden over there in the later afternoon, telling her cousin impetuously that she needed air, hotel life was becoming boring. Caroline took her word, because she was used to her sister's sudden change of moods. After Ariadne's departure, she tried to settle down for an hour with a book, found it uninteresting, then turned to needlework. But concentration on such mundane tasks was impossible. There was a restlessness in the air that filled her with a wild need for activity. The clouds were storm-tossed across a grey sky. Through the brown undergrowth a wind was rising from the sea, lashing white-crested waves against the cliffs, whipping the furze of hills to an uneasy creaking moan that tore the last leaves from bent trees and bushes. Gulls circled and screamed overhead. There was an elemental threatening quality about the atmosphere that drove Caroline to put on her cloak, saddle her mare, and take the moorland track from Lionswykka towards Treescarne. For too long now, she told herself rebelliously, she'd been denied access to the house by Joel, who had always had some excuse for her to keep away whenever she'd suggested going there. And why? It was her home. She wasn't particularly fond of it, but she knew her suspicions were not unfounded. Joel was up to something. Something in which she was to have no part.

'You wait, love,' he'd said, the last time she'd suggested it, 'when we go back you'll get a surprise.'

'What surprise? Are you having the place redecorated? When I saw it a week ago there seemed no change. Those awful sloes hadn't been cut or taken away, and there was no sign of anyone about, not even Mrs Magor—' She'd broken off, chilled by the anger in his eyes.

'I'd told you not to go that way,' he'd said curtly.

'I know.'

'And why did you?'

'Just *because* of that. You ordered me.'

'I see.' His voice had been grim.

'Joel—' She'd reached out to him pleadingly.

He'd taken her wrist, and staring into her face said coldly, 'When I made an order I mean it. If you persist in flagrantly disobeying me I'll have to lock you up. I don't want to, but I'd have no choice. So get that into your pretty head once and for all, understand?'

Without wincing or taking her eyes from his she'd replied, 'Yes.'

'Good.'

He'd released her and they'd parted, but with the light of battle still in their eyes.

Afterwards, although she'd not taken his threat seriously, the episode had remained in her mind.

Now, feeling suddenly apart, lonely, and anxious for activity, she rode quickly up the slope, crossing the narrow winding lane that led eventually past Treescarne towards the high moorland ridge stretching in a westerly direction towards Penzance.

She had only covered a hundred yards beyond the thread of roadway when a last ray of sunlight streaked from a gap in the clouds, briefly half-blinding her. It was only momentary. Seconds later it had died, but when she drew a hand across her eyes and looked round she saw something.

Something that froze her senses.

High above her, to her left, two figures standing by a clump of gorse, with their horses loosely held by the bridles, were outlined against the stormy background. Then as she watched, the man swept the woman into his arms, until they became just one shape, interlinked for an instant by an intensity emphasised by the tearing wind and darkening light.

The scene wasn't clearly cut. But Caroline, in a wave of disgust and resentment knew.

Joel and Ariadne.

For minutes, after the couple had parted and gone their different ways, swallowed up at last by the deepening vista of approaching storm, Caroline waited irresolutely, numbed and shamed by her own ignorance of the situation, of her refusal not to have recognised the truth earlier. She'd been forced to accept Joel's intrinsic selfishness, but had never doubted his faithfulness. That he'd had women in the past was no secret. He'd told her. But because she'd never known them, they'd not counted — had been mere stepping stones to obtaining his goal.

Ariadne, though, was a different matter. Her own sister! well-born, with a husband high up in society and able to give her all she wanted! — everything, she told herself bitterly, except Joel.

Now apparently, her beauty and sly ways had also captured him.

Disappointment and unhappiness slowly turned to mounting anger. Suddenly Caroline kicked her mare to a gallop, and was riding wildly under the crest of hills in the direction of Penjust. Past boulders and cromlechs, through thickening heather and undergrowth — over streams, narrowly skirting bog holes and jutting mounds of rising earth, horse and rider rushed, racing with wind, clouds and spatter of rain from the sea. Dark forces — the ancient legendary gods of the past seemed to drive and mock her as she passed. A menhir from primitive times appeared to lurch towards her, granite face leering mockingly through tangled brambles. At the first clap of thunder gulls screamed, rising with flapping wings to the sky. By a cut in the cliffs, the mare, with a shrill neigh of fear, reared, caught a hoof in a twisted branch of broken sloe, and threw her.

She lay in pain for moments, her face scratched, and bleeding from a knock on one temple. When at last she managed to rise, the horse had disappeared. She forced herself to her feet, and looked round. Twilight was quickly fading to angry evening. Slightly ahead of her, the dark shape of a ruined building – either part of an old mine-house, or a derelict chapel, loomed starkly above a wilderness of thorn and twisted trees. She recognised the place as one of evil reputation and strange hauntings. Few dared go there, except an occasional vagabond or thief wanting refuge. She, herself, hadn't believed in any ghosts or malignant spirits. Now she certainly needed refuge from the increasing rain and lashing winds. Her ankle had been twisted. Rest might help. She could at least tear a strip of material from an underskirt to bind it before making the effort to reach Treescarne or Lionswykka. How she'd do it, she didn't know, or how far she'd travelled over the wild sweep of moor. In the meantime, the horse, Diamond, might return.

Limping painfully she made her way to the overgrown gap of the door. A streak of lightning suddenly caught a holed window, giving it a fleeting look of malignant life.

She tottered once as she pushed thorns and twigs barring the entrance, then lowered herself painfully on to a lump of granite. There was a rustling as a mouse or some other wild thing scuttled by. Automatically she brushed the wet hair from her eyes, and at that moment a figure from the far corner lurched towards her. There was no way of distinguishing his features, but from the thickening smell of alcohol and the throaty chuckle of his voice, she knew that the man – whoever he was, was drunk. She pulled herself to her feet again, turned, trying to run, but her ankle gave way, and in a second she had fallen.

His heavy form was suddenly upon her, pulling at her clothes, his great body heaving upon her breasts and stomach. She clawed, scratched and kicked. The vile face came closer – closer and closer upon hers, until his thick lips were smothering her mouth, draining the breath from her body. Only one thing registered clearly before a great hand was thrust over her eyes – a jagged scar running from a temple to his jaw. As her skirt was pulled from her thighs, she managed to bring a knee hard against his stomach. He yelled and momentarily lessened his grip. Terror gave her strength. She searched the ground wildly and found a lump of stone nearby. He lurched again towards her but was defeated as the granite came hard against his head. With a groan he rolled over, the blood trickling to the damp earth.

Forgetting her strained ankle, not caring whether or not she'd killed her attacker, Caroline struggled to her feet, clutching at stones and tangled undergrowth for support. He hadn't managed to rape her, she thought wildly in a wave of relief. Thank God for that. But if he had it would have been Joel's fault. Joel, whom she'd trusted but who'd betrayed her with Ariadne.

She made her way blindly, by instinct over the rough moor towards Treescarne, occasionally resting to get her breath. By a broken half-circles of standing stones that had once witnessed pagan rites in a past age, she sat down with her back pressed against a leaning granite slab.

It was now eerily dark. From the distance odd lights seemed to twinkle for a moment then die again, blurred by rushing wind through coils of rising mist. All sense of direction was gone. Once she managed to form a tunnel of her hands and call bleakly. 'Joel — Joel—' until the senselessness of the effort registered. What was the use? Joel was with Ariadne. She was alone physically and in spirit, except for the ghostly mocking legions of those who'd once fought for existence and lived there — those primitive inhabitants of earliest Cornwall — the dark sturdy Celts of forgotten history.

As the grey air surged round her, forms took shape in her distorted imagination. The crying of birds and soughing of wind echoed desolately through her mind and heart. Her whole form felt chilled rigid, empty of purpose. She put an arm about the granite and half pulled herself upright. Then she fell back. She couldn't go back. She just couldn't. She was lying there when Joel found her, scratched and bruised, half-naked, and shivering with cold.

At first he could hardly believe his eyes. One breast was bare through her ripped bodice, her thighs, in the muddied torn pantaloons were half naked. She opened her eyes wide when he bent down and pulled her up to face him.

'In God's name what's this? What the devil's happened?' he asked, roughly because of the shock.

'Oh, Joel—' she answered, 'it was awful. He tried to – he tried—' She broke off, as he shook her.

'What?' he repeated. 'Who? Have you been—'

'No *no*.' The interruption was so wild and vehement he had to believe her. But a niggle of doubt drove him to continue ruthlessly, 'What were you doing up here?' He shook her again. 'Answer me. His name? Answer me or by God I'll—'

'Stop, *stop*. I don't know—' her teeth chattered. 'I was just having a ride—'

'What do you mean? A *ride*!' Anger was mounting in him.

'On Diamond. But she – she threw me and ran away. And then—'

'Well?' His voice was hard. 'Continue—'

But she couldn't. Suddenly the world seemed to topple, and go blank. Her figure fell limp against his arm. He lifted her up, staring hard through the misted night into her face. Her pallor even through the darkness was unmistakable. She had fainted.

Holding her firm against him, he made his way to a small thicket where he'd tethered his own stallion.

It was a mercy, he thought, that he'd had an assignation with one of his confederates that evening, otherwise he might never have found her. It didn't occur to him – there was no reason – that the man concerned had been Barney Swale, one of his gang, who was now, quite unknown to him, lying unconscious in the derelict ruin. Had he guessed the truth Joel might have returned and killed him with his two hands. But his one thought at the moment was to get Caroline safely home to Lionswykka. In minutes they were back, a little later she recovered consciousness and except for the hurt ankle and a cut by one temple, there seemed nothing wrong with her. Unfortunately she could answer none of Joel's questions. Details of the distressing incident had been completely erased from her mind. All she could recall was of riding away and seeing Ariadne in Joel's arms; of a fall, and then – nothing.

It didn't matter to her. Nothing mattered.

Joel at first did his best to comfort her. She turned away, and he, disgruntled, felt a dull stab of anger rising.

The seeds of jealousy had already been sewn, providing a pattern that was to alter the course of their lives.

7

The few days before Ariadne's departure passed quickly for Joel, but slowly for Caroline whose painful memories of betrayal drove all other matters from her mind. She lived in a dull world of disillusionment and disgust, allowing no intimacy at all between Joel and herself, keeping aloof from her half-sister, enforcing the brooding hatred for the beauty that had ruined her life. Or so she thought. Commonsense died into such a dark sense of failure in herself and distrust of Joel, that she could hardly bear to eat with them and had most meals in her room.

When Ariadne apologised hypocritically for her presence, saying she was afraid she'd caused disgruntlement, but would soon be gone, which was as well, Joel told her abruptly to stop talking nonsense. He needed her, not only as a woman, but as a partner.

'We shall be short-handed on Monday,' he said. 'I know I can depend on you to give a hand.'

'Of course, Joel.'

'The cargo should be delivered about nine by the cove,' he continued, 'according to the light and the tide. There should be no moon. I'll be short of a man, and daren't risk having anyone else involved. You know the ropes of the business well enough by now; there are a youth's clothes ready. If you're willing to take the risk — and there's always a certain amount — you're my man. But if you want to keep out I'll understand.'

'As if I would,' she exclaimed, with her eyes alight and her heart quickening.

'What?'

'Want to keep out.'

He grinned. 'I thought not.'

'And what do I get in return?' she asked. 'If it's a business deal, Joel, I've got a right to know.'

'You mercenary baggage. A small share of the profit, as I said earlier.'

'And what else?' She edged forward, easing her gown a fraction lower towards one white breast.

He pulled the dress into place again firmly.

'Enough of what you want to keep you satisfied when you lie with that cold fish of a husband,' he answered. 'But until then no games, understand? Keep your lusting heart and body to yourself, or you'll be out on your ear, the same as any other who plays me false.'

She flushed and said coldly, 'Why are you a man short, Joel? Did *he* let you down?'

'In a manner of speaking,' Joel replied sullenly. 'He got himself nearly dead through poaching on my own territory.'

'How?'

'What's that to you?'

She faced him stubbornly. 'As much right as *you* have to involve me in your illegal adventures.'

A smile of unwilling admiration lit his eyes. A quirk of amusement touched his lips.

'Maybe you're right.'

'And maybe you should have married *me* instead of Caroline,' she said boldly.

His face hardened. 'I think not, we're too much alike. Two of a kind — quite without conscience. You're a bitch — a beautiful one — but a bitch all the same. I wouldn't trust you an inch if I didn't know you'd too much to lose if you betrayed me. A word in Perryn's ear and the high-and-mighty lady business would be over as soon as he could contact his lawyers. Apart from that—'

'Yes?'

'Now you're in this thing you're damn well enjoying it. A spot of danger's just your cup of tea. *I* know it — you know it. So let's not discuss pros and cons any more. The fool of a man whose place you'll take is no matter. He'll be no concern of mine from now on. Contraband business needs cool heads and no drunks to see it through. Remember that.'

'I'll see to it,' she answered. 'So long as you remember *your* promise.'

The insolent minx, he thought. As though she could tie him down, or in any way jeopardise his life with Caroline.

Caro.

The memory of her aloof contempt momentarily set his senses alight. When all this business was over he'd get her to his bed again even if he had to beat her into submission. And then, by God! how he'd love her.

In the meantime at the appointed hour she'd be safely in the company of the devious vicar, and Reeves if he was in the vicinity at the time. He'd already had an invitation to the cleric's house for that evening, but had seemed doubtful. However, as Caroline would be there Joel had a shrewd idea the Captain would find it possible to attend. If so, all to the good. The plan was set. At eight forty-five precisely Joel had arranged to be called away on the pretext that a friend from the North – an engineer – had arrived at Treescarne to discuss with Joel the reopening of an old tin mine in the district. He would regret-fully take his departure, leaving his wife to be accompanied later by Reeves back to Lionswykka. The Captain could be depended upon to take special care of her especially in view of the serious shock she'd had so recently.

By the time he left the hotel, the smuggling operation would be over. Should the Captain not attend the vicar's little party, Joel would have to collect her. But he doubted there'd be the need.

This prediction proved correct.

Reeves, for once in his life, apparently, outwitted by Joel's devious and cunning plans, and increasingly fascinated by the flower-like Caroline Blake who from his first meeting with her had so stirred his imagination, could only feel a sense of relief when the messenger arrived at the rectory telling Blake of the unexpected visitor to Treescarne.

'He has to be gone before marnin', surr,' the man said sufficiently loudly for the Captain to overhear, 'Says he has to be at Redruth early, so's to get away again up North. Et sounded important — sumthen to do with that theer old mine.'

A minute later the parlour door opened. Reeves looked up, as Joel apologetically explained. There was no flicker of excitement on his face. His expression appeared completely normal and genuine, except for a frown of assumed regret that the party should be disrupted so early.

'Wonder if you could see my wife safely back to Lionswykka?' he asked. 'I *may* be able to fetch her of course, but I doubt it.'

'Oh, I think perhaps it would be better if I left now,' Caroline interrupted quickly. 'I'm a little tired still — from that — that fall I had. And—'

'Nonsense, nonsense,' the Reverend Barnaby Treverne told her, smiling benignly. 'The pleasure of young company, dear lady, is so seldom bestowed on these bachelor premises of mine, it would be most distressing to lose it before absolutely necessary. Do continue to grace my homely dwelling for a little longer. The Captain, I'm sure, as well as myself, will much appreciate the honour if you do.'

Uncomfortably aware of Reeves' eyes on her face, yet secretly flattered, Caroline half-heartedly agreed.

When Joel had left, and under the comforting influence of a glass of Treverne's specially brewed wine — Caroline at length relaxed, and began to enjoy the Captain's courteous attention. So different from Joel, she thought, who more often than not worked her up to a pitch of tension and excitement that left her feeling curiously depleted one moment, and the next transported to longing and ecstasy. Not that the latter had been the case recently, she told herself with a stab of bitterness. Since the 'accident', as she termed it, he had appeared more often than not angry and aloof, regarding her with unspoken condemnation that roused a mood of hostility in her. She knew he didn't believe her explanation of the attack on the moor, and in her turn she didn't accept his assertion that there was no serious relationship between himself and Ariadne. They had come to

an impasse — a situation that it would take a long time to
resolve, if ever.

Reeves, whose official 'nose' told him that despite everything
and the social mood, somewhere, somehow, something was
wrong, nevertheless kept his sneaking suspicions well hidden.
Duty and pleasure continued to war in his mind. But for the
time being he was content to let the latter take over. Without
positive proof he'd no excuse for leaving the lovely fragile-
looking young Caroline Blake to the unscrupulous attentions of
the portly lecherous clergyman, who was a dastardly character
if ever there was one, he told himself, eyeing the two of them
warily. For some time he'd doubted the cunning cleric's affability, had been positive of his duplicity and illegal methods of
imbuing his income. But so far there'd been no proof. One day,
though, he'd catch him. And if he was in league with Blake,
he'd have Joel as well. Would Caroline suffer by it? How much
was she in love with the jumped up stranger — the greedy adventurer she'd married? They certainly hadn't appeared on particularly amicable terms that evening, but the young wife's eyes
had strayed at moments to Joel's with something in them — a
yearning, longing and admiration that had sent a stab of envy
through the Captain's being.

He'd quickly diverted her attention, searching the lovely
languid eyes for some response. There was hurt in them — a hurt
which that buccaneer fellow Blake probably never even noticed,
damn and blast him, he thought savagely. In spite of the habitual
self-discipline of his rank, career, and age — the Captain was now
forty, and past calf-love — a wish to protect and cherish the lovely
young creature now left briefly in his charge, gradually deepened
in him to acute and aching desire. Yet he controlled the new and
bewildering emotion under a façade of polite friendliness to
which she responded innocently with charming frankness.

'Are you happy living in that magnificent hotel, Mrs Blake?'
he asked once. 'It's very picturesque of course and in the summer must be enjoyable. With the Winter coming on—' he
paused, adding a moment later, 'but there'll still be a few guests
about, I suppose.'

'We — Joel's — hoping for a busy time then,' Caroline answered. 'The trips to the Island will be stopped when the weather's bad. But the light here in Cornwall is beginning to attract quite a lot of artists and wealthy people. So I shouldn't be lonely. Anyway after Christmas we're retiring to Treescarne.'

'Are you looking forward to that?'

His glance was searching; her eyes were reflective, her voice dubious, when she replied, 'I don't know. Everything's so—' She broke off, and smiled before continuing 'I was going to say strange. But that's silly, isn't it?'

'Not at all. I'd use the same word myself. Your husband's a strong character, dedicated to his goal. There are naturally times when you find life quite a challenge. Well, there's nothing wrong with that provided other people don't have to suffer through it.'

Her manner instantly became defensive.

'Why should you say that, Captain Reeves?'

He shook his head slowly.

'You must know. I'm quite astute at assessing character.'

'But—'

He touched her hand gently.

'Don't misunderstand me. I'm not criticising — I just hope we can be friends, and that if ever you find yourself in a position needy of advice, you'll remember I'm at your service, and will help in any way possible.'

The faint colour in her face deepened to rose.

'It's kind of you to offer — and I — I *will* remember,' she told him, 'but I can't see any difficulties ahead, not really. It's just that—'

'Yes?'

'Oh nothing. You're really *very* kind. I do appreciate it.'

The short conversation was ended at that point by the vicar's return to the room, with a decanter of fresh wine on a tray.

'No need to be gloomy because that colourful and admirable Mr Joel Blake has most unfortunately been called away,' he said with obsequious affability. 'Do rest, dear lady. This home brew believe me, will help you to relax. It is, shall we say, of both medical and social value.'

'Oh no. Thank you — I'm not used to wine. And I'm rather tired.' She made an effort to smile naturally, 'It's kind of you, but soon I should be getting back to Lionswykka.'

The cleric threw up his hands, shaking his head. 'If you mean that, I have to accept it,' he said, 'but pray have no thought of departing so soon.' He turned a head to the window. 'The wind seems to be rising. I do hope we're not in for a gale. Horses can be temperamental sometimes in such circumstances, and the high lane is very bleak for carriages.'

'I imagine Mr Blake's horses are competent to behave safely,' the Captain said drily, 'and that the Lionswykka vehicle is completely in order. In my charge Mrs Blake will be safe. She has only to say when she wishes to return and I'm at her service.'

Caroline glanced at him gratefully.

'Thank you.'

He touched her hand briefly.

'No thanks are needed. I'll ride my own mount in case any cut-throats, or brigands happen to be about the moor.' He cast a fleeting glance at their host.

The Reverend Treverne appeared mildly displeased. 'We see few such unpleasant characters round here, sir,' he remarked shortly. 'Being in Holy Orders as I am, has an adverse effect on evil doers who make it their business to be away from my domain and surrounding land.'

Reeves gave a quick bow signifying nothing.

'I'm glad to hear it.'

The atmosphere had changed subtly from one of forced conviviality to wary defensiveness. Sensing it, Caroline remarked politely, 'Perhaps after all, I will have a little of your wine, Mr Treverne. But only a *very* little — just a taste.'

Immediately the clergyman was once more all bounce and good humour. 'Certainly — certainly. It's made of elderflower. Fragrant — a nectar of the gods one could say — very potent, so you shall have your wish: a mere taste to titillate your senses.'

The rest of the evening passed agreeably enough for Caroline

— not so much because of the wine, but because of the deepening feeling between herself and the Captain. He didn't allow himself to be too lavish with compliments, but at any available opportunity his hand contacted her arm or shoulder lightly for a fraction of time, and she was aware, confusedly, of a warm glow stirring her senses, including gratitude to him for making her feel a desirable woman again — something Joel had quite failed to do recently. Gradually as the minutes ticked by, she found herself not wishing to leave. If she could have been certain of a genuine welcome from Joel when she reached the hotel, circumstances would never have taken the trend they did. But she faced the fact that he would probably be only half aware of her presence on his return. She was becoming starved of attention and affection. His moods were so unpredictable she could never rely on a warm response when she needed it.

But John Reeves was in quite a different category. She suspected he was already falling in love with her, and knew that it would be very easy for her to turn to him in affection. He was a strong man, but understanding. *Kind*.

And she needed kindness just then.

*

Joel, meanwhile had reached Treescarne in the least possible time. His mind and senses were already alight with excitement, his will firmly under control, as he walked along the hall and took the bend up the stairs with the speed of a panther. Mrs Magor was already safely ensconced in her quarters, as planned. Peter Dory, wearing rough breeches, jacket, and high boots was waiting below in the cellars. At the bend of landing leading to a small arms room where Joel keeps guns, and other male weapons and articles useful for such secret occasions, a slim figure shrouded in a cloak, emerged from the shadows swaggering with an insolent air towards him. A woollen black cap covered the hair. Astonishment made him pause.

'What the hell—?'

He broke off as the cap was wrenched from the head. The cloak fell back. Tall, slim, clad in breeches, and seaman's boots, with her hair touched to pale fire in the glow of an oil lamp behind her, stood Ariadne, looking for all the world more like some legendary Rosalind resurrected from Shakespeare than a creature of flesh and blood.

'Hello, Joel,' she said.

Stirred by her beauty, but angry with himself for the rush of physical emotion that temporarily swept everything else into oblivion, he retorted gruffly, 'You were told to join Peter below then follow to meet the others. This isn't a game. Go on. Get away from here immediately, you minx—' He grabbed her arm, pulled her towards him and would have pushed her away, but she reached up and both hands were round his neck, her lovely taunting lips raised to his.

'Take me, Joel — take me, take me. You want it. I know it — just once—'

For seconds Joel stared into her eyes, his heart thumping with a wild untamed desire. The next moment his lips were on hers, not in love, but savagely, hungry as the rising elements of wind and driven rain from the storm-swept sky outside. Then abruptly, he released her, forcing her from him.

'You slut,' he said. 'You lusting whore. Stop it, Ariadne, before I have my riding crop about your back.'

She laughed in his face, white teeth gleaming, stubborn chin out-thrust, head thrown back defiantly giving the seductive lines of her figure added allure under the rough jerkin.

'You're a fool, Joel Blake,' she said softly. 'You need me as I need you — in *every* way. And don't threaten me. One day — sometime — I'll have you at my feet.'

His hand was suddenly smartly against a cheek — she drew back abruptly, and there was no longer any smile left on her lips.

'One day you'll pay for that,' she said. 'Tonight I'll—'

'Tonight you'll damn well do what you came to do and help remove those kegs,' he told her roughly. 'That's what you were hired for — trollop. Now — go on, get on down down those stairs, and tell young Davy I'll join him in five minutes.'

Mutely, half blind with fury, she pushed by, wrenching the

cloak from her shoulders and flinging it in his face. That she obeyed was from instinct only, the instinct for adventure, but some day, somehow, she knew she'd have revenge. The revenge of a woman humiliated to the point, almost, of madness.

By the time she reached the cellars and had entered the tunnel personal grievances had been allayed temporarily by the immediate business of the operation in hand. She worked tire-lessly and speedily as a man, aware only at moments of Joel's intermittent presence. Once through the darkness, the glimmer of a candle lit his eyes to sparks of fire. For a second they held hers, and she knew with a leap of triumph there was admiration in his glance. She turned away quickly, intent only on the laborious task of helping remove keg after keg to Peter and a more experienced confederate. There was no sound above the low rumbling of wood over stone, which with the moaning of wind and breaking of waves from the sea below held the menac-ing impression of an ever-encroaching thunderstorm.

By the time the bold operation was completely over, all signs of fitful moonlight had died over the black Atlantic. By then the small boats were safely away, the valuable cargo stored and effectively hidden in the upper cellars under the kitchens, and the men mostly gone their different ways through the darkness over the moor. Joel decided to remain at Treescarne for the night. In the morning, inevitably, he'd have to give some reason for his absence to Caroline. Well, he decided, mounting the stairs to the main bedroom, he had the excuse of the fictitious guest. She'd have to accept it, whether she believed in it, or not.

He almost forgot about Ariadne.

But when he opened the door she was there, already half naked, with her beautiful breasts bare, and the boys' breeches fallen to the floor. She stepped out of them, smiled briefly and said, 'Well, Joel dear, here I am. Quite successful, wasn't it? You really *are* a most daring man.' She moved towards him and opened her arms. 'Take me, darling.'

He paused, but only for a moment. Then he said, taking two strides towards her with a malicious smile on his lips, 'By God, I will, madam, and after it you'll never wish to look on me again.'

He ravished her effectively, and without love, uncaring of his abuse, as he would have raped any conscienceless whore who'd betrayed him.

Afterwards, bruised and smarting, she repeated her old threat. 'You'll pay for this, Joel Blake. One day I swear you'll pay.'

He laughed.

'I think not. It's *you* who'll foot the bill if there's any paying to do. But I don't imagine there'll be the need. I've had what I want of you. If you've any sense at all you'll make sure your so-useful Willie doesn't get to know anything of this unsavoury little episode. Now — get out if you please. Dress yourself, and before it's light see you're safely abed at Lionswykka. Go on, do as you're told before you find my boot at your so charming posterior. There are plenty of bedrooms at your disposal.'

White-faced, she fled from the room, hating and wanting to kill him. He stood motionless for minutes, a rigid hard figure, as though carved from stone. Then he shrugged his shoulders, laughed, and took a whisky flask from his pocket. To hell with all women, he thought. This one had only got what she deserved. As for Caroline — a faint tinge of shame touched him. He hadn't hurt her though; there was no reason why she should know anything about it. Men, after all, had different values from women; with which comforting philosophy he took a liberal swig of the neat spirit and flung himself on the bed.

It was some time before Joel had calmed down sufficiently to realise that he could have endangered his future through his contemptuous treatment of Ariadne. He knew enough of women to know that her type did not forget. A word in the ear of Sir William could easily put a stop to his remunerative occupation. But he hardly thought she'd take the risk. Eventually he, Joel Blake, held the trump card. Ariadne had as much — even more than himself — to lose by divulging a suspicion of the truth. Before she left Lionswykka, he'd play a subtle game of patience that would effectively write off any devious plan of blackmail between them. Then, when she'd gone, he'd make it his business to bring Caroline back to his arms again, not forcefully, as had been his intention at first, but using every male art he knew to soften and woo her.

To his surprise Caroline did not appear in the least anxious or tired when he met her the following morning coming from the conservatory with a single pink hot-house blossom pinned at her corsage, and with another in her hand. She was looking quite lovely in pale greenish grey that gave her a misleading ethereal quality, very different from Ariadne's striking beauty.

He cleared his throat before speaking, then he said, 'You look – rather nice in that thing—' indicating the gown.

'You mean my dress?' she smiled slightly, but her voice was aloof, composed. 'Yes. It arrived the other day – from London. I sent for it.'

Joel's eyebrows shot up. 'You did?'

'On my mother's advice. As a birthday present. She paid.'

'Your *birthday*? I didn't know.'

'How could you? I've never told you. There was no point.'

'Hm!' He paused before adding, 'Is it today then?'

'No. Another week yet. You've plenty of time, Joel.'

'Time?'

'To give me an outing. Truro perhaps? I need a new bonnet. Unless, of course, you have to economise.'

'Economise?' He looked bewildered. 'Why? What the devil do you mean?'

She gave a tinkle of laughter and passed him by with a show of amusement – of coquetry – he'd never seen in her before.

Glancing back she retorted meaningfully, 'Your little business deals must be – uncertain sometimes. Risky even. I wouldn't want to embarrass you.'

Now what did she mean by that? At any other time Joel would have followed her; but her unexpected change of mood, her perspicacity, took him quite aback. He stood watching her for a moment then turned on his heel abruptly and went to the study. Broodingly, he reviewed events of the evening. There was nothing to complain about. Everything had gone to plan; so far as he knew there had been no hitch anywhere. His picket had been reimbursed considerably, and it would be an easy matter to fool the vicar into accepting a far less percentage of the spoils than was his due according to the agreement. The lively interlude with Ariadne had eventually put her in her proper place. She knew where she stood, and wouldn't try any more devious tricks. Reeves, apparently, had proved himself gullible in the face of his — Joel's — cunning. Partly due to Caroline, of course.

Caro.

She was the one snag in his new adventurous career. Not because she could interfere in any future plans, but because — dammit — confounded nuisance as she was, he loved her. He'd thought the passion between them mutual, had taken it for granted.

Now here she was flinging airy suggestions in his face, indicating his wishes weren't, after all, so important to her as he'd believed.

A new bonnet indeed, and a trip to Truro! That saucy half defiant look in her eyes! What had she been up to? Reeves? Had they played about in his absence? Or was it that other licentious brute who'd tried to rape her on the moor? She'd put on a fine show of not remembering anything. But was it genuine? Had she really forgotten — or was it just evasion? There was no way of telling. She could have had a lover who'd gone rough on her. Women were secretive, cunning creatures, and he'd had so many things on his mind recently the thought of infidelity on her part had never occurred to him. When his first anger at the idea subsided, allowing him to face the situation more objectively, he saw she'd had cause to be fretful. But unfaithful? No. His own self-confidence and pride refused to accept it. She was cool with him simply because her nose had been put out of joint through Ariadne.

Well, Ariadne was leaving in two days; after that maybe he'd put himself out more to please and flatter his wife. A little outing could do both of them good, and he'd manage somehow to combine business with pleasure.

With facts neatly pigeon-holed in their proper places again, he put all emotional problems to the back of his mind, and gave full attention to hotel and other business.

One thing he had not foreseen — the full bitterness of Ariadne's hatred for him, or the fact that she would never rest until she'd had revenge for the humiliation inflicted.

8

During the brief time before her departure, Ariadne was outwardly non-committal and coldly polite to Joel, although plans to outwit him and somehow bring him to shame, or at least to his knees, were simmering wildly through her mind. Rejection and insulting behaviour from any man was a completely new experience to her. She hated him.

Strolling about the moor for a last walk before Willie collected her the following day, she was lucky enough to meet the Captain quite by chance, riding from the kiddleywink below, following a tip that shady business was brewing at the inn. He doffed his hat when he saw her, and stopped for a few words.

'Good afternoon, Lady Perryn,' he said, thinking how very smart and colourful she appeared in jade green velvet, with a small tricorne hat perched forward saucily on her pale hair. A veil floated from the back, light as gossamer in the rising breeze. 'Beautiful weather for the time of year. I'm surprised you're not riding.'

She informed him, with a note of regret in her voice, that her husband was expected during the evening, and that they were leaving Lionswykka in the early morning.

'I wondered if there was any sprig of heather still blooming,' she said, 'just a reminder of Cornwall to take back with me to dreary London. So I thought I'd walk.'

He dismounted and holding his mount by the bridle, asked, 'Have you enjoyed your stay here?'

Her eyes widened.

'Of *course*. I don't care for sophisticated life very much, and Willie's — my husband's — friends *are* rather boring.' She lifted a hand to her mouth in feigned embarrassment. 'Oh dear! how disloyal I must sound. I didn't mean to. But you see—' She paused, puckering her brows as though some problem was worrying her.

'Yes?'

She let out a sigh. 'There's something else. My sister. Caroline — Mrs Blake. I'm very fond of her.'

Reeves' face showed no trace of the sudden irrational emotion her very name evoked in him.

'Naturally,' he remarked. 'You'll miss her, I expect.'

'It isn't only that. It's — well, to be quite honest, Captain, I don't *entirely* trust Joel, her husband. If I knew you could keep an eye on her — in just a friendly way, of course, I'd feel so much happier.'

Reeves was puzzled.

'Is something wrong then? What are you worried about?' Before answering, Ariadne glanced round conspiratorially, as though to be sure no one was around, then continued in rushed half-whispered tones, 'I can't put a finger on it, *exactly*. But I believe—' She lifted her head higher, staring him straight in the face. 'In fact I *know* that in some strange way Joel Blake is playing a double game. No—' She lifted a hand. 'I've no way of proving it, and I don't want to make accusations that would cause hurt to Caro, but it's my belief that he's made fools of us all, and is making quite an illegal fortune out of contraband. It isn't my business to interfere, and I don't want my name mentioned, but if you're wise, Captain, you'll watch Treescarne *very* carefully, and keep an eye on the island too.'

She smiled sweetly, with the fading sunlight emphasising her brilliant eyes and flash of teeth.

'Now I must be on my way,' she added, 'and if I've spoken of things you don't wish to know, please forget I ever said anything. Good day, and good luck. It's been so very pleasant knowing you.'

She turned and walked on, a bright figure against the brown

moors and fading sky, hips swaying below the narrow waist of her jacket, and soft velvet folds of skirt.

'A beauty,' he thought, with brief admiration, but one he wouldn't trust an inch, although the thought suddenly struck him that there might be truth in her suggestive comments. He'd felt the same himself about the man from the first moment of meeting him. If it hadn't been for Caroline he'd have kept a tighter watch on things going on in the immediate vicinity. But he hadn't wanted her involved; so in a way he'd failed in his duty. Well, in future the situation could be remedied. No woman in the world — not even one he'd grown to care for so warmly, was going to restrain him from exerting his authority as an officer of the law.

If Blake was up to anything he'd see him in jail should the necessity arise, and good riddance on Caroline's behalf.

The decision made him feel better. A moment later he'd kicked his mount to a swift canter, and was on the way back to the inn to make enquiries about a suspicious character calling himself Black Dirke.

The landlord was at the bar when he went in. A conjurer — or witch — as he was known locally — was spinning a yarn about how a potion of his taken at sunset could cure warts and other malformities so long as his name was mentioned while the sufferer bowed three times to the west.

'Don' expec' a cure immediately,' he was careful to add. 'There weeks at most, an' all the devil's work on 'ee will be gone.'

One or two present believed him, others stared sceptically, but all listened. A sailor winked at a miner and said, 'Danny Figgins 'll be gone by then — half way to Ireland mebbe.'

There was laughter, but a few small coins dropped into Danny's hat.

Conversation and laughter died suddenly when the Captain appeared. An air of furtive caution and resentment descended. A prostitute seated in a shadowed corner on a seaman's knee, drew her bodice tightly over a bared ripe breast. One man, a tinner, wiped his mouth with the back of his hand, put his tankard down and left. A thin wind from the sea rocked the oil lamp hanging by the door as he went out.

'Black Dirke?' the landlord queried, after Reeves had questioned him, 'Never heard of 'im. There edn' no-one o' that name comes in 'eer. P'raps—' his small eyes glinted slily, 'someone's had 'ee on, maister. Rare enough wild tales gets abut, an' that's for sure.'

His remarks were confirmed by the rest of the inmates.

'No, sorry, Capn', the name don't ring a bell anywhere.'

'Can't say I ever seen nor eared o' such a chap.'

'Such characters doan hang abut 'ere, to my knowledge. Would 'elp you ef I could, but I never come across a Black Dirke anywhere.'

'Mebbe you'd have more luck Penzance way, or Falmouth p'raps. Them's the places for rascals o' that kind.'

'Well—' Reeves gave them all a hard glance. 'If you do happen to hear his name mentioned concerning any rascally deal — let me know, and I'll see you're the richer for it.'

One man started to speak, then hastily retreated into silence again. Realising no pact was possible, the Captain left, saying at the door, 'If I find out any of you have lied, there'll be trouble. Defying justice is a crime, so don't you forget it. I'll get my man in the end — *and* you, if necessary.'

There was the slam of the door, and presently the echo of horses' hooves had died into the booming of waves against the cliffs and moaning of the rising wind.

Black Dirke, no doubt, was lying low for a while, Reeves told himself. But a time would come when he'd be back at his dirty game again. If he turned out to be Blake, maybe it would be all for the best. There was no proof yet, only a doubting suspicion. Whichever way it was, he had a hunch that Caroline would be far better off without her colourful brigand of a husband. Poor girl! — poor? But she was lovely, warm and rich with potential for loving. Loving that at the moment was being wasted on that bounder, Joel. The man had guts, and certainly looks. He was daring, ambitious, quite immoral and without conscience.

Larger than life. A challenge to society and the law. He knew the type, though he'd never met one of Joel's calibre before.

If he could get him behind bars! – the suggestion sent a wave of determination through him. By God! life was only just beginning. Eventually if he had his way, he'd have Caroline safe and warm in his arms.

To that end he dedicated himself.

*

Ariadne's farewell to Caroline and Joel was hypocritically effusive. 'I do so *hate* leaving,' she gushed. 'It's been simply lovely seeing you two, but of course to be with darling Willie again means so much to me—' She glanced coyly at Sir William, whose fair moustache and beard partially concealed a weak chin and mouth, adding elegance and an air of nobility to his slight figure under the caped coat. Only a glimpse of the cream satin waistcoat could be seen. He wore a high collar over a spotted white starched shirt, and at the neck a gold necktie echoed his gingerish colouring. In his hand he held a tall black silk hat.

He smiled at his wife's upturned radiant face. If his narrowed pale eyes were a little cold, no one noticed it, except Joel.

'An odd fish,' he thought, mildly sorry, briefly, for Ariadne, 'but all the same, I'm not going to get on the wrong side of him.'

'Hope you'll both come one day,' he said cordially.

'Oh *I* shall – never doubt,' Ariadne remarked, with an acid glance at him. 'Nothing is going to keep me parted from my sister for so long again.'

Her smile was brittle, her composure complete. With a reflective quirk of wry amusement Joel recalled the abandonment of her passionate advances to him, and the humiliation she'd received. Oh, she'd not forgotten, and was not the type to forgive; he fully expected she'd make an attempt to get her own back one day, but couldn't see her succeeding. However, much as she despised her husband as a man, she was in awe of the prestige in being his wife, and knew she could go so far, but no further in her flirtatious games. Once Sir William caught her properly out, her role in his life would be over. He might turn a blind eye to her swarm of admirers, but as a cuckold, never.

So Joel felt completely free of her letting the cat out of the bag just to spite him and wound Caroline.

'Well,' he said to his wife, when the couple had left, 'that's over, and I'm quite relieved to see the last of them. For the time being of course.'

Caroline was standing by the window, from where they'd watched the chaise moving away down the drive. Her silhouette was exquisite against the morning light. Old desire rose in Joel to have her once again in his arms, to feel sensuous pleasure in possessing this lovely creature.

She half turned her head over her shoulder. A ray of sunlight glistened in a halo round the soft sheen of her light brown hair, touching it to gold.

'Oh?' she queried, 'I thought you got on extremely well with Ariadne.'

He moved up behind her, caressing her neck gently with the tips of his fingers, then kissed the faintly perfumed flesh.

'We understood each other,' he said. 'She's a type I know well.'

Her heart started to hammer.

'What type?'

'Beautiful, brash, and completely immoral,' he replied.

'I don't know why you say that — especially about my sister.' She shrugged. 'But of course with your great knowledge of women—'

He laughed, tightened his arm around her and swung her round. As usual and against her will, the contact made her faintly dizzy.

'Jealous?' he enquired teasingly.

She pulled herself free, and with her head up in a show of impatience, walked to the door, saying, 'Don't be ridiculous.'

In two seconds he was in front of her, and before she knew it had lifted her in his arms.

'Ridiculous?' he echoed. 'I'll soon show you what's ridiculous and what's not.'

He paused for a moment to see no servant was about, then carried her speedily on light feet upstairs to the main bedroom. In a show of indignation she rushed to the door, but found it already locked.

He approached her again, and his voice was quieter, yet more stern when he said, 'Don't try and escape, darling, and don't tell me you have a headache. For once, my love, you'll be sweet and obliging to your loving husband.'

There was little sweetness in her ultimate surrender, the tide of passion in her was too dark and strong, his mastery and power over her thrilling with a delight and despair she'd never known before.

When it was over and they lay at peace, he said, 'Now you know who's master here. And don't forget it, Caro. Nothing matters but us. You and I together, and nothing will come between — no woman, or man in the world. If he does, I'll kill him.'

She said nothing, just lay, staring at the ceiling.

His last statement had held a deadly ring about it and she knew he'd meant it. Knew too, that as far as she was concerned, for the present, anyway, he was the only man in the world for her.

She didn't admit to herself that she was also just a little afraid.

9

Caroline did not see Joel during the rest of the day following their passionate reunion. He rode away when she was vaguely selecting flowers from the conservatory for the hall and main rooms, leaving a message for her with Mrs Magor that it would probably be evening before he returned, and to expect him when she saw him.

What did *that* mean? she thought with a pang of disappointment — that having exerted his emotional and sexual prowess again she was once more to be regarded as the chattel and mere vehicle for his amusement and gratification when there was nothing better to do? Her first embarrassment at the thought of facing him again turned slowly to indignation. He could surely have explained himself — kissed her as any normal man would have done in such circumstances. Even a touch of the hand — some gesture of affection — would have sufficed. As it was she felt ignored and slighted. Oh, Joel had been very ardent, and convincing in his display of love. But then Ariadne had gone, and he'd wanted to assure himself he still had the capacity to charm his wife to his bed, even though she might be second best.

Second best! how shameful, the very idea. And how she detested Ariadne. Walking moodily about the house, jealousy gnawed her, with increasing humiliation. Obviously she'd been too responsive. She should have remained aloof, put on an act of chilling contempt, so that despite his forcefulness he would be aware of his rejection. Yes, rejection. The next time he attempted to make love she'd make her attitude quite clear. Perhaps then he'd regard her more respectfully or romantically.

'Aren't you well, ma'am?' Mrs Magor enquired once, when she'd called at the hotel with a bucket of fresh eggs from Treescarne. The old face with the bright button-like eyes in their wrinkled sockets of flesh held a shrewd, searching look.

Caroline lifted her head proudly.

'I'm quite well, thank you. What made you ask?'

'All this walkin' here, there, an' everywhere, with such a worried look on 'ee. I thought mebbe—'

'What?'

'Wi' child, are ye? 'Bout time, I'd say. Men like a son a'soon as possible, an' ee've bin wed long enough an' no mistake.'

'That's my affair,' Caroline retorted sharply. 'And please in future keep such thoughts to yourself. For your information', oh dear, she thought wrily, how pedantic she sounded, 'for your information, Mrs Magor, I'm *not* pregnant. And if any such rumours have got about you'll kindly deny them.'

The old woman muttered an adverse comment as she walked away, chin up, through the kitchens and out of the front door. Caroline, suddenly feeling weary and chilled, decided after all to go upstairs, rest for a time, then take a walk. The day was grey, cheerless, and uninviting, but maybe a whiff of fresh air would do her good.

She did not waste time pondering over the housekeeper's probing, but in a quarter of an hour had put on a blue fur-lined cloak and hood, and was making her way down again to the front door.

Once outside she took the path leading to the lane and high moors.

All was a vista of grey and brown now, bereft of human company, or movement except for the creaking undergrowth in the thin wind, and the curling smoke of an old mine against the distant hills — the mine in which Joel had invested sufficient capital to have it already working again. It stood only half a mile from the derelict workings bordering the vicar's land, and was obviously useful in other ways than in the production of copper. Joel had made it his business to establish himself as benefactor to families badly in need of employment and food for their bellies. A bond of understanding between them had taken root and was deepening every day. Secretly the natives had little liking for the devious and hypocritical vicar, but Joel was a very different matter. He showed at all times an approachable friendship, and it was known that he was never above himself, and was generally agreeable enough to offer a drink to employers who chanced to appear at the kiddleywink or any more respectable hostelry should he call in.

Rumours that the 'maister' — Mr Blake — even had dealings with 'Black Dirke' were accepted with a wink and a shrug. Most were sceptical, others knew. All kept their tongues guarded, having no liking for the law, and fully aware also which side their bread was buttered.

Caroline in a vague way was aware of the unspoken pact between her husband and natives of that wild part of Cornwall, and as she quickened her steps that afternoon she felt the strange spirit of 'place' envelop her. The great boulders and distant cromlechs, the twisted thorn trees and sloes crouching by dangerous bog holes and hidden ancient shafts seemed to emit a hidden secret life of their own — a little frightening, yet stimulating at the same time. As she climbed, the wind freshened. As she passed a lopsided centuries-old menhir protruding from entangling briars, her cape caught a branch that pulled her back suddenly, and she fell.

In an instant the shock touched some hidden recess of her brain, and she remembered; remembered the greedy lascivious face, the lusting hands that had attacked her. A fit of trembling seized her as a wave of nausea rose in her throat. She put an arm out to steady herself by the gnarled branch of an ancient elder. The face swimming in imagination before her eyes was of someone she knew — someone who'd called at Lionswykka more than once recently to bother Joel about work, a man called Barney Swales. Once when Swales had gone, she'd said, 'Who is he, Joel? That awful-looking man? Surely you don't have business with such a — such a—'

'Such a slimy unpleasant-looking customer?' Joel had given a short laugh, and continued, 'I deal with any who can be of use. This one was of help at one time, and got paid well. Now he's out. I don't employ drunks and if he bothers me once more the bastard'll have my whip about his back and be before the magistrates for trial.'

She shivered. 'Why did you have to have him at all — as a worker? What did he do? Mining, or — or something?'

He'd eyed her shrewdly. 'You ask too many questions, my business is my own affair, and none of yours. On the other hand—' his face had darkened '—I'd like to know why you're so interested.'

She pulled herself together abruptly. 'I'm not. It occurred to me though that it was rather out of keeping for you to interview such — creatures — at Lionswykka. As your wife I—'

'As my wife you also behave frequently in a way that isn't always reasonable or to my liking,' he'd told her sharply. 'You've not been exactly obliging with your favours recently, Caro. May I enquire *why?*'

'I don't know what you mean.'

'Oh yes you do. You know very well. Anyone else is there? If so I'd like his name before I have to force it out of you—'

'How *unfair* of you. And how stupid. You know very well I'm not that kind of woman.'

'Do I? What way have I of knowing? I'm away a good deal. Heaven knows what you get up to when you're left alone for a few hours. Finding you half naked on the moor, for instance, and your pretty story about forgetting what happened. Do you really imagine I'm so gullible as to have believed it?'

She'd stared at him, wide-eyed and shocked. 'You've *got* to believe it. I was dazed and frightened. If I could remember what had happened I'd have *said*. Don't you understand, Joel?' Her obvious distress had partially mollified him.

'I suppose I've no choice — at the moment. But if I ever find out you've deceived me, there'll be hell to pay.'

The discussion had ended there in an uneasy truce that had lasted until their passionate reunion. Now, recalling the lascivious attack, Caroline, after the first wild thought that she must tell Joel everything, knew suddenly she couldn't. He might believe her, he might not.

Whichever way it was he'd be so angry she daren't visualise the outcome. Besides, what need was there now? After last night, surely, the unpleasant past could be forgotten. When Joel returned everything would be different. He'd take her in his arms with trust and love. And maybe, soon, she'd be with child.

But things did not work out in the way she'd anticipated and hoped for.

Although Joel wouldn't admit embarrassment, even to himself, an unexpected innate core of shyness made him brusque and uncommunicative when he got back in the evening, to find her waiting for him hesitantly in the hall. He merely cleared his throat, gave her a light, casual peck of a kiss on the cheek, and flinging off his cape said, 'A tiring day. I shall be glad of a meal and a good night's rest.'

Chagrin, disappointment and humiliation churned in her. A second later she said coldly, 'The meal's waiting. I thought you'd be earlier.'

'Hm! have you had yours?'

'Yes,' she lied, 'all I want.'

'Good.'

That night they did not sleep together.

*

With the rift between husband and wife deepening, Joel occupied himself by another wild dream to take his mind off domestic matters. For some time he'd been planning eventually to start a steamship company which would not only bring in considerable extra income, but provide the means for a more adventurous outlet in contraband. The prospect would be hazardous, but risks could be overcome, provided he had trustworthy crews, and the essential monetary backing. His wealth, so far, was invested in the hotel and the mines of Treescarne and Lionswykka estates. It would be difficult to persuade shareholders of either concern to back another larger, more debatable concern. Someone else had to be found with sufficient collateral in his pocket and spirit of adventure in him, to take as partner on the scheme. A man of determination and courage possessing a knowledge of foreign parts. Yes, the latter could be very useful indeed. An American perhaps? In California and such faraway places they were mining for gold.

Gold!

That was it. Plunder from the other side of the Atlantic.

Once the idea had taken root, Joel could not shake it off. There would be the respectable trade as cover up, of course, and he'd see this was profitable. Naturally the plan would take time. A ship would have to be built — two probably, for both passenger and goods traffic, with sturdy, strong engines, and special wire rope and winches in case of unexpected contact with other vessels that had run into trouble, or those of a more hostile nature. But where, and from whom, could he obtain the funds?

Puzzling the matter over one day he suddenly recalled a character he'd known in the past — a Maltese who'd made a fortune from devious illegal means and who now ranked in the millionaire class. He'd risen, like Blake, from poverty-stricken beginnings with but one ruthless course in mind — to outwit the law for his own gain, and reign as king of his self-acquired domain. A rich wife whom he'd grown to dislike intensely, had helped him. He had a line of his own, which was his excuse for spending only a few months of each year with her. Under a veneer of politeness at such times the lust for fresh adventure still seethed in him. Success was not enough. He had to have excitement and other women to fan his self-esteem. Joel had heard that he had settled in America, but was now in Europe, and from France would probably visit Britain. His name was Ralph Sagor.

The very man, Joel decided, and immediately set about locating him.

When at last he did so, it was through a shipping company in Bristol. Joel, who had done Sagor a small personal favour in the past, before either had acquired success — set off straightaway for the City, and managed to contact him. Their dinner together that night at a reputable hotel, was a devious outwardly good-humoured affair, played nevertheless with the expertise of a complicated chess game. Sagor, small, thickly set with heavy jowls and brilliant penetrating black eyes set in mounds of flesh under fierce bristling brows, put on a show of conviviality which though a façade at first — for he was a shrewd character — gradually turned to genuine interest as Joel unfolded his plan.

'I'm rich,' Blake concluded, watching the other man's bland expression change, 'but not rich enough. I want capital which could be more than doubled in a few months once the trade gets going.'

'How do I know that? What guarantee? I don't take risks, Blake, unless I'm a hundred per cent sure of not being the loser if the project fails.'

'No one can be a hundred per cent certain. Ninety-nine and a half — I give you my word on that. *If* it fails—' Joel shrugged. 'There's the hotel. No gamble there. Anyway—' he winked and grinned, 'I thought a bit of risk might appeal to you.'

'So you did?' A stubby diamond ringed hand stroked the pointed carefully trimmed beard reflectively, then clicked open a gold case and offered a cigar to Blake.

With the comforting blend of rich smoke and vintage brandy enveloping them, the two men continued the discussion.

The conclusion of the meeting was in Joel's favour.

The verbal agreement was completed, and Joel, a few days later, set off to see a firm of boat builders at Falmouth, accompanied by Sagor. The following week he informed Caroline he had unexpectedly been called to Plymouth on business, and would be away for a week.

Her eyes widened. She stared at him under raised delicate brows. Her soft lips after a first expressive 'Oh', tightened.

'Why, Joel?'

'*Why?* Business, of course.'

'I see.' She looked away. 'Always business.'

'Yes, well — it won't always be the same,' he told her, uncomfortably recalling her proposed trip to Truro. 'I'm on to a good thing this time, Caro — we shall be rich—'

'Aren't we rich enough already?' she queried.

'No. A man of my kind's never rich enough. And you should be grateful I'm made that way. You can have anything you want — almost. The time'll come when there won't be a damned thing I can't give you — diamonds, furs, pearls — a trip round the world so folk everywhere can admire my lovely wife.' He came up behind her, took a hand and pulled her round to face him. 'Don't you understand, love? It's for *you* — all I do's got you in it somewhere. "This'll make Caro happy," I think, when I bring something back to you from one of my jaunts — you're never far out of my mind. Can't you get it into your pretty head that without you I wouldn't be grinding away here trying to think of new ways to make money? I'd be off finding new things in new lands—'

'I know. I *know*,' she interrupted before he could finish, 'and maybe that's what you *should* be doing.' Her voice hardened. 'It's been quite obvious lately, Joel, that I'm a hindrance and responsibility more than a wife. We never go anywhere together—'

'And seldom sleep together,' he pointed out. 'Whose fault is that?'

She felt her breath rising quickly; her heart quickened as she answered, 'I won't be just a commodity, Joel, something to be used and forgotten when you've had what you want. Another thing—'

'Yes?' The word came out with the sharp snappy sound of a pistol shot.

'You haven't even told me what this new business is – this fresh interest that's taking you to Plymouth – just as you've never taken me on that trip to Truro. Yet you had time to meet Ariadne more than once on the moors.' She broke off, putting two fingers over her lips hastily.

He frowned.

'I see. So you've been spying and following me around.'

'No. But I happen to have eyes in my head.'

'*And you happen* to have seen your lusting sister fling herself at my head. Isn't that the expression used?' He smiled sardonically. 'Well – I should have done a bit of that myself, shouldn't I?'

'What do you mean?'

'Been on your track more – on your trail when you had that low-down assignation on the moor.' He jerked her bodice at the neck and pulled her close, so her chin was raised painfully towards his.

'But I didn't – I—'

'You didn't *what*? What, madam? I haven't pressed the question until now. But I think the time's come, don't you? The pretence, the little act of not remembering – just a con trick, wasn't it? Eh?' He was half choking her. 'You had a lover there, didn't you? Some cunning devil who gave you apparently what I should have done long ago – and made you suffer for it—'

'No, no.' She struggled wildly, half choking. 'That isn't true – I – Joel, Joel. You must believe me.'

He released her suddenly; she fell back against the table. He wiped the sweat from his collar, adjusted his neck tie, and when he glanced at her again his expression had changed – become harder, cold.

'There's no must,' he answered. 'I'll try, for both our sakes. But don't ever dare cuckold me, madam, or I'll see you wish you'd never been born, so help me God.'

'And Ariadne?' she asked miserably.

'What about her?'

'Is it going on?'

He laughed shortly.

'No one can predict the future. But for your information – your so aristocratic half sister is no more than a high-class whore, a breed I've no liking for – except as an antidote for other things – for what I lack. Do you know what I'm talking about?'

'I don't know. I—'

'Of course you do. Think about it, my love, and maybe if you behave, and I can forget certain things, we might have some sort of a future together after all.'

With which unsatisfactory statement the bitter interlude was temporarily ended.

For a time there was an almost silent truce between them, and when the day came for Joel's departure for Plymouth, he kissed her dutifully on the cheek before turning briskly with a brief, impersonal wave of the hand. Caroline watched him stride to the main drive where the chaise was waiting, then she sighed and went back into the house.

It was early December; against the leaden sky the leafless trees were networked dark in a cold wind. The moors stretched bleakly to the rising line of grey hills. All, suddenly, seemed hopeless to her. She climbed the stairs to her room, wondering whether to get down to letter writing, or have a canter on Diamond. The latter seemed preferable; there was no one to talk to at Lionswykka except the servants or the one remaining guest of the season – an elderly lady who bored her. For Christmas more would arrive, but until then her own presence there seemed futile. She was preparing to change into her riding habit when t`e` threat of faintness swept over her. Once or twice recently she'd been feeling overtired, at times quite exhausted — the result, she'd told herself, of her worry and anxiety over Joel and Ariadne. That morning, however, the nauseous sensation became so overwhelming she decided on the spur of the moment to change her plans and visit Penzance to see the doctor. Joel would not like it — he always wanted to know the reason for the carriage being used. But the old man, Isaac Penvane, who had once been head groom at a large estate and who now worked part-time at Lionswykka stables, would drive her and keep his mouth shut. No one would say anything if she asked. In any case, as mistress of the household she had a perfect right to have an outing in her husband's absence.

So it was arranged, and presently the vehicle set off, containing Caroline as the only passenger — a very charming-looking Caroline, clad in soft blue velvet edged by grey fur, with a shoulder cape, and a small fur bonnet hat tilted very slightly forward over the silky fawn hair. Two spots of excitement burned in her cheeks. By the time they reached Penzance all trace of feeling unwell had vanished.

It was market day. The town was busier than usual, not only because of farmers and smallholders and those who'd come from outlying parts of the countryside to sell, buy, or barter goods, but because a ship had just berthed in the harbour and French sailors thronged the streets.

When the carriage was deposited in an inn yard and an ostler given charge of the horses, the elderly coachman went inside for a mug of ale leaving Caroline, unescorted, to make her way from the cobbled yard up the main street. Near Market Square she took a side turning leading downward again towards the harbour. The doctor's house, she had been told, was on the right; no one could mistake it, it had a brass plate outside.

She located the square-faced building easily, and was fortunate in finding Doctor Marsley on his premises.

After a comparatively brief examination, he eyed Caroline shrewdly for a few moments, blue eyes twinkling knowingly under a balding head, and said, 'Well, Mrs Blake, I can find no trace of sickness in your condition, in fact—' he smiled broadly, coughed and resumed, 'You are a very healthy young woman, who should have no difficulties whatsoever in bearing a fine child.'

Caroline gasped, 'A child? But—'

He put his stethoscope sharply down on the table, 'You're pregnant, my dear young lady, which I rather guessed at a first glance. Come and see me in another month, and confirmation will be complete. The faintness and sickness are merely symptoms of your condition. There now! I hope you're pleased. Your husband, I'm sure, will be delighted − or should be?' His voice died questioningly into silence. Caroline pulled herself together abruptly.

'Oh yes,' she answered, with more conviction than she felt just then. 'We both want children. It's just that − well, I hadn't considered it − not lately. We've been married for two years, and I was beginning to think—'

A friendly hand patted her shoulder. 'It's as well for a young couple to have time together before starting a family. In the meantime I'll give you a few pills and some medicine, in case you need it. Follow the directions carefully, take gentle exercise, but plenty of rest also, and avoid being agitated over the forthcoming event − or anything else. Tranquillity is invaluable during the months before a confinement.'

In a kind of dream Caroline watched as the doctor went to a cabinet, took out a number of bottles and some small packets, hummed and hawed to himself, wrote a few words on small labels, then returned and handed two neatly wrapped white parcels to her.

'There you are, my dear. And remember what I've said − quiet, exercise and plenty of rest.'

A few minutes later Caroline was in the street again, on her way back to the inn. Her thoughts were dazed, at one point filled with faint doubt, the next risen to heights of elation. Joel would be *pleased*. He must be, she told herself firmly; for so long, in the past, he'd taunted her about her childlessness. Two years seemed long to a man wanting an heir. Perhaps now, his recent moodiness and casual attitude to her would change. In any case, he'd have other things to think and dwell on, than the memory of Ariadne. The picture of her and Joel standing interlocked in each other's arms, returned for a few dark seconds like a shadow clouding Caroline's mind. And this was followed by another — the recollection of the hateful man who'd attacked her on the moor. She wished she'd never remembered or recognised him, wished desperately that Joel could have let the matter rest and trusted her. It was wrong — so wrong — that two incidents should cause such havoc in their relationship.

It was unfair of him to have believed, for one moment, she could be capable of such treachery. Other men of a different nature, would have taken her word. Men like Captain Reeves. Remembering his courtesy gave a lift to her spirits. It was so comforting to have as well as an exciting husband an understanding friend, who, whatever her faults, always managed to see her virtues, and compliment her when she was feeling low and in need of self-confidence.

By the time she was back at Lionswykka any apprehension she'd previously felt had disappeared, and she had already started planning how she'd convey the news to Joel when he returned from Plymouth.

Mrs Magor was not deceived by Caroline's alternating moods. She came of a family of miners, and possessed a prophetic tendency of sensing joy or disaster ahead. Resenting her young mistress's refusal to confide in her, she nevertheless made it her business to mutter a number of superstitious warnings and advice on the chance occasions when they met. To put a mug of milk outside the back kitchen door for the small folk when the moon was full, would mean good luck for any tiny stranger about to arrive. Never, she said, wander the moors near the mines when the Buccas were enjoying an evening of revelry, and always to keep a sprig of white heather under the pillow. 'You heed what I do tell you,' she said more than once when Caroline smiled, faintly amused. 'An' doan you laugh, mistress, at Cornish truth. You look fairly bemused and wayward these days, to be sure. But sometimes—' She paused, pushed her gnarled old face forward from her bent shoulders, 'sometimes ted'n so good is it? That's always the way when young wummen be in your state.'

Caroline was about to make a sharp rebuke of denial, but thought better of it. Mrs Magor *knew*.

What about it, anyway. What did it matter? Joel would soon be back, and when he heard he'd be sure to spread the news proudly wherever he went.

Unfortunately, her optimism wasn't justified.

Following her breathless statement shortly after his return, Joel merely said in cool matter-of-fact tones, 'That will be nice for you, won't it? Women generally like to have a child around. Congratulations.'

She was silent for some moments, standing with condemning eyes, her face set and suddenly bleak, by the dressing table of their bedroom. He hadn't even kissed her. As he took his bag towards the dressing room, she rushed forward, and forced herself between her husband and the door.

'What do you mean, talking like that? Aren't you pleased? You've always taunted me about not starting a family. Well, now it's happened—' She broke off, dismayed by the unyielding expression on his handsome face.

'So you've told me. And I've already congratulated you.' His voice was dry.

'But—'

'Oh, Caroline, can't you see I'm tired and not exactly in the mood for emotional scenes? I've had a busy, complicated week. There's been much to discuss and settle—'

'And what about me? What do you think *I've* been feeling?'

'I'm not a woman, so I just can't imagine. In the morning I'll probably be able to listen more understandingly. Not that it should be necessary; bearing children is a wife's natural occupation, and I'm sure you'll be adequately able to deal with it.'

Indignation flamed in her, holding as well, dull disappointment. Her face whitened. She bit her lip.

'I'm so *sorry* I've bored you,' she said coldly. 'I'll see it won't happen again.'

'Caroline—'

He put out an arm, she brushed it aside, and pushed past him, walking sharply to a chair where a shawl was lying. She put it round her shoulders, and not looking at him continued chillingly, 'It's quite all right. I understand, Joel. I know how important and demanding your business meetings are. And as you say — bearing children is a woman's concern. I just thought you ought to know.'

She flounced out of the room with a flurry and rustle of silk. She hated Joel, briefly, for his callous indifference to her needs, and for his preoccupation with making money. Money! — *money*. In the few disillusioned moments she doubted that he'd ever really loved her at all. Perhaps he was incapable of any of the finer emotions. He had married her in the first place because she had not been entirely without means, and because of the prestige in being her father's daughter. So she should have been wiser, from the very beginning of their union, not to betray her feelings so naively. Had she held herself aloof Ariadne might never have intruded upon their relationship

Ariadne! the very thought of her now, was offensive. If she could help it, her sister would never set a foot in Lionswykka or at Treescarne again. The months before the baby's birth must be spared at least that humiliation.

Very slowly the nervous tension in her eased, giving place to a cold reserve and determination to plan efficiently and as far as possible — unemotionally — for the approaching event. Joel meanwhile after a few unsuccessful attempts to make his wife 'see sense', as he considered it, gave up trying, telling himself in time she'd come round.

Eventually the obsession for his new project deepened and took precedence in his mind to the exclusion of anything else except its ability to provide further wild excitement and gain.

Gold!

He saw no obstacle to the possibility of his plan. Under the guise of respectability, sufficient of the precious ore could be smuggled through the customs to have him a millionaire.

His own initiative and ambition had already made him rich.

But riches beyond his wildest dreams so far now loomed as the future reality. Diamonds too maybe. Why not? A diamond king! With the contacts and finance now available nothing was beyond achievement. He'd heard a story when he was young of precious stones being hidden in horses' hooves. The importation of horses was possible from abroad, and the diamond fields of South Africa were flourishing. The more Joel considered the suggestion the stronger his confidence grew. But one fact registered clearly − the necessity for a respectable façade. This meant an end to the dashing cunning figure of Black Dirke, and to any small deals he'd previously considered.

Lionswykka's prestige must be enhanced, tempting the wealthiest and most honoured clientele, not only from every part of Britain, but from abroad. His own name would be beyond reproach; he knew people. This was one of his crowning virtues − learned so assiduously from his humbler beginnings as kitchen boy and chef − the capacity to recognise the fads and fancies of those with the means to pay. His name was already becoming a byword on the Continent. With his growing social background it was hardly likely that when the new line came into being his reputation would become linked in any shady way likely to interest revenue officials. From now on he just had to be careful, that was all. The necessity, the sense of outwitting such a cunning breed of men gave fire to his imagination.

So Caroline's coolness at that particular time didn't really worry him. Motherhood itself was gratifying, and Caroline's could have given him considerable pleasure if he'd been able to accept he was the coming baby's father.

But he wasn't sure. Until the night when he'd found her, half naked and distraught on the moor, he'd had no cause to doubt her faithfulness. Now all was different. Women were weak, and Caroline quite likely was no different from the rest of them. Whichever way it was he'd be legal father to the offspring, thank God. But when, if ever, he discovered he'd been deceived, he'd make her pay, in one way or another. In the meantime, let her sulk and flaunt her airs in his face; he had far too much of importance on his mind than to worry over a passionate moody

woman's whims. One fact above all others remained hard and
invincible at the back of his mind. She was *his*! Just as the new
line would be. A possession symbolising power and prestige to
the world. 'Caroline Carnforth' — he could almost hear the
words whispered in his imaginings of the future. 'An aristocrat,
don'-cher-know? One of the best families in Cornwall. When
Joel Blake married her he knew what he was doing. A beauty
too, in her way. Wouldn' mind being in *his* shoes, by Gad!'

That was true enough, too, he thought with growing pride,
they'd be damned envious. For that matter already were. So he
mustn't let the wild adventurous streak in him let him down
before the scene was ripe and set for the really big operation. No
more hazardous small deals. No risks. For the time being Joel
Blake had to prove himself an aspiring honourable benefactor
to the district and county; to which end he temporarily dedicated himself.

Reeves was puzzled. Outwardly, during the weeks that followed Joel put no step wrong. He attended any social function
where he could be of use, backed charities needing ballast and
money, hiding his chagrin at having to do so under a mask of
cheerful goodwill and bonhomie. All, superficially, was gener-
ously straightforward, yet the Captain still doubted the man,
considering him a buccaneer of the most devious and dangerous
type. Ariadne's words had made their mark. He didn't trust her
one inch, she was a headstrong character — impetuous and wayward, who could be wildly jealous under certain circumstances.
Her remarks concerning Joel had held a bitter sting; could they
have been lovers? Possibly, and her statement a mere lie con-
cocted by a jealous mistress to make trouble. On the first
meeting with Blake he'd suspected the man — sensed undercurrents in his nature that were hard to pinpoint. Contraband
certainly would appeal to him, but so far nothing tangible had
been discovered against him.

There was, as well, Caroline to consider. Reeves well knew
she wasn't happy, and he was loth to make accusations that
would add to any private worries she had, unless they could be
proved.

Proof! this was what he wanted — the essential factor before he took action. He was quite prepared to wait and watch events secretly, until the opportune moment arose to catch the wily bird in operation. It wouldn't be easy, but for Caroline's sake he had to curb his impatience.

Time passed.

In the spring of 1883 Lionswykka was almost filled by guests again, mostly by the artistic elite and the wealthy upper classes wishing to indulge in a life of leisure and new interests far removed from the wars and rumours of wars that seemed forever to be threatening Europe. To most of these visitors, General Gordon — 'Chinese Gordon' as he was known — was a mere name, as was the bickering between the General and Gladstone. Events abroad held little fear for the majority of Britain's population. The small island was gradually expanding its power over the whole world leaving the well-to-do classes basking in an aura of glory that was well content to leave the plights of the poor and underprivileged disregarded.

In Cornwall miners were still emigrating to America; throughout the county the copper and tin industry was slowly decreasing, although new mines were still being exploited by knowledgeable men with sufficient brains and wealth to make them operable. Deeper shafts were being sunk. Anyone with a nose for such matters, was aware that ore still lay in considerable quantities hundreds of fathoms down. Joel suspected that a tidy future could still be made from the discovery of new levels running through Lionswykka land, but he made no attempt to investigate such possibilities. He had sufficient on his hands already, and was shrewd enough to conserve his energies for the one wild dream. None of his workers, anyway, had cause to complain. Already Wheal Marion, which was in a sorry state when he built Lionswykka, was fully employed again. He was continually winning approval from the natives. Trust in him from such a quarter was important. Co-operation could be a deciding factor in any future crisis concerning the Revenue men.

To hell with the latter, he told himself frequently, and smiled to himself. He, Joel Blake, would prove himself the winner, and then Caroline would come to heel. He'd no doubts whatever that he could either tame her, or woo her to his bed again. But the child! Whenever he visualised Caroline as a mother, doubt and jealousy consumed him. Only one thing could be the answer. As soon as possible following the baby's birth he'd see she conceived another — one indisputedly his.

This decision made him able temporarily to put her out of mind once more.

Meanwhile Caroline, resentful of his preoccupation, coldness, and apparent indifference, became increasingly friendly with Captain Reeves, meeting him either by chance or intent, at places where they could talk in private without arousing any gossip or speculation. Joel was away so frequently that she was able to journey to Truro occasionally and have a meal with him at a certain hostelry patronised by the select and well-to-do. Both of them realised there was a certain risk in such a situation. But the Captain was careful to have a plausible explanation ready should questioning arise from any quarter, and Caroline was genuinely entitled, in her condition, to visit a Penzance doctor or Truro specialist whenever she felt the necessity.

Affection between them deepened. Resentment at Joel's neglect, hatred of his devious business projects and the memory of his involvement with Ariadne made Reeves' friendship all the more important. For the first time she accepted that her marriage to Joel had in many ways been a mistake. He was not of her world. If she had married the Captain — or someone of his type — always at such a point she abruptly ended the conjecturing. There was no point in 'ifs', 'whys', or wondering. Joel was her husband. Nothing could alter it, unless — unless something happened; something terrible. And she didn't want that. The mere suggestion of there being no Joel in her life always caused her distress. This was the trouble. Hate him she might sometimes. There were moments when life with him seemed intolerable. At others she simply couldn't visualise never seeing him again.

By the end of February, in spite of careful corseting and

cunning flouncing adapted to the fashion of the period it became apparent that Caroline was *enceinte*. A little of her inherent vivacity had vanished. Instead of showing happiness as many women did at such times, she frequently seemed languid and over-tired. Under other circumstances she could have blossomed. But Joel's neglect intensified her growing fears that he now disliked, rather than desired, her. This increased her growing closeness to Reeves.

Early spring was already feathering the trees with palest golden green, when, on a late afternoon before driving back to Lionswykka, she strolled for a short walk with him by the river. Both were unusually silent until the Captain stopped and said in quiet but forceful tones, 'Caroline, I must speak to you.'

His hand touched her arm, sending a wave of frustrated emotion through her. She glanced up; his grey eyes were warm and discerning on her delicate face, the feeling between them mutual. Never had she appeared more appealing, or more in need of sympathy.

'Yes?' There was a faint smile in the question.

'You're — with child, aren't you?'

She nodded. 'I didn't think it was too noticeable yet. I would have told you, perhaps I should have, you've been such a good friend to me. But women don't generally speak of such things to men. Even—' Her voice faltered.

'Even to anyone who cares as much as I do?' Though controlled in manner, the sincerity, the anxious undertone did not escape her. She freed herself gently.

'We mustn't speak like this. It's wrong, isn't it?'

'Why? What's wrong in admitting what we both know?'

Over the surface of the river shadows trembled and as suddenly disappeared again. Fleeting as the changeful emotion of her bewildered inner self.

'Because I'm Joel's wife.' She spoke sadly as though a risen ghost divided them.

'I know. I'm sorry to have intruded. I've no right; no right at all.' He stiffened and made a gesture of turning back the way they'd come. 'It's late. I suppose we should be getting back.'

On impulse, she clutched a sleeve lightly. 'Oh, Rupert — Captain Reeves — I mean — please understand. It was true what I said, about being Joel's wife. But — but you haven't intruded. What I should have done without you I don't know.'

'Do you mean that?'

'Yes.'

He shook his head, felt for her hand, held it a moment, then resumed, 'Why did you ever marry that brigand, Caroline?'

'Brigand?' She forced a laugh. 'Oh, he's not exactly that. Adventurous and exciting yes. And I suppose that's why I fell in love with him.'

'I see.'

'Do you? I don't. I can't understand myself at all. I think I knew that life would be unpredictable with him. What I *didn't* expect was the loneliness.'

'That and other things.'

She flushed. 'What do you mean?'

'I don't have to tell you. It's more than loneliness. You're unhappy.'

'No.' She lifted her chin and started to walk back in the direction of the town. He followed automatically. 'I'm not *really* unhappy,' she continued. 'It's more a feeling of complete uselessness. Joel doesn't need me, and that's the truth. He only needs his ambition and work.'

'Which is?'

'Hotels of course, and making money. The rest I don't know. He keeps everything from me.'

'And you'd like to share more.'

'Naturally I would. Oh, I don't mean I'm interested in business and stuffy finance, but we seem to be drawing further apart every day. There's no *contact* any more.'

'Maybe after the child comes it will be different?'

In the gradually fading light he didn't notice the instinctive tightening of her lips. But he was shocked when she said, 'No — I don't think so. He doesn't particularly want the baby. You see that's one of the troubles — he thinks I'm — he suspects he's not the father.'

'What?'

'It's true. That's what's so dreadful — for him to believe I'm that kind of woman.'

For moments Reeves did not speak, then he said in dangerously quiet tones, 'He must be off his head. The blackguard. I'd like to have a few words with him. Or a man-to-man punch-up. Maybe the last would be better.'

'You mustn't, Rupert. You must keep away. *Please*, for my sake—'

He stared at her doubtfully.

'Very well, if you wish. But if he ever lays a finger on you, Caroline, just let me know and I'll deal with him in the way he deserves.'

Shortly afterwards the personal subject faded into more ordinary channels. But following the meeting Caroline had to accept the fact that she was already more than half in love with the Captain, and that no-one — least of all herself — could foretell the future.

*

At the beginning of April Caroline received a letter from Ariadne containing the information that her sister was expecting a second child.

Of course Willie is delighted. He's not the demonstrative type of man, as you must know. But *fearfully* proud underneath, and a second son would ensure a direct family heir in case anything happened to Jasper. Not that there's much likelihood of *that*. Jasper's such a lusty little boy — if you can *call* him little. He's too bouncy for me to control, and I'm rather thankful we have such a good Nanny. Still, a young brother will be of help — I *hope*. If it's a girl it will be disappointing for Willie, but I'd rather like a daughter myself — someone to cuddle and dress up in pretty clothes. Oh dear I expect I sound selfish and vain, and incompetent, so unlike *you* darling, who are a born mother. Any signs yet of making Joel a proud daddy? Do let me know all the news. A little later when the weather's warmer I hope to join you again for a time at Lionswykka. Willie's all for it, and I'm dying for another glimpse of Cornwall.

Remember me to Joel.

As ever your loving sister,

Ariadne.

Caroline put the letter down with a sense of rising hostility and impatience.

The thought of the three of them, Ariadne, herself, and Joel, under the same roof so soon following the last visit, filled her with depression. In a wave of revolt she told Joel she wanted more peace, and insisted on returning to Treescarne, adding the news about Ariadne.

To her surprise, he agreed.

'Very well,' he said, 'if that's how you feel, go — for a time. But don't expect me to be available at the hotel to play host to your arrogant sister. During the next month or two I shall be away frequently at Falmouth, and will certainly have no time to fuss over the whims of pregnant women.' He threw her a shrewd assessing glance, adding placatingly, 'Except you, of course, on occasions.'

'Thank you.' She turned away, chilled by the last sentence, which although meant to appease, nevertheless held no shred of feeling. It seemed at a time when she most needed sympathy and understanding there was no one except Rupert Reeves to turn to; and after all, opportunities to talk with him were rare, and mostly had to be carefully contrived. It was all wrong, she decided, wishing desperately he was there beside her, to soothe her tired nerves to peace again.

Joel didn't care for her.

He never had — except to use, and possess her when he needed a woman. He'd taken all she had, subtly contriving to mould her to his will. If she'd known — she told herself passionately — she'd never have married him, *never*. At the same time she recognised such an assertion was a lie. From the start Joel and she had been meant for each other. But for how long?

Like a shadow the question hovered and clouded her mind, providing no answer.

There was none — yet.

Only the future could tell, and the future also was partially bound up with Rupert Reeves.

10

Caroline wasted no time in replying to Ariadne's letter:

It would be better if you came later. Joel is away a great deal at the moment, and I'm returning to Treescarne. For how long I don't know. I'm feeling tired and want some peace. Really, Ariadne, with us both as we are I'm sure it's more sensible for us to wait until we've had our babies. If you insist on leaving Willie so soon, why don't you go to Papa's for a bit? I'm sure he'd be glad to see you. You know how concerned and interested he is in little Jasper. And it's a long time since he saw you.

Ariadne's reaction was brief and to the point.

If you imagine for one moment I'd demean myself by staying under the roof he shares with that smirking common woman Agnes Poldew, you're quite mistaken [she scrawled in her bold hand-writing]. It was awful the last time, having her gushing and throwing her airs about just as though she was mistress of our old home as well as him. She's a greedy, lusting creature — you can see it in her eyes — even when she smiles in that flattering soft-soapy way. She thinks she has Papa by the ear, of course. But she hasn't. You *see*! — when he dies she'll not get a penny. There probably won't be much to leave anyway, except debts and the house. So as you obviously don't want me, Caro, I'll do what you say and put the visit off until a later time.

Sorry to have bothered you.

Yours

Ariadne.

Caroline put the letter down on the table. It was the first time she and Joel had had breakfast together for more than a week.

Joel glanced at the envelope. He recognised the hand-writing.

'From your sister, I take it?' he said, with no expression at all on his face.

'Yes. I wrote to her telling her I was returning to Treescarne and that it would be better for her to come and see us later.'

Joel shrugged. 'It's your affair. Remember though, that having Lady Perryn at Lionswykka is a good advertisement for the hotel.'

'Oh, bother Lionswykka,' Caroline said shortly.

He stared, amazed.

'Do you know what you're saying?'

Her glance at him was defiant.

'Perfectly. It seems to rule our lives, or *did* — until you took on other responsibilities. We agreed I should be free of it while you're so concerned with business developments and — and those projects you won't talk about. Having Ariadne calling on me whenever she liked — which would be often, without you there — would be a nuisance. She tires me.'

'Can it be that you're still the slightest bit jealous?' Joel's voice, though curious, was slightly amused.

'Of *course* I'm not jealous. Not any more. I suppose I've grown used to your — peccadilloes.'

He laughed outright and pulled her to him. 'I like you when you're in a rage, Mrs Blake,' he said, 'it gives me something to do.'

'What do you mean?'

'Wondering how to tame you.'

She sighed.

'You've done that already and you know it. But just now I don't feel like games, neither do you. I'm merely a diversion — and don't try and deny it, Joel — from your real aims. It doesn't *really* matter to you whether I'm at Lionswykka or Treescarne — for the moment. And I don't believe you're bothered about Ariadne either. There's something remote and cold about you, not quite human. It's not people you want, but things.'

'What a damned lie. Sheer nonsense.'

'No.' She walked swiftly away from him. 'It's obvious.'

He sped after her, and kissed her hard on the lips. For the first time during their marriage she felt no response. He was aware of it, and might have forced her into acquiescence and ultimate submission, if he hadn't suddenly seen her face.

The expression there was unfathomable and chilling.

'The little vixen,' he thought; one day he'd show her. When the pregnancy business was over he'd have her defenceless in his arms again, at his mercy, and reunited in passion. For the present let her spit and scratch. He didn't really need her at that particular point. To a man like Joel Blake there was always a willing woman somewhere around if necessary — a woman who wouldn't attempt to chain or possess him.

Instinctively his mind wandered to Ariadne. Then as lightly he dismissed her. Too dangerous. And what on earth use could she be, except an encumbrance, if what Caroline had said was true? — that she was expecting Willie's child?

'To hell with all women,' he told himself, 'there are far more important matters ahead to worry about.' That same week he was to attend a meeting in Falmouth concerning the building of the first boat for the new line. An estimate had already been given of £15,000. Not bad; less than he'd expected, and Sagor had told him of another — secondhand, cheaper, but sturdy.

He was going into both possibilities thoroughly, and Sagor would be there. A very satisfactory arrangement indeed.

By the time Caroline had closed the door behind her she was almost completely out of his mind.

But he was not out of hers.

*

The following day, as she was leaving by a side door for a walk across the moors, Caroline saw a sturdy figure cutting up from the stables towards the back of the house. Her heart lurched a little. She paused, recognising him immediately; the man was Barney Swales who'd molested her in the bracken down by the ruin months ago when she'd sprained her ankle. Her first impulse was to rush back into the house, tell Joel who was in the library, revealing his identity so that her husband could deal with him as he wished, and get rid of him for ever. The next moment she'd changed her mind, and when the bulky figure had disappeared she had cut quickly across the moors and was walking sharply along a narrow track skirting the base of the hills. The air was sweet and fresh, laden with the mingled scents of sea, heather, gorse, and springing young bracken. Physically, it was one of her good days. The nausea had not troubled her recently, and the knowledge she carried a young life within her gave happiness and buoyancy to her step — in spite of Joel's attitude.

Joel.

She could be as passionately in love with him as ever, if only he was kinder and showed a little interest. Surely there was some way of dispelling his suspicions about the baby? That awful man, Barney! — if she *could* find sufficient courage to reveal the truth, her husband would be forced to believe it. But again — suppose he didn't? Suppose he considered her story merely a lie to protect some other lover? Someone more suitable, like Rupert? No, she decided, after all, it was better to keep her mouth shut. Trouble of any kind would be upsetting. All she needed in the world was to be free for a time from jealousy and bitterness and the continued taunts so frequently flung at her. By a strange coincidence, as she reached the end of the track which curved gently upwards to the lane, she saw a horseman riding from the direction of Port Ia, towards her. All thought of Joel was dispelled in a wave of rising happiness.

Rupert.

He quickened his pace, and in a few moments had covered the distance between them. Swinging himself from the saddle he went towards her and took her two hands briefly in his. Then he smiled.

'Must be telepathy between us, Mrs Blake,' he said. Then he added, 'And how I dislike calling you that.'

'You don't always; not now,' she reminded him.

'No. And I wish your surname could be mine.'

She flushed slightly.

'Isn't it unwise riding so near Lionswykka?'

'It could be, if I hadn't arranged a business call at the kiddleywink below. Another of my men could have been allotted the task of course. But I hoped very much to get a sight of you. And now I have, I—'

She lifted a hand. 'Please don't say it,' she begged. 'It isn't any use. As I keep pointing out I'm married to Joel, and nothing can alter that.'

'Oh yes it can.' He spoke grimly. 'And although I don't want you to suffer, Caroline, I'm much afraid you'll have to — in the end. And when that time comes I hope I'll be there. You can always count on me.' His expression changed, became anxious, a little strained. 'You believe it, don't you?'

'I know you mean what you say,' she replied warmly, 'and I'm grateful. But—'

'Damn it, I don't want your *gratitude*. I want your *love*, woman. What's more you want me too. I know it's impertinent of me — but I happen to be made of flesh and blood, and you're not a cold character. Maybe I've burned my boats in speaking too soon, but that's the way it is. I shan't press anything or attempt to force the issue until your child is born. After that you should know your own mind and face it. Then we can come to proper terms. If you still want to cling to that dastardly husband — and that's what he is, Caroline, make no mistake about it — I'll take off somewhere where you'll never be troubled by me again. It's a promise. Understood?'

'Yes,' she agreed faintly.

'Right. Only be honest with yourself. For both our sakes.'

She nodded mutely. He didn't attempt to hold her, and a few minutes later had passed on and was cantering at a sharp pace down the slope.

She watched him until horse and rider had finally disappeared, then, with a curious sense of loss and loneliness, she turned and started walking back towards Lionswykka.

Joel meanwhile, was in confrontation with Swales.

'I've no intention of taking you on again,' he was saying in forceful yet controlled tones. 'Drunks and layabouts have no place in my plans. Anyone who let me down as you did that day is out for good. So that's all there is to it.'

Swales' dark face was thrust forward towards Joel's aggressively. 'Is it now? It is indeed? Strikes me you need to think a bit more, mister. There's things I could go spreadin' about the district as wouldn' exactly go down well wi' the Revenue — specially that stuck-up captain as seems so taken wi' your lady wife!' he leered slyly. 'You wanter watch out there, Mr High-an-Mighty-Blake.'

Joel's face whitened. An arm shot out and caught Barney's jacket fiercely under the throat. 'You bloody swine,' he said. 'Any more of that and I'll kill you, by God—' he jerked the man's neckscarf tight. 'Understand? I mean it. Now — look sharp and get out. And if any of your dirty lies are spread, I'll see you in hell! — or down a mine shaft. Maybe that would be the best.'

He let the man go suddenly, and dealt him a blow across the cheek. Blood slowly oozed from one eye. Swales lifted a hand and mopped it with the corner of the torn scarf. He went towards the door, turned and said thickly:

'Doan' think you can rid o' me that easily. I've got a wumman to look—' he broke off, gasping.

'I've heard about the poor creature,' Joel replied. 'If she gets rid of you I'll see she doesn't suffer. Let's hope the luckless slut has some sense enough left to do it.'

'She'll do what I say,' Swales replied, 'stick by me she will, or get the stick about her backside. Knows which side her bread's buttered my Liza does. Not like some – the haughty breed you fancy—' Before Barney knew what was happening, Joel had sprung after him, raised his boot, and sent the man sprawling. A string of curses and oaths issued from the bruised mouth.

Joel turned away with a look of disgust on his face. 'Get out,' he remarked contemptuously, 'and don't ever let me see you near this place again.'

The man said no more. As he lurched down the hall and out of the first available door, he saw Caroline coming towards him down the drive. They passed each other without a word, but his glance was lecherous and obscene.

Her spine stiffened apprehensively. She quickened her pace, and was slightly out of breath when she entered the house. Joel met her at the foot of the stairs.

'Where have you been?' he asked abruptly.

'Out. For a walk. I wanted air. Is there anything wrong in that?'

Burning with a fresh stab of jealousy, Joel replied, 'Not so long as you keep yourself decent, and remember you're my wife. In other words keep your body to yourself and free of any lusting wanderer of the moor. Understand?'

'I think so.' Her voice was cold, cutting. 'And I think – you're a beast, Joel Blake. Sometimes I hate you.' She shuddered, remembering the lumbering bruised shape of Swales down the drive.

'Yes, and I hate you too, madam. But for the sake of the hotel and its reputation, I suggest we keep the knowledge to ourselves. And by the way—' he paused, eyeing her not only with anger but mounting desire, '—I'll be waiting your presence in the connubial bedroom tonight.'

One of her hands clutched the neck of her bodice protectively. 'Oh *no*, Joel. Not now. I—'

'I well know the delicate state of your health, and it doesn't deceive me one bit. You're fit as a fiddle, and quite able to bear a few husbandly advances for a change.'

He turned on his heel and walked sharply away.

She shivered. Did he mean it? How could he, after suggesting such terrible things. No, he couldn't. It was just bravado.

But she found later it wasn't. And when the painful passionate ravishing was over, and Joel had left, she lay for a considerable time with the lashes wet on her cheeks, longing for Rupert and his sympathy.

11

Joel's meeting with Sagor and a possible wealthy investor Paul Verne in Falmouth, proved more successful than he'd contemplated; although he kept his satisfaction controlled under a veneer of half grudging speculation. 'As chief shareholder and owner of the new line,' he pointed out, 'I take the risk and stand to lose more than my partners if anything should go wrong. Not that there's much danger there. I've never been a loser in any worthwhile deal. But the Cornish side — the timing, landing, storage, and final disposal of contraband would be mainly in the hands of myself and my own confederates. And where gold is concerned there'll be heavy payment at the other end. So the cost of shipbuilding must be kept at a reasonable minimum. You, Verne, say £15,000 is cheap. *I* suggest five hundred less. As for the secondhand steamer — with cash down — ready payment — a tidy sum should be knocked off the asking price. Another thing—' he raised a finger significantly, '—remember any reasonable profit will take time. For the first year it'll be evens at the best — straight business and passengers. The Blake Line has to be proved beyond reproach to any suspicious watching Revenue Johnnies—' he chuckled. 'No goods carried except the legal stuff. And no arguing, if the Preventive want a search. *Toujours la politesse* as they say.' He winked. 'Got me?'

As the talk continued, the few men present realised that Joel had everything pigeon-holed, possessing not only the rare gift of swaying listeners, but of calculating methodically a pattern of possibilities and action foolproof as any venture ever could be. His magnetic personality and single-mindedness, combined with his splendid physique and looks eventually won the day, proposals of shipping experts and boat builders were brought into practical perspective, and a further meeting in two days was arranged, followed by others, which meant the Falmouth visit would be postponed.

When Joel eventually arrived back at Lionswykka he was in high good humour, and further gratified to find the hotel almost full, and that the new guests included a Lord and Lady Beckersley, both very wealthy eccentrics with a passion for nature and the ever increasing popularity of the art of photography. Under Joel's flattering charm, Adela Beckersley simpered and fawned; she was a thin plain woman with a weak chin and long aristocratic nose. Joel made her feel beautiful. He well knew from their first half-an-hour's conversation she and her husband would become regular visitors. And thank heaven she *had* a husband, he thought, when he'd finally escaped for a stiff whisky in the library. Women were such fools, and those with money the worst. To have been chased by Adela Beckersley would have been an ordeal. If she'd had looks – but she hadn't. And that was one of the queer quirks of life. The richest and most accessible of females all too frequently had nothing else to commend them.

With such uncomplimentary assessments of the female gender swimming vaguely through his mind, he thought of Caroline. Hiding away at Treescarne of course. Keeping herself aloof as usual, the little chit. Well, he'd soon put an end to that. Dammit all, she was his wife and had duties still, even though she was 'expecting'. Maybe he could sweeten her sour mood if he went out of his way to charm her.

So after a meal he changed, saddled his horse, and was soon riding up the slope to the dip beneath the fold of the hill, where the house stood in its nest of trees.

'She edn in,' he was told by Mrs Magor, when he enquired about his wife.

'What do you mean – not in? She's living here.'

The housekeeper nodded sourly.

'She sleeps an' eats here – *mostly*, sur. But she's other places to visit too.'

'Do you mind explaining?'

She shook her head. 'I dunno nuthen. Only that the mistress gets these wild ideas of ridin' 'bout the place now an' then. Sometimes she takes the carriage to Truro, an'-isn' back for a whole day. It's *my* belief—'

'Yes?'

The old woman's jaws snapped to belligerentiy. 'I'm not saying. I don't want trouble. People in her condition get funny ideas sometimes. Only it's my opinion, master, she shud have more comp'ny of the right sort. *Yours* perhaps. There's always those around — *men* of the wrong kind — ready to take advantage of a ladylike critter such as she be.'

Instantly a flame of hot anger rushed to Joel's head. He reddened, turned abruptly and said, 'It would be better for you if you kept your thoughts to yourself, Mrs Magor. Still, under the circumstances, I'll take note of what you've said.'

The woman went away, grumbling, leaving Joel to his dark thoughts. Her implications had not escaped him, and jealousy burned him angrily, like a hot flame, kindling lust from desire, certainty and condemnation from suspicion.

When Caroline arrived ten minutes later, flushed from her canter, and still wearing her riding habit, he met her coming up the hall. She stopped when she saw him, overcome by a tumult of emotion.

'Where have you been?' he demanded in a dangerously hard voice.

'Out. I wanted exercise. Why Joel?' Her eyes had widened, staring at him with the innocence apparently of some lovely child.

Assumed innocence.

'You've no business to go riding in your state.'

'I asked the doctor. He said—'

'What the doctor said's nothing to me. Balderdash.' He took a step towards her. She backed.

'You heard what I said,' he continued, still in that formidable cold voice. 'Up those stairs, madam. I'll talk to you where the servants can't hear.'

To hide her fear, she laughed derisively.

'What servants? Mrs *Magor*? The girl — who's already left, or the stupid stable boy?'

'Do as you're told.'

She shrugged, and passed before him proudly, skirt held in one hand above her boots, her hat in the other.

When they reached the bedroom he closed the door behind them, locked it, took her by an arm, pushed her on to the four-poster and said, 'Take these things off, Caroline, and try and behave decently for once, even if you're not.'

'*How dare* you talk to me like that?'

'Melodrama?' he questioned, raising his eyebrows mockingly. 'You're quite an expert. But after so long I find your moods damned boring, understand? For once you'll come down to earth and we'll have things straight. I haven't a clue what's been going on in my absence — yet, but I'm getting the truth this time.'

'I don't know what you mean.'

She started to get up. He pushed her back. 'Oh yes you do. Your lover, Mrs Blake. His name if you don't mind.'

She made another effort to pull away, but his face was close, his eyes hard, boring into hers.

'I have no lover. I never did have—'

'The child's father. What about him? It was all a put up job wasn't it? Leaving you there on the moor as though you'd been attacked? — a trick to burden me with his bastard when the time came?'

One hand grabbed her jacket and forced her head back, half strangling her. She fell choking against the pillows.

'Joel, please — please—'

'His name? That stuck-up Reeves — your fancy man! — was he the one?'

Terror seized her. '*No*. Of course not. We're — he — he's never touched me. He—'

'Then *who*? You tell me, or I'll beat the hell out of you.'

'It was *him*,' she cried desperately. 'That man who worked for you. Swales. He — he—' Her teeth were chattering, she couldn't finish.

He suddenly released her. '*Swales?*'

'He was drunk. He happened to be there when I went in. There was a storm—'

He'd gone very white.

'Another lie is it? To protect your precious captain?'

Life returned to her.

'Why should I protect him? He's done nothing wrong.'

'But that other filthy rogue *did*? That's what you're asking me to believe? It's *his* bastard in your womb?'

'*No!*' she shouted. 'The child will be yours, Joel, if it's ever born.' Tears forcefully held back until then were suddenly released; she broke into a fit of sobbing that angered rather than unnerved him.

He brought the palm of a hand smartly against her cheek. 'Stop that. And no more tricks, d'you hear? I've had more than enough.'

She put shaking fingers to her smarting flesh.

'It's not a trick. If you don't believe me I've no proof. But it's true.'

'We'll see about that.' He strode to the door, turned, and said grimly, 'I'll find him. And when I do—'

'Joel.'

'In the meantime you'd better say your prayers, madam, and let's hope your God hears. I know men — most of all cowardly brutes like Swales. When his answer comes it'll be genuine, I promise you that. And if I find you're still lying — by heaven, I'll force the truth from you in a way you'll never forget.'

She shuddered. A second later he'd gone. Never in her life before had she been so frightened or upset, never had she seen such deadly anger in any man's face or voice. She had a wild desire to escape, to run away somewhere where he'd never find her, although, in her condition, she recognised the impossibility.

How could she ever have thought she loved such a man? Yet when the first fit of nerves was over she knew that if the past could be relived she'd act in exactly the same way. His power over her was so wild and primitive it both terrified and stirred her to a pitch of despair and longing beyond any realm of reason or commonsense. Those threats! Had he meant them? she wasn't sure, but decided when she'd calmed down that he couldn't have − they were simply the wild bitter reaction of a man goaded to fury through jealousy. To have taken him seriously would have meant that she could not possibly have gone on living with him. And eventually surely he would come to recognise the truth and accept her word.

Joel, meanwhile, after taking a stiff whisky, and bracing himself for what lay ahead, went out, cut down the side of Treescarne to the back of the house where the stables were, saddled a young stallion, Lightning, mounted him, and set off for the Swales' cottage. There was no wind; the air had become heavy with the threat of approaching thunder, the sky a sullen yellow above the dark line of hills. Between dark clumps of heather and furze, early bluebells poked their speared heads, emitting a sweet almost cloying scent, mingled with damp earth smells where fronds of springing bracken curled.

Huddled from straggling briar and undergrowth great granite boulders crouched, beastlike, in the fading light.

Joel was only half way to the cottage when he saw Swales with a bundle of wood under one arm lurching along in shadows thrown by a derelict mine. He looked up menacingly as Joel came to a halt, dismounted, and after slipping Lightning's bridle over the twisted trunk of a dead tree, stepped smartly up to the man.

'I want a word with you, Swales.'

'Me? Agen? Want a go at me, still, do you? Edu' you satisfied?' The thick lips took a sneering twist. 'What about, mister? Tesn' often men of your so mighty state demeans 'emselves 'want talk wi' my kind—' His mood was taunting, swaggering from the drink he'd taken. A hot whiff of spirits clouded the atmosphere. Distaste and hatred thickened in Joel's throat.

He stepped closer, the riding whip raised threateningly in one hand. 'No games, Swales,' he said, 'no lies, I want the truth and by God I'll have it, or kill you with my two hands. What happened with my wife? You attacked her, didn't you?

You filthy scoundrel. It was *you* that day. By God, if you don't speak—'

Swales' large head took an ugly thrust forward.

'An' if I tells you, maister, think yu'd like et, eh? I tell you this—' he was breathing heavily, 'ef she was my wumman I'd tie 'er up an give 'er such a hidin' she'd not walk or sit for days without screamin'. That's what she needs — a strap across 'er backside.' He wiped a great hand across his mouth, his eyes were small fiery slits of red in their pouched creases of flesh.

Joel shot an arm out and sent the man reeling. He clutched his stomach, fell back on a clump of gorse, narrowly escaping a stone, tried to get to his feet, but was knocked back again by the attacker.

'Look 'ere—' Swales gasped. 'You edn' no right to act this way. She edn' worth et, Maister Blake. I tells you—'

Joel grabbed the collar of his jacket, and pulled him up.

'You tell me *just* what happened, you swine, and I shall know if you lie — see? Then you'll wish you'd never been born.'

He waited for Swales' reaction. The man didn't answer at first merely watched slily, top lip drawn snarlingly up over his ugly teeth, small piggy eyes blazing with hatred and fear. Joel suddenly let him go, but before Swales could properly escape, brought his riding crop against the broad shoulders and bull neck, and in renewed fury kicked out sending Barney once more lurching into the tangled furze and undergrowth. For a moment Joel paused, then went after him.

Swales turned once, yelling, 'You won't never know now, will you, maister? Won' never know now whether I took the bitch or not—' He was laughing and leering, his broad face gone an angry purple.

'You daren't—' Joel shouted. 'I'll—' He was on the point of coming to grips again with Swales when the man cut away with sudden speed to the left, and was lurching with increasing speed past rocks, bog pools and clumps of gorse, heedless of where he went, uncaring of the danger ahead, or of hidden mine shafts where darkness yawned beneath brambles and overgrown weeds. This was a particularly bad spot of moor for both human beings and animals. Many had been trapped there and never seen again. No one ventured to walk or ride that way any more.

But Swales went on.

'Come back, you fool,' Joel shouted. It was imperative to him the man should live to either allay his suspicions or confirm them. Barney took no notice. His figure now could have been that of some wild creature – badger or fox, nosing to a hidden lair. Only a dark shape could be seen, bent and half crawling.

Screwing his eyes up, Joel watched.

Then, suddenly, the scrambling figure disappeared. There was a yell – and what sounded like a distant thud, as Swales pitched down the gaping shaft-hole, down and down, to crumple in a few seconds broken and blackened by slime and weed into the murky waiting water. There was a curdling and swirling, a claw-like thrusting arm through the blackness. Then complete silence.

Joel waited hesitatingly for a time wondering what to do. Eventually, very cautiously, he made his way to the shaft. Broken briar branches and stems of torn weed marked the place where Swales' body had fallen. There was also a shred of Barney's coat. The hole loomed dark and terrifying – a yawning hungry chasm of darkness and certain death.

Nothing could be done for Barney Swales. Rescue was impossible. Joel turned and made his way back to where his horse was tethered. Good riddance of bad rubbish, he told himself unfeelingly. The man had been a brute and a liar, and the world was well rid of him. He determined to keep his mouth shut about the whole affair. It was only later that he was forced to recognise the one unfortunate angle of Swales' death. He, Joel, would never now know the answer to the vital question – had such a filthy lusting drunk sired the child that in a few months his wife, Caroline, was to bear?

His whole being was suddenly consumed by contempt.

One day he'd find out, dammit. A slip of her tongue in a weak moment, a glance at her eyes, a refusal to give a straight answer to a direct question – oh, he'd force the truth out of her somehow.

Spots of rain were falling when he passed through the hall. Neither of them spoke. A pall of despair seemed to hover over Treescarne. Anguish was in Caroline's heart — not only because of the tension between them, but over her longing for the comfort of Rupert Reeves' arms about her.

Never had the future appeared so black.

12

The next few months were busy ones for Joel, which made it easier for both him and Caroline to put up a front of normality before servants and any occasional visitor calling at Treescarne. Joel was more often away at Falmouth or Bristol than at home, and Caroline's condition didn't encourage callers. In herself she felt curiously remote from the outside world; Joel's business affairs no longer interested her, and he was apparently indifferent to any emotional undercurrents in her nature of antagonism or longing. Since the day of his scene with Swales on the moor and the man's fatal fall down the abandoned shaft, he'd controlled his first wild instincts to force facts out of her, needing temporarily to forget the whole business. He hadn't killed the man, but it was better he was gone, although a lingering resentment remained in Joel's mind that he'd taken the truth with him to his grave. There, Barney had won. None could bring him back to life. In this lay both Swales' victory and his defeat. One day possibly his body might be found, but it was unlikely. He was missed by no one. His wife even was more relieved than sorry for his disappearance.

So the days passed for Caroline almost without incident.

Joel made no advances to her; she was free to take reasonable exercise, and found a strange inner companionship with the wild creatures of the moors and lonely vista of hills where cromlech and ancient stones of the past reigned.

During the short period before the baby's birth Rupert contrived to see her only once, making a devious excuse to call at Treescarne. Although heartened by his presence, she was embarrassingly aware of her bulky figure, and regretted he would not see her at her best.

'I don't like looking so — so clumsy,' she admitted, 'I shall be glad when I can be a normal woman again.' Her delicate face was thinner, a little strained, her eyes had dark rings under them, emphasising their size. But to him she had never appeared more beautiful.

'I shall be glad for you,' he told her. 'I only wish—'

'Sh!' she lifted a warning finger. 'Don't say it, Rupert. The baby will be all right. Joel's child. We mustn't forget.'

He stared at her intently. 'Do you want it? The baby?'

She turned away.

'Of course. All women want their children.'

'No. Not *all*. The primitive type perhaps, and to those like you needing care and love—'

'You don't know me, not properly,' she interrupted. 'If you did you mightn't like me at all. You see, I'm not one of your gentle delicate types, Rupert dear. I *am* primitive — in a way—'

'And so am I.' His voice was gruff. 'That's why I'd sometimes like to get my hands round that bastard's — Joel's — neck, and throttle him. He doesn't deserve you.'

She smiled faintly, trying to make light of things.

'And you do? Maybe. You'd find me an awful trial.'

'Caroline—' He'd have taken her in his arms, but she pushed him away.

'Please don't. I mean it.'

He frowned. 'I'm sorry. For trying to force the issue at such a time, I mean.' He picked up his hat and went towards the door. As he opened it he turned for one long last look at her. There was a pause during which her strongest instinct was to run and fling herself into his arms. Then he said quietly, 'Things will work out one day, Caroline, I'm sure of it. One day, as I've said before, you'll need me, and I'll be there.'

She was still standing motionless, watching him, when he went out. There was a snap of a latch followed by another and the dying echo of his footsteps on the gravel outside.

Lethargically, as in a dream, she moved and went to the window. Horse and rider had already disappeared round a corner of the wooded drive, leaving only a fading shadow behind.

*

Towards the end of June when gorse flamed gold on the hills, and roses bloomed richest, deepest red about the garden of Treescarne Caroline gave birth to twins, a boy and girl. Neither bore any particular resemblance to Joel or their mother. The girl was dark, with already a tuft of rich chestnut brown hair emphasising the greenish hazel eyes and rosebud lips. She was neither skinny, red, wrinkled, or creased, as most babies were, but from the first day promised great beauty later. The boy was more fragile and delicate and unfortunately had a slight spinal defect.

'Nothing to worry about,' the doctor said, 'with good care and food, and special medical attention for a time he should grow into a fine boy.'

Joel's first glance at the children was enigmatic, holding little feeling except a grudging admiration of the girl. The boy's pale frizz of hair — almost white — and light eyes, combined with his high pitched wail, mildly affronted him. He surely couldn't be of his begetting, he thought, and instantly once more recalled the fair-haired Captain Reeves, and Barney Swales, either of whom might have sired the children. Still, for the sake of convention, he pretended a fleeting interest, said politely to Caroline, 'Congratulations! You appear to have got through the ordeal pretty well.'

Caroline looked away. 'I'm all right. Just tired.'

'Oh well, that's natural.' He coughed, kissed her dutifully on the forehead and said, 'I must be going. Not much use here anyway. The doctor and Mrs Magor will see you have all that's necessary.'

Inwardly Caroline sighed. All that was necessary! But these were her children, Joel's and hers, and he didn't care one iota.

'I quite understand,' she said. 'Don't bother about me. I'm sure you have far more important matters to attend to.'

Disregarding the note of sarcasm, Joel turned on his heel and left. His faint look of contempt when he'd glanced at the little boy had not escaped her, and from that moment she determined to make up to the child with all the love and compassion that was in her. The little girl would be healthy and strong. Already character and intelligence were alive in her face. But the boy! Instinctively she reached out and held him close. He was *hers*, and always would be — a special charge needing unfailing devotion and care.

Later the babies at Caroline's request were named respectively Holly and Luke. Luke, because, during the first weeks of his life — although he remained physically frail in comparison to his robust sister — he showed signs of an unexpected understanding and dawning knowledge which later was to prove his strength. Holly, because of her rosy cheeks and sturdy vitality. Joel didn't care for the name and said so, preferring something more exotic. But just for once he gave in.

Joel could feel no affection for Luke whatsoever.

For the girl he felt quite differently: Whatever she was — either his own, or of some other man's begetting — she was a beauty, and would bring pride to the name of Blake. He'd keep her as his own, whatever the truth of their blood relationship. Luke, on the other hand, was Caroline's responsibility. Let her do what she liked with him. He couldn't care less.

Caroline was bitterly hurt by Joel's attitude; because of his indifference which sometimes showed as more than that — definite dislike — of the little boy — she continued her passionate devotion to the child, giving him extra affection as compensation for his father's neglect. Treescarne became more than ever, at that period, a place of divided loyalties and misunderstanding. If Caroline attempted in any way to curb Holly's volatile temperament, Joel would counteract by spoiling the baby in every possible way.

'Don't you dare lay a finger on her — *ever*,' he said once to his wife when she'd given a light tap on the little girl's hand. 'If you do there'll be trouble, and it's *you* who'll suffer.'

'I never touched her,' Caroline retorted indignantly. 'As if I'd *slap* a baby.'

Joel's face was dark.

'I'm just warning you.'

Caroline could not help remarking tartly, 'If you could pay a little more attention to *both* children, Joel, Holly wouldn't scream so for what she wants. And Luke would be more responsive. He watches you often. He knows you don't like him.'

'*Like* him? He's just a *baby*. A—'

'So is Holly,' she interrupted.

'She's different. Lively, strong. The boy's a weakling.'

Caroline's lips tightened.

'I see.'

'And what does that mean?'

She felt suddenly tired, 'Oh, nothing, Joel. Nothing except — you'll never change. You just go for what you want giving no thought to anyone else at all.'

'Thank you. Thank you very much *indeed*.' His lips curved sarcastically above the strong chin. 'Go for what I want, do I? Well — maybe you're right. And it's high time you gave a thought to your own words. On the whole I've been extremely patient for far too long where you're concerned. You've shown considerable subtlety lately in keeping your delectable body to yourself. A taste of it now and again wouldn't go amiss. Remember that.' His mouth hardened. 'And be prepared in future to share your bed any moment I feel like it.'

He left her feeling tense and strained, in a conflict of emotion which held undercurrents of resentment, longing, and also faint fear.

Joel, however, in the immediate days following, showed no sign of fulfilling his threat or promises, and at the end of the week Caroline's thoughts were diverted by another problem — a letter from Ariadne.

Dearest Caro [she gushed] you knew I'd had my baby of course — a fortnight following your twins. *What* an accomplishment! — to have two babies at once, I mean. And isn't it thrilling for us to be mothers at almost the same time? Willie's naturally glad to have another boy, although he hides his enthusiasm too much sometimes. I suppose he thinks showing emotion is bad form. Oh dear! if only he could have a touch of Joel's adventurous streak, and Joel be just a *little* more restrained — (I'm *thinking of you*, darling, when I write this). It would be useful if we could put them both in a great bag and shake them up, wouldn't it? But of course I'm talking nonsense. Just like me. The point is, Caro, I'm thinking of coming to Lionswykka for a bit, if you have room at the hotel, and bringing Marcus with me. Marcus is a family name, you know. I thought it would be so wonderful to be real sisters again, two proud young mamas gossiping about their offspring. So I've written asking if I can have a room in the middle of September. I do hope that's all right with you, and that you won't be away or anything?

My love to you, the twins and of course to Joel.
    Ariadne.

'Oh botheration!' Caroline said to herself after she'd read it. By now the letter had probably been received at the office, and the booking accepted. What would Joel's reaction be? When Caroline told him he appeared to have little interest in the proposed visit, simply answering, 'Why not? I'm sure you two will have much to discuss.'

His voice and manner betrayed nothing.

No one could have guessed the seething irritation behind the hard exterior.

13

Ariadne arrived at Lionswykka in September, and after the first gushing, forced greetings to her sister and Joel, proved to be less of a social encumbrance than Caroline had feared. She visited Treescarne only three times during the first fortnight, and appeared to avoid Joel's company rather than seek it. Except for occasional overt glances when they met, he was merely casually polite to her, although Caroline sensed undercurrents of bitterness or desire — she could not decide which — that were subtly disturbing. She told herself she no longer cared for Joel, therefore his life was his own — only Rupert mattered. Rupert and Luke. How the pattern of their lives could eventually be resolved she'd no clear idea; only that she was not prepared to live forever with a man who could be passionately possessive one moment, the next treat her with contempt as though she didn't exist. She'd learned that his cruel manner of speech sometimes was mostly bravado, but there were depths to his character that still disturbed her. When he was about, his energy and volatile presence seemed to electrify the whole atmosphere, and she found herself tensed up, and frequently caught up between laughter and tears.

Yet the wild streak in him still intrigued her, like the adventurous spirit of a much younger man intent on conquering the world. In a rare moment he had revealed and discussed the new shipping line with her. 'Next year we shall have two ships under steam,' he'd said. 'You'll be able to have anything you like then — *anything*! Diamonds, gold—' His eyes had gleamed.

'Oh, Joel, I have enough jewellery,' she'd told him. 'Just—'

'Well?'

She'd mean to say, 'Just love me a little, make me think you care for me as a woman and not a possession, a showpiece.' But she'd held her tongue. 'Just be patient with me when I can't keep up with your plans,' she'd finished lamely.

He'd laughed, 'Who expects you to keep up? My aims are my own. A man's aims. Yours are in the nursery.'

After that the conversation had died, as it usually did when any reference to the babies was made.

Ariadne, who'd brought her young son with a nanny to the hotel, remarked on Joel's apparent lack of interest in his son, as the two women chatted together at Treescarne one afternoon.

'He seems devoted to Holly,' she said speculating, with a questioning glance towards her sister, 'but not Luke. Why?'

The abrupt question took Caroline aback.

'You must be mistaken. Although Mama says men are generally more fond of daughters than sons, once they've got an heir.'

'Hm!' Ariadne frowned. 'Neither of the babies are much like Joel, are they? *Or* you for that matter.'

'It's a good thing. Children should be personalities — themselves.'

'Think so?' Ariadne laughted shortly. 'Maybe you're right. Jasper takes after Willie of course, thank God. But Marcus so far's a cuckoo-in-the-nest — or *could* be. I mean, look at him!'

Caroline glanced down at the robust baby lying in her sister's arms. The nanny had gone for a few minutes to join the twins with their nursemaid in their own quarters. As she stared into the grey clear eyes of the little boy, he broke into gurgling laughter, lifting a tiny hand towards her. Caroline was startled. Although so young, the gesture of grasping at life, of unrestrained vitality, reminded her suddenly, acutely of Joel. She looked quickly away, aware of Ariadne's eyes intent upon her face.

'Well?' her sister insisted. 'What do you think?'

'What do you mean?'

'Who does he resemble? Willie or me?'

Caroline forced her voice to be calm. 'No one can tell. It's impossible to say, at such a young age.'

'Yes. That's what I told Willie.'

'Did he want another son like Jasper?'

'I expect so. Why shouldn't he? Most great families want the family line to show. Family *line*!' Her mouth curled contemptuously. 'Ridiculous really, isn't it? Who'd want a string of little Willies crawling about the nursery! But this one's different, aren't you, darling?' She kissed the baby on a fat cheek below a tuft of dark reddish hair. 'This one's unique.'

The baby suddenly gave a kick and started to cry. 'Oh botheration.' Ariadne got up, smoothed her skirt, and carried the bouncing infant to the door.

'*Lydia*, you're wanted. Come here, quickly.'

The girl appeared and took the child almost instantly. When they'd gone Ariadne sighed, glanced in the mirror, patted a few bright curls into place, and relaxed on to the sofa with her lovely face turned upwards from a blue velvet cushion. How handsome she was, Caroline thought with a stab of envy. Delicately made, yet vividly arresting. No wonder Joel had been captivated. There was the baby too. So dissimilar to her own small son. Very like Joel must have been when he was a child.

Joel!

Dark suspicion flooded through her. Could it be? Had fate been so cruel as to play such a monstrous trick upon her? During the days that followed Caroline did her best to allay her doubts. But the shadow remained, and she avoided contact with the little boy as much as possible. Joel showed little interest in the children except a certain fleeting glance of admiration whenever his eyes lighted on Holly. This, though, was seldom. His growing concern with matters involving the new ships took him so frequently away, either to Falmouth or Plymouth that moments with his family were rare.

Ariadne and the baby stayed on. Caroline became not only irritated but puzzled.

'Doesn't Willie *want* you home now?' she queried tartly one day. 'I should have thought you'd want the children to be together anyway. Surely Jasper should be with the baby? When you get back they'll be like strangers again, and small children can be jealous.'

Ariadne's glance held a hint of mockery. 'Oh no. There'll never be cause for Jasper to be jealous. My dear husband will see to that. Jasper's his glory and his heir.' Her lips curled in quick scorn. 'A true Perryn. I must admit though—' Her tone changed subtly. 'I felt a bit affronted at first – Willie's reaction wasn't *quite* what I expected.'

'How? When?'

'When he first saw Marcus. He was pleased it was a boy, as I told you. But he was critical. "How very *large*," he said. Just imagine it. It was as though he resented being the father of such a beautiful baby.'

'Yes. It does seem strange,' Caroline admitted. Her voice was calm, but beneath the short sentence her mind was in a whirl of tormenting confusion. She had a wild instinct to confront Joel with the blunt question, 'Is Ariadne's child *your* son? I've a right to know.'

Had she though? Was she imagining the likeness? Was the idea simply a concoction of her own distorted imagination? She tried to believe it was, but as the days passed she found her resentment to Joel deepening. On a rare occasion when Rupert met her in Truro, he sensed it and felt both enraged at Blake's casually cruel attitude to the woman he, Reeves, had come to care for so deeply, yet gratified she was beginning to accept the truth – however bitter. The sad situation could not endure much longer. She, Caroline, knew it. The break was inevitable, and would cause hurt and harm all round. His own reputation would suffer badly. He might have to resign his official post. If that happened he was prepared for it. Caroline's happiness came first.

Joel meanwhile avoided for a time becoming involved again in any emotional tangle. But one afternoon, when he was studying maps and routes in the library at Lionswykka, there was a light tap on the door, and Ariadne entered. From a side stained glass window the light touched her hair to fiery gold. She was wearing pale green muslin, and looked entrancing.

'Joel?' Her voice, though light, was rich and musical. Her lips curved upwards in an enticing smile.

'Yes?' His tone was abrupt.

'I'm sorry to disturb you. But − can you spare me a few moments? Or is it too difficult for you? − are you *very* busy?'

'Yes, very.'

'Oh,' she pouted. 'I'm sorry. Very well then; we can meet some other time. But I simply *must* talk to you.' She made a gesture as though to leave. He stopped her with a wave of his hand. 'No, if you've anything to speak about go ahead. Better get it off your chest. I'm a busy man. Sit down, Ariadne, for heaven's sake and don't dither.'

Her smile, then, was brittle. She seated herself opposite to him, and as his rather heavy brows arched questioningly above his clear eyes, she said, 'I'm in rather a difficult position, Joel.'

'Difficult? What do you mean?'

'With Willie.'

'What has Willie to do with me? Surely that's your own affair.'

'Oh yes. And I'll have to deal with him. But I—' her voice faltered before she continued, 'I need money, Joel. Rather a lot, I'm afraid. I've been a stupid woman, and Willie's found out. At least he *suspects* − and I have no fun any more, none at all, I've got into debt, and—'

'And you damn well come to me expecting I'll pay for your frivolities. Well − make no mistake, I'm not doing a thing. I owe you nothing; it shouldn't be difficult for a woman of your type to find some rich fool willing enough to put his hand in his pocket.'

Ariadne's wild rose complexion turned to deep crimson.

'Don't dare to talk to me in that fashion, Joel Blake. And don't think you can shrug off your responsibilities so easily—' She broke off, breathing heavily.

'*Responsibilities?*'

'Yes. And you know what I mean. Don't say you haven't *guessed*?'

There was derision in his voice.

'Guessed? Guessed what? What the devil are you talking about?'

'That Marcus is your son. I need support for him, and you're going to give it, Joel. If you don't the whole district and London will know the truth. I'll see to it. How will you like that? You won't, will you? You're very proud of your rising reputation, and very *very* ambitious. A bastard son isn't going to help, though. And Caro certainly won't like it.'

Joel's face whitened. He strode towards her, gripped an upper arm savagely, and shook her. 'Don't you *dare* mention a word of this to my wife — or to anyone else either. And don't think you'll get a penny out of me, madam, by your lying tongue. I'm not the man to be blackmailed. So see you keep your mouth shut. That lusty brat of yours may not be your precious husband's, but he's certainly not mine. And you know it.'

'Do I?' Again the acid-sweet smile. 'Just look at him, Joel, the first chance you have. He's the spitting image of you. And that's funny, isn't it? But Fate's a great joker. If you denied the truth not a soul in the world would believe you. You should have been more careful that time you raped me.'

For a moment or two he merely stared at her, then he suddenly slapped her face smartly. 'You *whore*!' he muttered.

She put a hand to her burning cheek, gave a short derisive laugh, went to the door, and before leaving said, 'Think about it, Joel. But not for too long. When you've considered everything I think you'll see I'm being extremely reasonable. Five thousand pounds — for your son's well-being and Caro's peace of mind. Cheap, considering, especially as you're so well able to afford it.'

Without another word she lifted her head haughtily, turned, and was gone.

Joel stood for some moments stunned and at a loss.

All his life he'd considered himself master of the situation where any woman was concerned. But this one appeared, for once, in danger of getting the better of him, simply because he accepted, secretly, that her son *was* of his begetting, and if the knowledge reached the ears of the Perryns could cause considerable trouble, and also endanger further his life with Caroline.

14

After his scene with Ariadne Joel half expected her to return to London either ostentatiously with a threatening glance in her eyes, for him, or quietly and suddenly, leaving him in doubt concerning her intentions when she confronted her husband once more. He wasn't unduly perturbed about the latter. Seeing he, Joel, meant to stand firm over the distasteful situation she'd hardly risk a break with Perryn. But Caroline was a different matter. He wouldn't put it past Ariadne to make trouble there. Sarcastic innuendoes, hints and sly comments — a jealous thwarted beauty like his sister-in-law would use them as effectively as possible to cause a proper rift. Not that the rift wasn't there already. He couldn't rid himself of dark suspicions towards his wife. What a mix up! Ariadne accusing him of fathering her blood bastard, and he under the cloud of not knowing whether Caroline's children were his or not. Why the devil couldn't he be left in peace, he thought whenever he came face to face with either woman? And why on earth was Ariadne lingering on?

Finding no satisfactory answer he shut his mind firmly away from both problems, and concentrated his full attention on the business and practical problems of getting the Blake Line under way, cargoes and routes pigeon-holed with contracts already under discussion.

Ariadne, meanwhile, made a point of being agreeable to the remaining guests at Lionswykka, conducting herself with the polite but charming hauteur expected of Lady Perryn. Beneath the façade, though, she was afraid. Afraid she had gone too far with Joel, and most of all afraid of the developing uncanny likeness between the baby and Blake. Ineffectual in many ways

Willie might be. But she recognised he was already tiring of her moods and many affairs. Before leaving London there had been an angry scene between them in which the odious word 'divorce' had been used. So far there was no actual *proof* of her infidelity; but bills were mounting up. She was desperate for money. Willie would not give it to her, and if he saw Marcus and Joel together — but he must not.

She must think up some plan that would take her away for a time, to the Continent perhaps, on the pretext that her health demanded it. Her son could go with her, accompanied by the nanny, and when they returned her husband would surely have been able to turn his suspicions into trust again. Marcus would be a fine son to him. After all — and she rejected the thought instantly, as though it was some sort of ritual — all babies looked in some way a little alike. She would find some characteristic in the child that could be magnified and eventually accepted by Willie as a likeness to him — a *family* quality proving he was undisputedly a true Perryn.

She sent a friendly letter to her husband, telling him she was deeply sorry for the quarrel, and that when she returned to London, which would be soon — he would be delighted to see how Marcus had grown and improved. 'He reminds me so much of your father, sometimes,' she wrote, 'and although I realise that Jasper will always be your favourite, a fine second son like darling Marcus will be a credit to us both.'

Willie's reply was terse and to the point.

'. . . for your sake I'm glad you're so proud of the boy, but you know my feelings on the matter, or should, by now. I thought I made them quite clear before you left London. I'm not really interested in your offspring's ancestry, or your tawdry if elegant affairs. We should not have married, Ariadne, there's no real point of contact between us, or ever has been. If you'd been more discreet maybe we could have kept up the charade; but discretion is not one of your characteristics. I refuse to be dubbed a cuckold, and have already consulted my lawyers. Everything will be achieved as quietly and efficiently as possible. You will receive a certain allow-ance, eventually. In the meantime I'm sure your jumped-up hotel owner will see you have a roof over your head. *He*'s the one, isn't he? Then see he pays.

Please don't write and say I have no proof. I've gathered plenty during these last two years — excluding Joel.

Yours,
William S. Perryn.

Ariadne was outraged.

How dare he! How *dare* he! she thought contemptuously, in the first heat of her anger. A dull colourless character with nothing to commend him but his name — a man who was accepted socially simply because he happened to have been born a Perryn. It was she, his wife, who gave him publicity and colour, who was always being alluded to in the press. And now to be talking again of divorce! It was ridiculous, a trick con-ceived somehow to shame her because he was jealous of her popularity. But as her rage gradually quietened, she knew, with a sinking heart, that Willie's words were no trick. He meant them.

Gradually slow fear in her welled up. Fear that turned to hatred. Joel was to blame for her dilemma. Joel, who had so viciously humiliated her when he'd taken her body in lust and then abandoned her. It was rape, no less. And Marcus was the outcome. Marcus! whose name should be Blake and not Perryn. And so it would be, one day, somehow. She'd see to that.

Eventually, after how long she couldn't guess, her natural resilience returned, and she forced herself to face the future squarely, with facts as they were. Willie *knew*; so did Joel. There was nothing she could do now to win Willie's forgiveness, but Joel must be made to face his responsibility. In spite of her husband's many shortcomings, Willie kept his word, and she knew that both for his own sake and hers, any forthcoming divorce would be kept as quiet as possible revealing few un-savoury details.

There would be gossip, of course, but in time, if she went

away, abroad perhaps, tongues would cease wagging. She could lead her own life, have fun — even perhaps find a nice rich husband who would give added glamour to her existence. She was beautiful still; everything she wished for was possible — provided she had sufficient finance. Her family had none to spare. Willie would keep any allowance to a minimum.

Only Joel was the answer, and the stumbling block there was Caroline. Caroline was sure to do all she could to thwart any generosity on his part to her sister. *Sister!* Well she was — half, anyway. Therefore it might be best to prepare her — convey the news herself that Marcus was her husband's offspring, and that she, Ariadne, expected him to do the right thing in shouldering responsibility.

Caro naturally would be hurt and very offended; that would be an advantage. Joel was not the type of man to be brow-beaten or scolded by any woman alive. Any tantrum of hers would only tend to send him, if not exactly into the arms of his paramour — but certainly into a more sympathetic mood. That he had threatened and abused her — Ariadne — so viciously once, didn't mean he would do so a second time. Wifely hysterics could even enhance any sensual allure Joel secretly felt for his sister-in-law.

So! it was settled.

With resolve firmly planted in her mind Ariadne confronted Caroline the following day in the large parlour, shortly after breakfast. She put the truth boldly and simply, showing neither antagonism or undue feeling.

'I'm sorry it had to come out this way,' she said with a wry glance, and a shrug. 'But you know me well enough, Caro, to realise I never beat about the bush. It was *partly* my fault I suppose, for ever becoming so friendly with Joel. But I didn't expect him to act the way he did. He *raped* me, and that's the truth. Willie guesses, of course. If I could have kept the truth from him, I would have. I've enjoyed being Lady Perryn. But it's impossible now. So you see I *have* to have Joel's assistance — financially. And I shall expect him to take responsibility for Marcus.'

She paused, watching her sister closely. Caroline had gone very white and was gripping the arm of a chair.

'I don't believe you,' she said in a faint, ice-cold voice. 'You've made it all up. Just to cause trouble. It's been the same always—' Her eyes closed briefly, and for a moment Ariadne thought she was going to swoon.

'For heaven's sake Caro, don't faint. Heavens! You were never such a weak ninny. Here—' She grabbed a decanter and poured brandy into a glass. 'Take this, pull yourself together. You're not a fool. You must've known from the beginning what Joel was like. It's not the end of the world.'

Caroline's eyes opened again. She pushed the glass away, spilling most of the liquid on the carpet.

'Caro—'

'I don't want it. I don't want anything from you. See Joel if you like. Tell him what you've told me. I don't care. I don't care a damn about *any* of you.'

She turned suddenly and rushed, with a flurry of skirts, from the room. Her world seemed to be toppling around her. She was too upset, too bitter, even to cry. When at last she reached the bedroom she went to the window and stood staring at the expanse of bleak moors, brown and gold now under the rising autumn sun. She shivered, feeling cold and bereft, as though seared by a biting wind. Deep down, of course, she'd guessed, but not wanted to admit it. Now there was no way out for her – nothing she could do, except leave Treescarne and Joel for ever – unless a miracle happened.

She was still standing there when her husband entered the room half an hour later.

'What's the matter?' he enquired, noting her rigid stance.

Caroline turned, looking straight at him. The bold lines of his face showed clear and strongly carved, although her own countenance was in shadow.

'I hear that Ariadne's child is your son,' Caroline answered. 'It's true, I suppose? And please don't lie to me.'

There was a deadly silence before Joel answered, 'Who said so?'

'Ariadne. And I believe her.'

Joel's hands were clenched at his sides.

'The bitch!'

'Yes. She always was. You're two of a kind, Joel.'

At that point he didn't attempt to deny the truth but after saying, 'I'll talk to you later,' left, slamming the door behind him, and went downstairs to confront Ariadne.

She had left the parlour, and was waiting for him in the library. Without a word he beckoned her autocratically, opened the door, and when she'd passed through, directed her to his study. Once there they stood confronting each other for a moment before he said, 'Sit down.'

'No, thank you, I'd rather stand. I realise this isn't a friendly interview.' The sarcastic smile held no guile, no pleading. She was wearing pale grey, which emphasised the ice-cold quality of her present mood.

'You're quite right — it isn't. If you were a man I'd kick you out of the house. As it is — after what you've just told my wife I can only order you to pack your things and be away in an hour.'

'Really?' The faint amusement in her voice added fuel to his rage.

'I've known some pretty cheap characters in my time, from lords and ladies to scheming prostitutes, but none to compare with you.'

'Of course not,' she remarked with a brittle smile. 'I'm a perfectionist.'

'You—'

'I know. I know — I'm under no illusions where you're concerned, Joel. We've got each other's measure pretty well by now, I think. I'm in a difficult situation — owing to *you*! remember that. I want money — you've got it. If you won't afford a little on your own son's behalf — and he *is* your son, Joel, you know that yourself — I'll make your name dirt through the land. No one will want to know you. *No* one.'

She paused, breathing quickly, watching a flicker of doubt cloud his eyes, then continued, 'Womaniser, low born adventurer of illegal deals in contraband, seducer, thief! Oh dear I'm afraid your fashionable world would soon collapse if I revealed all I knew.'

He smiled grimly.

'Blackmail doesn't go down with the law.'

'Oh, but it wouldn't be blackmail, Joel dear. I should be considered merely as the wronged woman — a colourful character no doubt — nevertheless one who had been ruthlessly misled, and let down by both her husband and unscrupulous lover. Imagine it! to be abandoned, and with a young baby. No doubt I could cause quite a sensation, and make a tidy little income from interviews with the press. But it would be so much nicer, and to your credit, don't you think, to behave with dignity? With me out of the country — and I promise I'd go as soon as I had sufficient in my pocket, the scandal would soon die.'

'And Marcus?'

'Ah!' Ariadne tapped the table speculatively with her carefully manicured white fingers. 'That's the problem. I would want to be free, naturally. To be burdened with a baby would curtail my — chances considerably, of making a fresh start.' Her chin took a sudden thrust. 'It isn't that I don't care for him — I'm not completely selfish. But as I said, I want the best for him. A good education which you can afford — and I hope — a father's pride.' For a fleeting second or two she appeared warmer, almost human. Her lip trembled.

'At first I thought of taking him. That's why I wanted so much from you. Now — I'm willing to reduce the sum quite a lot.'

'How very considerate of you.'

'I suppose I'm thinking of myself mostly,' she admitted unexpectedly. 'Security to live decently. Oh, for God's sake, Joel, after the way you treated me can't you for once see my point?'

'After what you've done to Caroline?'

She averted her eyes.

'I don't think Caroline will ever be happy with you, Joel. I haven't spoiled anything. Only speeded things up.'

'In a disgusting manner. You're a calculating—'

'Bitch,' she interrupted fiercely. 'Yes, I am. If I wasn't, I wouldn't get anywhere, would I? And don't tell me to go to hell. I've been there several times already. It can be quite amusing, at times. But as a permanency? No. For a change I just want relaxation in pleasant circumstances, that's all.'

The interview was ended abruptly by Joel striding to the door and saying with cold contempt, 'Get out, Ariadne. I'll think about what you've said. Not for your sake or because I owe you anything. I don't. But to have you out of my life once and for all. In the meantime, hold your tongue and keep quiet, otherwise—' his eyes glinted dangerously — 'I'll have to resort to other means.'

What those means were he had no idea at that moment, and she well knew it. She passed him with her chin high and a rustle of silk. There was triumph in her every gesture. She thought she'd won, the vixen, he told himself, as the latch snapped to. Well, to a certain extent she had, but only within limits. The sum mentioned by her would never be at her disposal to squander willy-nilly. As for the boy — poor little bastard — to be brought up by a woman like Ariadne seemed, somehow, unthinkable. If Perryn would have nothing to do with him — and Joel had a shrewd idea he didn't intend to, then somehow he, Joel, had to have a hand in the boy's future. The whole problem loomed before him, like a tiresome and boring game of chess.

For a week he conjured and played with various possibilities, and at the end of it made his decision clear to Ariadne.

'I will make you an allowance which will be sent to you every month by my solicitor,' he told her, naming a certain sum. 'You'll get nothing more out of me — not a single penny, so forget your greedy ideas for living in luxury on the Continent. On the other hand, what I am proposing will enable you to take a room permanently in some quite respectable hotel in Plymouth or Bristol. If you preferred it you could find a cottage somewhere.'

'A *cottage*? A hotel?'

'Why not?' He smiled coldly. 'Either, providing you never *never* come within fifty miles of Lionswykka again. If you take my advice you'll choose a hotel, so much more opportunity to stroll the streets at leisure and snap up some rich lover—'

Her colour deepened.

'You bastard!'

'No. I'm not,' Joel remarked, beginning to enjoy the game, 'which is quite surprising, considering my lowly beginnings. But I can assure you I was born in wedlock.' He paused, then continued, 'You will sign a paper I shall have prepared discrediting any lie or adverse statement you have made about me, and take an affidavit giving your word not to slander me in any way in the future.'

'I see?' her mouth tightened. 'And Marcus?'

'Marcus can, and will remain with me. So you will forego any right of contact or to interfere in the future.'

She gasped.

'My own *son*?'

Again the hard smile on Joel's lips.

'And mine, I believe. You've said it, and I accept it. I've eyes in my head.'

Eventually the deal was completed.

Ariadne commenced making plans to leave Lionswykka, and Joel, wanting to be free of the atmosphere and of Caroline's incessant questioning and dark moods, left for a few days and took himself off to Falmouth, not realising one quarter of Caroline's distress.

She hoped, prayed, desperately tried to believe, that Joel, in the end, would refute Ariadne's claims concerning Marcus, knowing, deep down, that he wouldn't. He wasn't by nature a liar; she herself guessed the truth. When she thought of their life together in the days ahead, everything appeared empty and impossible. If only he'd send her sister and child away immediately, there might be a chance for their marriage — outwardly. But apparently he was determined to refuse such a concession, which not only shocked, but humiliated her beyond bearing. Before Joel set off for the Falmouth visit he'd told her of his decision concerning Ariadne.

'I was a fool,' he admitted, 'she means nothing to me. I took her in a spirit of revenge as I would any whore set out to trap me. She'll never bother us again though, I'll see to that. But the boy's my responsibility.'

'Why?'

'Because I sired him — presumably.'

'So you admit it?'

'Haven't I said so? There have been quite a number of by-blows in high class society, before this one. Youngsters without names — foundlings placed in foster homes, neglected without proper care or affection. Well — this one won't. You may consider me all kinds of a rake and rascal, but I don't aim for any boy of my begetting to grow up without a chance. So he'll stay here.'

'*Here?* — with Holly and Luke?'

'They won't be contaminated. Marcus is strong and healthy.'

'Unlike your legal child Luke,' she'd said bitterly, 'and mine.'

'Obviously. But don't take the blame. It's not your fault.'

'My fault? — *my* fault? How *dare* you!'

Her hands had been clenched at her sides, her eyes wide and bright above the flaming colour staining the high cheek bones.

He'd given a derisive laugh. 'Oh, Caro, don't be so melo-dramatic — *dare*?' The tone of his voice changed suddenly. 'Don't challenge me. I make the decisions here, and don't you forget it. You'll be reasonable, and behave, and accept the presence of another defenceless baby in our menage without trouble, or I'll know the reason why. Do you understand?'

She'd faced him defiantly and answered coldly, 'Yes, I under-stand. The trouble is — you don't understand *me*.'

She'd turned, and walked away. He'd watched her moodily, thinking, 'Let her scratch and claw. She'll come round.'

In the first two days of Joel's absence Caroline and Ariadne didn't speak to each other. Then, feeling desperate one after-noon, Caroline went to Lionswykka to see her.

Ariadne was in her bedroom sorting out clothes and nick-nacks ready for her approaching departure. She looked up as Caroline entered without knocking, feigning surprise.

'Caro! how nice. Or shouldn't I say that? Should I offer my

hand begging forgiveness. If so I'm afraid you'll be disappointed. I'm in a hole, thanks to your no-good husband, and about to take off for good. But, of course, you know that. You've won, Caro, if you think it an achievement to be chained to such a greedy cold-blooded tyrant as Joel Blake. But let me tell you this, and I mean it, I wouldn't be in *your* shoes for all the tea in China — that's a ridiculous expression, isn't it? Still — if you're willing to be a doormat it's *your* affair. *I'm* not though. He's a lusty lover, and can be diverting at times, but I prefer to be the one and only in any man's life, which I sadly fear will never be your lot — not with Joel.'

Before she properly realised what she was doing, Caroline stepped forward quickly and slapped Ariadne sharply on the face. 'You're rotten,' she said, 'Joel was right. He—'

Touching her burning cheek lightly, Ariadne said in bored tones, 'Oh, leave me alone. I can guess what Joel said. Believe him then, I don't care. I'm sick of you both. Thank heaven I shall soon be away from this moribund place. I detest it, and I detest your puritanical mind. You bore me utterly.' She turned away with a curl of the lip. A moment later Caroline, without another word, left her.

That evening she wrote to Rupert Reeves:

. . . I can't stay here any longer. I'm just too unhappy and miserable to put up with things any more. I don't quite know what to do, or where to go. Is it possible for me to see you tomorrow, Rupert, before Joel gets back? He's at Falmouth for a few days. You've always been so kind and sympathetic to me — my only friend except for my father, and I'm afraid he wouldn't be free to give proper advice concerning mama's attitude. I hate having to burden you with my affairs, but if ever I needed you, it's now. And just to guide me a little, that's all.

Your devoted,
    Caroline.

She sent the letter by early post to Bodmin, where Rupert had his headquarters. He replied immediately, saying, he would arrive at Treescarne the following day as soon as possible to discuss things. He also told her to be prepared to leave with him. Caroline waited all morning in a fever of anxiety for his arrival, desperately hoping Joel would not appear first. She had a case packed and ready in the hall. In it were a minimum of clothes and accessories for herself, and all that was necessary for tiny Luke. Mrs Magor was belligerently disapproving, although Caroline had insisted she was only departing on a short holiday, and would be visiting her parents in the meantime.

'Captain Reeves is coming to escort me,' she said. 'I've already given orders at the stables for the carriage to be ready.'

'Oh! so that's et. Another *man*! Well, ma'am, your life's your own. I only hope your husband knows.' Her small eyes grew smaller. 'Back sometime today or tomorrer, edn' he? For your own sake mebbe it'd be better if he gets here first. Not the kind of man I should say who'd 'preciate a young wife tekkin' off without so much as a word, an' in *such* circumstances. Another thing—' she sniffed, 'what about little Holly? Desertin' her, are you?'

Caroline's colour fled. 'That is not your business, Mrs Magor. Holly is her father's pet. He'd be extremely put out to be separated even for such a short time.'

'*Would* he now! I shouldn't have said so. Seems to me it's *you* he's concerned with, an' no one else.'

Defiance suddenly drained from Caroline's whole being.

'You're quite wrong.' Her voice was very tired. 'And please stop questioning me. It isn't your place to do so.'

'No one seems to know what anyone's place is in this house any more,' the harsh old voice stated ironically. 'Lady hoity-toity whatsername at Lionswykka now. She's another one who's up to something. She and that — that screamin' brat o' hers. Of course, 'tisn't *my* affair to suggest anythin' where the master's concerned, but one look at the boy's enough — if you get my meanin' — that's *why* if you've any sense, you'll stay here ma'am, an' see you get y'r rights. I don't approve of what you're doin'; two wrong's don't make a right. But I c'n understand, in a way. I'm not without sympathy, though you may think so. It's just I'm not a fool, and can't for the life of me see any good comin' of your runnin' off.'

'I'm *not* running off. And I told you — it's none of your business.' Following a few more words of argument the old woman went away leaving Caroline feeling more ill-at-ease and anxious than ever.

Half an hour later the Captain arrived. In an instant, Caroline, hardly realising it, was in his arms. After the first embrace and sudden flood of tears she explained as lucidly as possible, her humiliating circumstances, adding, 'Ariadne's going away of course, and leaving the baby, Marcus, behind. I *won't* and can't stand it any more, Rupert. You've told me time after time to contact you if it was necessary. I didn't want to — at least I *did* — but I wouldn't have, if Joel had shown me the slightest affection or consideration for his own son. But he hasn't and never will. He's never really cared about me, I can see it now. There's something cold and brutal about him—'

She dabbed her eyes with a lacy shred of handkerchief. His arm tightened about her shoulders. The affectionate pressure gave her renewed strength. She eased herself away, and asked simply, 'What am I to do? What do you advise?'

'You know that; you've known it for some time. You must leave him. I suppose a visit to your parents would be the conventional and right thing — for most women. But I know you don't get on too well. Also — I'm thinking of myself.' His glance warmed her. 'Not immediately though. First of all you must have somewhere comfortable to live. I suggest you staying with an aunt of mine near Exeter. There all proprieties would be observed, and I should have every chance of seeing you when duty allowed. Do you understand?'

It did not take Caroline long to agree. In five minutes time she and tiny Luke were on their way in the carriage to Penzance station with Rupert riding a little way ahead. From there the Captain managed to get a message through to his aunt.

They were lucky to find a train due to start almost immediately for Devon. It was only when they were comfortably away in their own compartment that Caroline asked, 'Has it been

difficult for you, Rupert? Will you be blamed for – for neglect
ing your duties or anything?'

His hand enclosed hers.

'Let duty go to the devil,' he said lightly. 'Just for once. You're
the most important thing in my life now. I may even give up the
service later. Who knows? The fact is, I love you.'

And I love you, she thought, at the same time wondering at
the wild brief sense of loss in her, when she so hated Joel. She
was thankful to be rid of him. But life would never be quite the
same again. It was as though a fire had raged and suddenly
died, leaving her exhausted and spent, unable yet completely to
envisage the new life ahead.

Life with Rupert and Luke. Yes, eventually they would be
together for all time. A faint smile touched her lips. The
Captain was a good man, and kind. She could trust him.

Never, *never* would she regret the decision to leave Joel. With
which thought her eyes slowly closed, and she was asleep. The
baby wailed faintly. Rupert very gently removed the child from
her arms and managed to quieten him.

'Damn glad there's no one else in the compartment,' he
thought, and for the first time realised what he was taking on.
She was worth it though. And he wouldn't let her down. She'd
suffered; a woman of her type didn't lightly break a marriage,
leaving one child behind, into the bargain. His hand touched
hers compassionately. She stirred and glanced at him. It was as
though the thought of Holly had somehow penetrated her consciousness, forming a mental bridge between them.

She sighed. 'You must think me rather callous, leaving one
baby behind.'

'You did the practical thing. From what you say she's her
father's child more than yours.'

'She didn't respond to me at all,' Caroline said. 'Jane, the
nursemaid, and Joel are the only ones who count with her. It's
odd how different the two children are. Twins are generally
close, aren't they? But from the first Holly dominated poor little
Luke. When she wants anything she screams until she gets it—'
she sighed, then added, 'Joel will spoil her, when he has time. If

he ever does — that's what makes me feel guilty, that she'll grow up not knowing what family life is.'

'You're being too pessimistic. A little later we can see about having the child with her brother. If I know men as I think I do, Blake won't care much whether she's with him or you — if there's a court case over a divorce.'

'I don't want that.'

'Neither do I. But you're facing a new future, Caroline, which will have to be legalised sometime.' Noting her reflective, sad expression, he continued, 'Don't worry, love, *please*. For my sake as much as yours.' He rested his lips briefly against her cheek. The train jolted as it drew up at a station. The tiny baby woke, breaking into a wail.

Rupert smiled. 'You'd better take him, I think he needs attention. I feel a certain dampness—'

Caroline blushed, reaching for the child. 'Oh, Rupert, how awful. I *am* sorry.'

He touched his breeches, grinning. 'No harm done, you're just in time.'

Caroline made her way with Luke down the corridor. When they returned, the baby had stopped wailing and looked comparatively happy.

By the time they reached Exeter the light was fading, giving the silhouetted buildings and hills beyond a dream-like but faintly menacing look. A thin mist, which later might turn to fog, was rising. The busy station was damp and bewildering to Caroline, a changing macabre scene of furry dark figures, swaying fitful lights, and porters, of shouting as luggage trucks passed and the cloying smell of steam and smoke. Shrill whistles penetrated the thick air at intervals.

Loneliness briefly engulfed her. What had she done? Where was she going with this kindly loving man she cared for, but who nevertheless was almost a stranger? As though sensing her trepidation, Reeves took her arm, and with a porter carrying what luggage they had, urged her to the barrier.

'My aunt's chaise will be waiting outside,' he said. 'Don't worry, darling. You must be tired, but we'll soon be there.'

Still feeling in a daze, Caroline walked automatically by Rupert's side through the barrier and out into the street. As he'd said, the family vehicle was waiting. Assisted by the Captain, she stepped inside, and a short while later they were off, driving through a medley of streets to the outskirts of the city. Caroline's nerves relaxed. The baby, to her great relief, was content and asleep.

By the time they reached Greenvale, a small mansion situated in a dip of hills and pasture land, it was almost completely dark. Squares of windows sent lights streaking across a drive leading to the front door. The house was of Georgian architecture obviously, but to Caroline the fact was of little interest just then. All she felt was relief at last of reaching a tangible destination where she and Luke could rest, at peace.

15

Joel was enraged when he returned to Treescarne and found Caroline gone. But he kept his temper outwardly under control.

'What do you mean — *gone*?' he demanded after questioning Mrs Magor.

The old housekeeper eyed him shrewdly, with a touch of belligerence in her manner.

'Just what I say,' she replied, 'took off in that theer coach thing an' couldn' tell no one where she was goin'. That man was with her.' Her lips primped meaningfully. 'Ridin' I mean — aside her, as though he was some kind o' guard. The baby too. Little Luke.'

'What man?'

'The Cap'n. I did say sumthen' 'bout en, to you afore.'

Inward fury drove the colour from Joel's face; his lips were grey and compressed.

'Thank you,' he said abruptly.

He strode to the stables where he confronted the groom who'd driven the chaise.

'What the devil do you mean taking my wife on a journey without my permission? And where did she go?' He enquired tightening his jaws. 'Tell me, you oaf, or I'll have you out on your ear—' He grasped the man's jacket at a shoulder. After a second the man freed himself.

'All I know is she got a train at the station, surr – up-country. An' I couldn' ask your permission to drive her because you warn't there.'

'And the Captain? It was Captain Reeves presumably?'

'Yes. That was him. The Revenue Officer.' His voice was expressionless, the blue eyes blank. 'I know nuthen' of the circumstances, surr. But there was a man took the Cap'n's hoss away. So I reckon he went with her, Cap'n Reeves did, on the steam train.'

Blake turned on his heel and returned to the house. His mood had changed to sombre, ugly bewilderment. So his suspicion had been right. Caroline had deceived him. The children were of that sly devious Captain's begetting. If he could get his hands on him at that moment he'd have killed him and be damned to the consequences. But why the devil hadn't she taken the girl too? Holly.

He went to the converted bedroom where the child was sleeping. The nurse – or 'nanny' to use the high-falluting term – was sitting in an easy chair reading, from the glow of an oil lamp burning on a small table nearby. She hurriedly jumped to her feet when he entered.

'Do *you* know anything about it?' he asked bluntly. 'Were you in any plot to assist the disappearance of my wife – and son?' The last word came out haltingly, with considerable distaste.

'No, I wouldn't dream of such a thing.' Her voice held veiled contempt. She was an ordinary but comparatively well-educated young woman who'd been chosen by Caroline, but cost far more, in Joel's opinion, than she was worth. 'You were in a position of trust,' Joel said shortly. 'Why did you allow the twins to be parted?'

'How could I stop Mrs Blake wanting to take her little son on a — holiday? His own mother.'

'Hm! His own mother. No. I suppose it was difficult. She did say a holiday then?'

'That's what was implied.'

'And you don't know where?'

'No.'

Dissatisfied, feeling suddenly thwarted and noting that none of the servants were either able or willing to help him, Joel went sullenly to his private sanctum where he drank more whisky than was good for his health or any logical reasoning power he had left. His brief spell in Falmouth had been successful. The Blake Line would open in the New Year. The first cargo was to be general merchandise shipped between America and Britain, the name of the boat *The Golden Star*. A number of passengers would be included on the maiden journey.

Everything so satisfactory, except his marriage.

Gradually Joel's ill humour turned to grudging acceptance. Bemused by the spirit, he thought, 'Well, what of it?' As far as he was concerned marriage had more than fulfilled its purpose. If the young madam wished to take off with her fancy man, he couldn't care a cuss. She'd helped get him where he wanted, but of late had been more of an encumbrance and scold than anything else.

He was unsteady on his feet, with a fiery glow in him when at last he made his way to the bedroom. By then it was dark outside but a chink of light slid under the door, streaking across the landing floor. He fumbled with the knob, then managed to turn it and went in. Half stumbling he approached the bed. Then, with a start that brought a brief shock of sobriety to his befuddled senses, he saw someone standing by the dressing table. A white, luscious naked figure, standing with her arm partially extended towards him, her pale gold hair lit to silver about her shoulders.

Ariadne.

He gasped, feeling the lust stir in him through a wave of revenge. Yet drunk as he was, he managed to say, 'Get out, you slut—' knowing he no longer meant it.

She moved towards him. 'Oh, no, Joel,' her voice was low and throaty, rich with desire and promise. 'Not now. You need me more than ever. Two of a kind. Remember?'

Her smile was warm, the scent of her body overpowering with heady perfume. 'You can have anything you want of me,' she whispered, 'Body, spirit — everything. Life can be an adventure, Joel. Together we can achieve anything you want.'

Achievement — yes. Perhaps she was right. Her face swam on a sea of half oblivion before his eyes; but her flesh, as he reached and fondled it, lit a fire in his veins. Suddenly in reckless shame he took her to him, wrenching his own clothes apart before savouring the opiate for Caroline's rejection.

When it was over, they lay for a time at peace until he suddenly got up, jerked her to full consciousness, and said roughly, 'Now get up, dress yourself, and be out of his house before I lay a whip about your shoulders.'

Her mouth opened uncomprehendingly at first then as the truth registered — he could mean what he said — her eyes widened in alarm; she half rolled out of bed; he gave her a push, reached for her clothes from the floor and flung them at her. 'Get out, you—' The filthy word never left his lips. By then he was sane enough to realise Mrs Magor already might be lurking about.

With a little cry of hatred and fear, Ariadne clutched her clothes and rushed to the dressing room. She was shaking and still only half coherent but seeing a brandy bottle on a shelf, grabbed it and put it to her lips. The alcohol temporarily revived her and cleared her head. She pulled on her gown, cape, and a pair of boots — not hers, they were far too large, but some visitor's maybe or a servant's — and with the hood of the wrap pushed well forward to hide her face, plunged downstairs and out of a side door.

It was very dark outside. What thin moon there'd been was clouded by mist. Bushes, rocks and occasional standing stones were dwarfed and contorted beyond recognition, rising as great lumps suddenly out of the tangled ground. Tiredness once more dulled her senses. She tried to recall the shortest way back to Lionswykka, the route she'd taken when she'd heard Joel had returned, but no proper sense of direction registered, only one fact — down, down. She must continue towards the dip in the moor before the headland rose dark and jagged, stretching into the Atlantic. Twice she stumbled, drunkenly, and lay for moments crumpled and breathing heavily. Then she got up again and went on. Brambles clawed. Evil faces seemed to peer from granite lumps mockingly. And always behind her, she fancied Joel in pursuit, wanting to kill her.

Kill! Kill! But there was life ahead. At the hotel she'd be safe if only she could reach it. She continued breathlessly, and stopped briefly, searching the pocket of her cape for a brandy flask. Usually she carried one, but it wasn't there. The heavy boots tugged at her ankles and feet; every step she took now became heavier and more laborious. 'I must get these things off', she thought, half falling on to a stone, and tugged at one. But the effort was useless. Her head became lighter. The world spun round. She dragged herself up, and scratched and bleeding went on once more, not realising the yawning pools of dangerous bog ahead.

Suddenly she pitched forward and fell. Yawning, sticky blackness claimed her. She was sufficiently sober by then to realise what was happening. She screamed but no one heard. As though her feet were lead blocks, she sank, inch by inch into the greedy sucking ground. As the dank filth closed over her chin, then her mouth and eyes, a frail hand clawed upwards helplessly, then disappeared. The moon cleared momentarily from its belt of cloud, spreading a wan light over a broken circle of black bubbles that eventually settled again into shining blackness.

A bird screamed as it rose from a stunted tree to the night sky. Then all was still.

Ariadne was no more.

*

If Mrs Magor had heard anything that went on between Ariadne and Joel that fatal night she staunchly held her tongue. In answer to the inevitable enquiries concerning Lady Perryn's disappearance, all she said was that she had paid a visit to Treescarne early in the evening, and had then left, alone. She knew, because she'd watched her go.

'She was a very energetic, restless lady,' she told the police, 'always comin' an' goin'. The master asked me if I'd seen her when he came back, an' I told 'en she'd gone without so much as a goodnight or anythin'. In my opinion—'

'Yes?' the officer enquired.

'She's just lost 'erself down one o' them hidden mine-shafts, or took off wi' them gypsies. I don' put nuthen past 'er.'

The gypsies were questioned. One or two known open shafts were investigated as closely as possible. Neither gave any clue.

Whether dead or alive, the mystery was never solved. Neither Joel nor anyone else was blamed. The sudden disappearance of Ariadne, the beautiful Lady Perryn, became in time just one of those inexplicable macabre events occurring at rare intervals in that remote wild part of Cornwall.

16

During the immediate days following Ariadne's death, Joel
became at first sullen and silent, then worked himself to fever-
pitch concerning the opening of the Blake Shipping Line. He
was irate with workers at the estate and upset miners by threats
of further unemployment unless a larger quota of tin and
copper was produced. Above everything else he was furiously
mortified by Caroline's desertion, and determined to get her
back even if it was by force. He received a letter from his wife
after a week with the Captain's aunt, giving her address but also
informing him she would never return.

. . . I don't know quite where I shall live in the future, but I
am not coming back to you. It would be useless. You never
loved me, or you would not have behaved so unspeakably
with Ariadne, or flaunted your relationship and her child —
your child, under my nose. I've borne your threats and
cruelty in the past because I cared. Now I don't. You've
spoiled all that for ever. I hope you will be civilised over everything and not come here trying to bully me into returning.
Joanna — Miss Reeves — is very kind, I am well, and so is
Luke. Not that you mind about him. You never did, did you?
Although he, also, is your son. Another thing — I was never
unfaithful to you, Joel. The twins *are* yours, whatever warped
ideas you have. About Holly! I'm sure, in time, when matters
are settled, you'll see that the best thing is for me to have her
with me so she can become more close to her brother. I only
left her with you because you've shown interest in her in the
past, and I didn't want to upset you unnecessarily, and

because, for the time being I felt unable to deal with the two children.

I will write more later when you have thought things over and come to see reason.

This isn't a hasty decision.

I *mean* it.

Caroline.

Joel was stunned, then violently angry. He wrote a short reply, tore Caroline's letter up, and despatched his own immediately:

. . . you've behaved outrageously [he wrote in his bold hand-writing]. And I shall certainly not agree that you contact my daughter in any way until you return and behave in a rational manner. I could divorce you for taking off with that sly mealy-mouthed official, but I'm not going to. You'll never be free of me, Caroline, neither will I pay you a penny for your support or that of our weakling son — if he *is* ours. Reeves can fork out if he cares to, more fool him; but if he does, by God! — I'll ruin him. He deserves a horse whip about his shoulders. As for you — don't talk about me threatening you, madam — unless you come to heel and do your duty as a normal wife you'll meet with more than threats. . . .

The letter ended on a more conciliatory note,

. . . come back, Caroline. I may be a tough character, but I want you.

Your husband,

Joel Blake.

Caroline didn't answer the communication, and three days later Joel arrived at the Reeves' residence. The Regency house stood in a slope of parkland on the outskirts and overlooking the City. There was a short straight drive leading between elm trees to terraced steps and a porticoed front door. From a window of a parlour Caroline, glancing out, saw him walk smartly from the cab in his usual arrogant fashion, top-hatted, wearing fawn breeches and cut-away brown coat. Her heart quickened with the familiar sense of excitement and fear Joel's presence always roused in her. She had a wild wish to run away and hide — somehow avoid the confrontation. No good would come of it — only pain for both of them. But she recognised it was impossible. The servants knew she was in the house. Miss Reeves was already in the hall arranging flowers. She would not consider it right to turn her husband away when he had come so far. If only Rupert was here! Rupert, though, was in Plymouth for two days, so she had only Joanna to rely upon.

After a quick glance through the mirror and a pat on her curls, Caroline heard voices, and the next minute Joel was shown in.

'A visitor for you, my dear,' Rupert's aunt said in controlled tones. 'Your husband, Mr Blake.' She stood by the door until Joel had passed through, a tall, stately woman, dressed well, but simply, in dark green, with a high-necked bodice that emphasised the clearly cut stern features and air of strength about her erect well corseted body.

'When you have finished talking,' she said, before closing the door behind her, 'just ring, Caroline, and I will see you have some refreshment.'

She left.

Joel stared at Caroline hard before speaking. She didn't flinch, but her face was white when he said coldly, 'What do you mean by this ridiculous play-acting? This — this farce.'

'I'm not acting, Joel. I thought by now you'd have understood.' She walked to the window, then turned and faced him again. A rim of sunlight outlined her slender figure. She was wearing pastel blue that emphasised her ethereal quality and remote attitude. He took a step towards her. She lifted a hand haltingly. 'No, Joel, don't, please. I meant what I said — it's over.' In spite of her resolve there was a quiver on her lips. 'Oh, please don't argue. I'm so tired of your dominance, selfishness

– your – your overpowering, aggressive way of getting what you want. I'm sorry. I really am. In many ways I'm—'

'You're my wife,' he interrupted harshly, and before she knew it he had grasped her wrist. 'That's all that matters. Just remember it and listen to me. I'm not giving you up – to *anyone*. Least of all to any smarmy, sly-tongued Revenue official.' His eyes burned into hers, reviving for an instant a spark of the old flame between them. 'If he was here he'd soon know where he stood. *And* you—'

'Joel.'

'Don't Joel me, don't plead, don't try to be so damned rational either because you're not. You're as wild and wanton underneath your prim manner, as—'

'Ariadne?' The name was a stab that shook him.

'She's nothing to do with us. Leave her out of it.'

'How can we? The mother of your child? Your – your bastard. And where is she, Joel? What happened? As her sister I think I've a right to know.'

'If I had a clue I'd tell you. Ask your lover. He's got a nose for mysteries, I believe, for sniffing about like a bloodhound into other folk's affairs. As far as I'm concerned—' His grip loosened a little.

'Yes?'

'She can go to hell.'

'A pity you didn't think of that before.' She loosened herself abruptly, and continued in cold tones, 'Go now, Joel. I'm *not* coming with you, and I think it would be far better if you accepted the fact that anything we had together is over now – for good. All the same, you should understand that Rupert – Captain Reeves – isn't my lover and never has been – yet. One day, perhaps, who knows? But that won't be your concern.'

Her arrogance goaded him to quick action. He slapped her face sharply, pointed to the door and said, 'Go and get packed. I'm waiting here till you're ready.'

Caroline reached for a bell on the side table, and rang it with vigour. Almost instantly the door opened and Joanna appeared. Her dark brows were drawn together in a puzzled frown. There was something both noble and formidable about her that momentarily subdued him.

'Joel is just leaving,' Caroline said, in level tones.

'Really? A *very* brief visit.' The firm lips showed a faint hard smile. 'Still, I am sure Mr Blake knows his own business best. Crowther?' She glanced back over her shoulder. The figure of a man servant emerged from the shadows. He looked immensely strong, and Joel, whose first instinct was to lunge out and push the fellow aside, noted in time, the indignity and doubtful process of the attempt. He took his hat and cane with a savage gesture. There had been a plot, obviously, to get him away as soon as Caroline gave a clue.

With icy sarcasm he smiled at Joanna.

'Your household is very efficiently ordered, Miss Reeves. I congratulate you.'

She inclined her head slightly. 'Thank you. I'm sorry you won't stay and eat with us. But under the circumstances—'

'The circumstances will be different next time, ma'am,' Joel cut in, smiling acidly. 'My wife and I have several matters to discuss yet, so I look forward to your hospitality in due course.'

Stifling an impulse to put Caroline over his knee and shame her then and there before the astonished eyes of the prim virginal Miss Reeves, he turned on his heel, and without a shake of the hand or chaste kiss on his wife's brow, strode quickly past the footman to the front door and out down the steps to the drive.

Joanna touched Caroline's arm tentatively. 'It's all right, my dear. He's gone now. He can't hurt you in any way,' she said reasoningly. 'Not a nice man at all.'

No, Caroline agreed inwardly. Not nice. A hard man, incapable of making any woman truly happy. Why, then, did she suddenly feel so flat and alone? So bereft of sparkle and the joy of living?

'Rupert will be back in a few days,' she heard Joanna saying, as though through a dream. 'You'll feel better then.' There was a sigh. 'I don't really approve, dear, of women leaving their husbands, and I must confess that when my nephew confided to me his feelings for you, I was doubtful — doubtful and disappointed at first. Then, when I grew to knew you, I changed my mind. Well, I had to, didn't I? Seeing how things were, and knowing my nephew. He's a very loyal character. If you are ever free to marry him I'm sure you'll be a devoted couple. But be sure of yourself, Caroline, my dear. Be *very* sure before you embark on a new life. It would pain me very much to see Rupert hurt.'

'I'll never willingly do that,' Caroline answered, and meant it.

*

For the first few days after his unsatisfactory meeting with Caroline, Joel made an attempt to shut all emotion from him, dedicating himself fanatically to business matters. In a comparatively short time the first ship would steam out of Falmouth under the Blake name for America with a number of passengers and with legal cargo. It could be lucrative, and the return passage more so. Pride still goaded him, the true and more adventurous undertaking lay in the future. But inwardly he was bitter. His life was not clean-cut any more. Although his inherent commonsense told him no woman was worth fretting over, the fact remained that with Caroline he had failed. One day, he told himself, in the rare moments when he allowed his thoughts to dwell on her at all, he'd get her back. No man — not even the suave-tongued Reeves, would have the better of him for ever.

In the meantime, his opiate and true objective was work. He became morose, and more short-tempered which did not help his failing popularity with workers and inhabitants of the district. Through his initiative and determination he had procured employment for men who before had been out of work, but some had suffered and lost their livelihood. Whispering started. What was the rich buccaneer up to? Oh yes, he worked all right — and was a real devil at getting others to go along with him. But what happened when they didn't? And wasn't it a bit odd that more than one connected with him had disappeared? Swales, for instance? And now that stuck-up Lady Perryn who according to rumour had been on considerably more than friendly terms with him? Where was she? She'd been with him the night she took off? As for the baby she'd left behind — one look was enough to show who'd sired him. Another thing — his wife wouldn't have taken off for nothing. Oh, he was a dark one all right. And so the rumours and whispering went on.

Joel was only half aware of it. In any case he didn't care. He'd had no hand in the misfortunes of either the rascally Swales or the greedy luscious Ariadne. He cursed himself for ever having had anything to do with her, that was all. But the children were a mix-up. He'd no liking for his legitimate son, but if Caro thought she could keep him for ever she was making a great mistake, which she'd realise soon enough when he got down to brass-tacks, either with the assistance of the Law or not.

Marcus was a different matter.

One day, seeing the child and Holly in a large carriage together which had been specially made for the twins, he went over and had a look at both. A flicker of admiration lit his eyes. Holly day by day was growing more beautiful, but it was the boy who arrested his attention. So strong and lively, bright-eyed and radiant, chuckling as Joel put a strong finger at his stomach, tickling him. A stab of amazement seized him. What Ariadne had said was perfectly true. A miniature Joel lay there, greedily grabbing a finger with his tiny fist.

'*My* boy!' Joel thought with more than a hint of pride. 'A son to follow in my own footsteps and one day control the Blake Shipping Line. My God! no fool of a Perryn will get a hand on *him*. I'll see to that.'

His glance strayed to the little girl, Holly. 'And you too, my lovely,' he said aloud. 'A real Blake you'll be, and a fine lady. The toast of society. Maybe even a duchess—'

He turned to the nursemaid who had stood apart as he examined the babies. 'A fine pair, aren't they?' he enquired of the nursemaid.

'Oh yes, sir. And a handful too,' she smiled.

Joel nodded. 'I know that. I can see it in their faces. More than a bit of a devil in them both. Well—' His disarming grin appeared for the first time in weeks. 'What good would any human being be, or life for that matter, without a bit of original sin in it?'

'No sir,' she agreed meekly. He patted her shoulder, and he walked away feeling he'd achieved something, though he couldn't decide what.

The following day Sir William Perryn appeared unexpectedly at Lionswykka.

'I have to inform you, Blake,' he said, when the first preliminary greetings were over, 'that you will be named among others, as co-respondent in the divorce action I'm taking against my missing wife. My lawyers naturally, will contact you officially in due course. Only I felt it my duty to confront you openly, and tell you why I have not sent for – my son. He is still legally that, I believe, until proved otherwise, which I can assure you will not be difficult.'

He paused.

'Yes?' Joel enquired. 'And what else? I gather there *is* more.'

'Certainly. I'm not satisfied with Lady Perryn's disappearance. Neither, as you well know, are the police.'

'Nor I,' Joel agreed coldly. 'But you must accept, sir, that your lady spouse was an extremely unpredictable character. She appeared at my private residence on the night in question, uninvited, and certainly unwanted, which I demonstrated quite clearly. She left on her own, unobserved, except by the housekeeper. That's all I know, and *did* know until the following day.'

'And you allowed it? Knowing—'

'Knowing her secret addiction to the brandy bottle? Is that what you were going to say? Or weren't you aware yourself? Hell, sir! Then what've you been doing during the last few years? It seems to me that if you'd kept your eye on her more effectively and seen she knew her place, the whole sorry business could have been avoided. In other words – your wife was a trollop, whom you were short-sighted enough to marry and then left her to go her own way plaguing other men.'

Sir William's expression turned to cold contempt.

'I've no intention of becoming involved in a vulgar slanging match concerning my wife's character. Neither do I wish to hear a commentary on past mistakes. The objective for all concerned surely is for such errors to be rectified as soon as possible. Another thing, Blake—' He paused, while Joel waited, chagrined for once to find himself intimidated by the suave manner of a man so physically inferior to himself, simply because he had background and a handle to his name.

'Yes?'

'Don't expect an entry into any organisation social or otherwise connected with my name. Money accrued from gold fields or lucrative shipping lines can buy much — but not necessarily an honourable reputation, and if you attempt to trade on contacts, you may find yourself in the tricky and humiliating position of being politely but bluntly debarred entrance to any respectable club in town. In short — you are to me an outsider of the most despicable order. Good day to you.'

The slim, almost puny figure in the impeccably tailored grey jacket and drain-pipe trousers, turned, and without a shake of hands, walked smartly to the door. Joel, fuming inwardly, touched a bell. A servant appeared almost instantly. 'The gentleman is leaving,' he said curtly. 'Show him out.'

A minute later the sound of wheels and horses' hooves from outside grew quickly fainter as the carriage was driven away. Joel moved then. 'Blast the fellow,' he thought, pouring himself a stiff whisky. This time the pip-squeak of a swaggering little aristocrat might think he'd got his way — but he hadn't. Not for good. One day he, Joel, would pay the fellow out. No one — *no one* in the world must be allowed to get the better of him with such insulting behaviour. Clubs be damned! he'd no liking for such places or for the gossipy chit-chat of old men content to live in the past, behind their newspapers in brandy-soaked dreams. Life was for living.

Life!

Suddenly the desire for action shook Joel from resentment to a new mood of defiance and lust for adventure.

Respectability! For the time being he'd had enough of it. The hotel was thriving, the first Blake ship was soon to sail the ocean waves. These were facts. Solid achievement that couldn't be halted now by a taste of personal danger. He'd thought to plan his course carefully, discipline himself to the conventional requirements of society until the first big scheme could be launched. But there was no need. One more little adventure was the tonic needed to reimburse his own pride and self-confidence. And by God, he'd have it.

So be damned to them all: the nobs, the Perryns, the sneaky sly Revenue officers, the women — the whole lot of them, luscious whores like Ariadne and the hoity-toity Caroline!

With the first whisky gulped almost immediately, he took another, followed by a third. After that he felt better.

The next day he contacted Marty concerning a suggestion put to him recently by an Irish man, which would involve a Maltese vessel carrying, with legal cargo, a quantity of tobacco and other contraband.

'Light stuff, sir,' Marty said. 'I've had it official like. 120 pounds of tobacco covered by canvas, some of it as lifebelts. Ingenious. That's the word, I b'lieve. Cou'd be took from the barque by smaller ones and hid on th' island for a time. No one'd suspect — not even that theer Cap'n Reeves. Been quiet for a long time now. If you ask me he hasn' any suspicion at all any more.'

Joel was intrigued. The idea was unique and titillated him.

'I'll think about it,' he said. 'And let you know, tomorrow probably.'

Marty winked and grunted acquiescence. Neither had the remotest idea that Captain Reeves had already had a tip, and was hoping Joel would be tempted by the project. His business was to watch.

This, with careful planning, he managed to do, unobserved.

17

Rupert was away from Greenvale for three weeks. During that time Caroline heard nothing from Joel, but inwardly she remained tense and uneasy, half expecting him to appear again, or for a communication demanding her return and that of his son to Treescarne.

When Rupert heard of his visit, and once more assured her of his support and love, the relief was so great she almost broke into a flood of tears, but controlled herself sufficiently to say haltingly, 'Are you *sure*, Rupert — *really* sure?'

'Of what?'

'That you want to go on with it? Us? I mean—'

'Of course. Now just what are you worrying about?'

She drew herself from his arms.

'Joel.'

'Be damned to him. He hasn't a leg to stand on. Apart from neglecting you, and fathering another woman's child, there are a whole lot of other things coming to light that will get him behind bars once they're proved. You've no need to fear him, Caroline love. As for us — we know where we stand. We love each other — it will take time, but once you're free we'll start a new life together with the children, and you'll be able to forget this dark episode.'

'No, Rupert.' Her voice by then was controlled and firm. 'I shan't ever forget — completely. I *do* love you, but no one can cut the past out of a life like — like losing a limb, a finger or toe—' She tried to smile, 'And Joel *is* Luke's father. Holly's too. I suppose he'll have certain rights. He may not ever let Holly leave him.'

'He'll be forced to, I promise you, when I've finished with him.'

There was a pause, then she continued, 'What did you mean about other things coming to light? And having Joel behind bars?'

Rupert hesitated before answering:

'He's involved in contraband, Caroline. But surely you must have known.'

'No, I *didn't*. I suspected. I guessed his business matters weren't only to do with his Blake Line and hotels. But I never had proof, and I haven't now.' Just a hint of defiance underlay her voice. 'And *you* can't be sure, can you?'

'Pretty certain,' he answered, watching her closely. 'In the first place he's over-alert and ambiguous when certain official matters are discussed in public. He's too much of a good fellow to ring true. Hale, hearty, and a hell of a good liar. An actor, too, if ever there was one — a man in shady games not only for his own profit, but because he likes to cock-a-snout, as they say, at the law. The adventurer.'

'Joel always was. He gets bored without a challenge. That's where our marriage has failed, I suppose. If I'd been wilder, like Ariadne—' A swift picture flashed vividly through her mind as she recalled her sister locked in Joel's arms on that fateful evening when she'd seen them by chance on the moor.

Rupert went towards her determinedly, and put an arm round her, drawing her once more close.

'Forget Ariadne, love. All that's over. For her, as well as you.'

A slight shiver went through her. 'What do *you* think happened to her? Do you believe she's alive? — or dead?'

'I've no proof, but I'd say the latter.'

He could feel her body trembling.

'I didn't *want* anything like that. I *had* begun to hate her, but I wouldn't have—'

'I know. I *know*.' His lips brushed her hair briefly.

'And Joel, wouldn't have either,' she said with such conviction he released her, staring hard into her eyes.

'He may be mad and reckless,' she continued, 'but half the

things he says are just bravado. He wouldn't kill anyone. I'm certain of that, Rupert.'

'Hm! well, I must say you seem to be doing your very best to defend him. Why? Are you still yearning secretly for that braggart to have his arms round you?'

'Rupert! Oh *no*. Please believe me. I was just being fair. We've got to be, haven't we? Both of us. It's no good — just because *we* care — wanting other people to suffer. And I *was* in love with Joel once.'

'Were you?'

Her eyes widened. 'Of course.'

'Yes, I suppose so,' he agreed grudgingly. 'The point is, are you quite certain a bit of it doesn't still remain?'

Was she? At that moment she couldn't be sure. Obviously Joel and she weren't suited and were no use to each other. Their values were completely different; she hated and feared most things about him. All she truly needed and wanted was the support and enduring affection of this honourable brave man she had come to care for.

She smiled.

'A bit of my *past*; that's all, darling,' she replied, reaching out a hand to touch his face. 'The present's here — with you. Don't spoil it, Rupert. Questions are so bewildering and somehow useless.'

'You're right.'

He kissed her gently, and there, for the time being, the subject of Joel was dismissed.

*

Joel meanwhile, was going ahead with plans for the tobacco run.

The operation was planned for an evening in March, before the hotel was crowded, yet with promising weather ahead to lure a number of visitors to the hotel. This would entail certain activity with the pleasure boats round the island, causing, therefore, no suspicion with the Preventive, should an unexpected small craft be spotted. The cargo was to be deposited

in the cave until exactly the right and propitious time arrived
for having it removed to the mainland.

Dangerous? Hardly, Joel thought, as Marty Werne outlined
the plan. All the same, sufficiently titillating to add spice to life
at that period when he was so at odds with his private affairs.
The memory of Caroline still niggled him in quiet moments,
therefore he had to have action — assume a different facade
than the go-ahead practical Joel Blake — a swaggering dramatic
character that could have been in a play — Black Dirke again!
the true buccaneer and plunderer of the seas. A rebel set to
outwit law and order and prove himself master of both.

Yes. To prove himself.

Before the actual day of the event he locked the door of his
study one morning, donned his dark attire and the black beard,
and regarded his blurred image through the glass of the
window. He thrust his chest out, swaggered to and fro for a
minute, feeling laughter — the rumble of triumph — shake his
chest and throat. Already he felt better a completely new individual freed from the chains of domesticity and all women.
Damn women! what did they know — any one of them? — of the
hunger and demands of a man like himself? — a man who must
have a challenge ahead, whatever the odds? Ariadne perhaps —
she'd grabbed at life and thrown it in his face. In hating and
fighting her he'd come very near to knowing his real self. But
she'd proved to be a tawdry combatant, cheap and greedy. The
first fire of her had turned only to loathing in him and self-
contempt. In becoming Black Dirke he could be purged of the
past, and maybe win Caro again. Caro! his loins hardened. He
was doing this for her; proving he could be greater than any
puny smirking Revenue Officer. He'd win all right. Black Dirke
would win! self confidence intensified in him. He took a flask
from a table and held it to his mouth. After that he removed the
beard, wig, and smuggling attire, combed his red locks into
place, settled himself at the table and wrote to his wife:

. . . in a week or so I shall see you, after conducting a little
project — and then we'll have everything straight between us.

So be ready to return with me to Lionswykka. In the meantime, keep your gentleman lover at bay. Better still, see he's not around at the time or he'll maybe have a dagger through his guts. You're mine, Caro, and you know it. Nothing will ever part us.

I'm a man of my word. So see you behave, and no monkey business.

As ever,
     Joel.

Rupert happened to be staying with his aunt when the note arrived. Caroline showed it to him immediately.

'I think he's — I think he's planning something,' she said. 'He goes like that, kind of reckless and adventurous — when he's on to what he calls a "deal", or "project", or some secret business. Not a word about Holly, or divorce, nothing to do with normal life. I wish—'

'Yes? What do you wish?'

'I wish it hadn't come. I'm *afraid*, Rupert.'

Reeves' lips hardened. 'Why? There's no need to be. I'm not surprised by your bit of paper. I've been expecting something of the sort. Your buccaneer will hang himself yet, my love—'

She shivered. '*No*. Not that.'

He pressed her ribs. 'Not exactly. Metaphorically speaking, I should have said. But why are you so concerned?'

'I'm not any more concerned that I would be about anyone else walking into a trap.'

But was she? She didn't know.

He shook his head slowly, in bewilderment.

'I believe you've got a soft spot in your head for the fellow still.'

'I was *married* to him, darling. I feel somehow — guilty. Oh I know I shouldn't,' she added hastily. 'But in some ways he's like a child—' She broke off, realising how ridiculous the description was.

'And what about me?' Rupert's voice had hardened. 'Am I always to be plagued by sentimental reminders of a past relationship? Listen, Caroline. You came to me for help. I've given it. I would have in any case, whether I'd fallen in love with you or not. But I *do* love you, and I very much hope you haven't changed?' His words faded into a question.

'Of *course* I haven't. Would I be here with you now if I had? Only please, Rupert, you can't expect me to be rational all the time. It's not been easy, walking out of my home, leaving a husband and one of my own children just as though they'd never happened. I know it's stupid of me—' a lump of emotion rose in her throat, 'but sometimes I wonder if—' She hesitated.

'Yes. Go on.'

'I wonder if I'm being fair to you. You must have had real chances of happiness in your life, known other women so much more suited without all these entanglements—'

He placed both hands on her shoulders.

'Yes. That's true enough. And I've been in love, and on the verge of marriage. But *never* — I swear it — have I *loved* a woman before, truly, deeply, as I love you. As for entanglements — we'll have them sorted out one day. That is, if you stop this silly nonsense about not being fair, and really want to go on with me.'

She relaxed suddenly. A quick flooding of peace encompassed her as though she'd come to the end of a long tiring road. She recalled Joel's selfishness, his callous indifference, overbearing dominance and changeful moods, and knew that with this man there could be no more of it. She could have security, affection, consideration of her needs, and following a period of peace and recuperation, the capacity to put the past completely behind her. She could bear his children and together their future would be emotionally stable, rich in mutual understanding and the art of giving and taking.

'I do love you, Rupert,' she said, laying her head against his breast, and at that moment it was true.

The subject of Joel's letter was dismissed, and Caroline forced herself not to think of it. With Rupert it was different. He had obtained useful clues of the planned event from a social source, and by the tone of Joel's communication he was more than ever convinced what he'd heard was correct.

So on the appointed evening his men were hidden and on the watch at points of the mainland, while he himself waited in a small customs' boat that had been secreted cunningly during a mist in a gully of the island. There was no way the Maltese vessel could have been seen. Nothing was suspected by Joel or Marty Werne and his gang. Reports had been confirmed that Revenue were concerned with a raid up the coast. The tobacco run appeared a surprisingly simple operation.

Except for over-confidence on Joel's part, and a few flamboyant remarks, Reeves' plans indeed could have been foiled.

Unfortunately for Joel, complete disaster ensued. Just as the official cutter appeared to intercept the vessel containing the illegal cargo, which was already being unloaded into smaller boats — two of the Maltese crew got into an argument resulting in a shindy.

Shocked and dismayed, Joel, as Black Dirke, flung himself into the foray, at the same time cursing himself for not having stayed on the coast at the receiving end of the 'run'. There were shouts and oaths, followed by one shot, then another.

When Reeves and his men boarded the boat, Joel was found lying on deck, with an arm almost completely amputated, wig and beard torn away, his chest covered by a stream of his own blood.

Rupert gave formal orders for his removal to the mainland where he could have expert medical attention. Whether Blake died or not he did not much care. His main problem would obviously be how to tell Caroline the news. Even through the confusion that followed he was filled with foreboding. Part of him rejoined in achieving his goal and arrests. But he knew that moral victory might not necessarily bring happiness, and feared that in capturing the rascally Blake he might lose the one woman he loved.

Caro.

*

'Where *is* he?' Caroline demanded after Rupert had told her the news. '*Tell* me.'

'At Lionswykka temporarily,' Reeves answered. 'Later he'll be removed — naturally.'

'To prison?' Her face was white, her voice shrill and cold.

'Not yet. Hospital first.'

'You mean he's seriously ill? Dying?' She gripped a sleeve of his coat.

'No, darling, *no*. He's a tough customer as you well know. He's wounded pretty badly, but I have seen men pull through worse.'

She moved abruptly, and with her head high, chin thrust forward determinedly, said, 'I must go to him.'

'But, my dear love, *why*? You've gone through enough already. Why prolong the agony? After all we've done to have you free, it doesn't make sense—'

'Sense isn't everything. He's still my husband.'

'Is he? I wouldn't have said so. Or is it that you've changed your mind? It's *him*, you want — not me. Be honest, love—'

'*Don't* say such stupid things.'

'But I must, Caroline. For my own sake as well as yours. If you're determined to cling to the rascally Blake in spite of everything, I—' he broke off shrugging his shoulders helplessly, '—well, I can't keep you by force. God knows I want you. But in the end you have to make your own choice.'

She softened and reached out to him. '*Please*, Rupert. There *is* no choice. It's made already; you *know* that. He's nothing to me, not in the way you mean. I may be old-fashioned — perhaps I've got a mistaken sense of duty. But unless I go I'll feel wrong about it always. These things are important. When we're married — and I do *want* to marry you — it must be with no blame anywhere. No niggle of conscience. Can't you understand?'

'Maybe, with my mind,' he conceded grudgingly. 'I still think you're making a mistake, but if you're determined, I'll arrange it. He'll not be a pretty sight, I warn you. So be prepared for a shock.'

'I am,' she told him tight-lipped.

And so shortly afterwards the journey began. They travelled by coach and did not reach Lionswykka until the early hours of the next day.

The first glimmer of pale sunlight was lifting over a motionless sea when Caroline entered the hotel and went upstairs to the familiar bedroom that had been the background to so many scenes of stormy passion between herself and Joel. A nurse had evidently been in attendance and was on the point of leaving. At the door of the room she told Caroline in an undertone that Mr Blake's pain had been eased somewhat, soothing drugs had been administered, and it was hoped he would be able to have rest before the surgeon and specialist arrived to do whatever was necessary.

'What do you mean by that?' Caroline asked.

The nurse waited for moments before replying, then she said, 'One arm will almost certainly have to be amputated, Mrs Blake. There is a fear of gangrene. It was hoped for his removal to hospital. But the journey, as he is, would be too dangerous. The facilities here are comparatively good, which is lucky for the patient — *and* for us. A special room is being prepared for the operation.'

She gave a brief humourless smile, and left.

Joel's eyes were closed when Caroline entered the bedroom. In spite of the dimmed light his bold profile was outlined clearly against the pillow, the red hair swept back from the arrogant brow, giving him the semblance of an already dead Caesar from by-gone history.

Caroline stepped forward quietly. 'Joel,' she said, almost in a whisper.

He didn't stir. She repeated his name twice before any response came. At last he opened his eyes. No trace of emotion flickered over his face. His eyes stared at her, cold and enigmatic as pale glass. She stretched out a hand. 'I'm so sorry,' she continued, 'about the — about your arm—' A glance of disdain seemed to flicker momentarily over the set features, then he said faintly, but in icy clipped tones, 'Go away. I don't want you here.'

'But, Joel—'

'Get out.' The lids closed over his eyes again, leaving only a twist of bitterness on the hard lips.

'But—'

He managed to turn his head from her, muttering, 'Don't stand there, you fool. Just *go*.'

Hurt and humiliated, she obeyed, and with a sudden feeling of complete exhaustion, drained physically and mentally to the roots of her being, she went out, closing the door quietly behind her. Strangely, for the time being, all sense of pity and compassion had deserted her.

Rupert had been right, she told herself, as she went down the stairs, she should never have come. Joel was just the same as he'd ever been — ruthless and cruel in sickness, as he'd been in life. She hated him. But the tears were thick in her throat when she met Rupert who was waiting for her in the library. One look at her face told him of her distress.

'I was afraid it wouldn't be easy,' he said, touching her shoulders comfortingly. 'Try and forget now. They're bringing us something to eat and drink in the breakfast room. We can talk there, and arrange what to do next. There's your daughter to think of now.'

Yes, of course — Holly.

From that point Caroline allowed Rupert to take charge. At the end of the week, following the successful amputation just below the elbow and assurances from the specialists that Joel would eventually recover she set off with Rupert for Greenvale, taking Holly with her. If her husband had shown any desire for her presence she'd have remained for a time. But he'd resented even a brief appearance of her slender form at his bedside. The mention of her name had inflamed his temper to such a pitch that she'd been advised to keep away.

Caroline was not sure. She was not sure of anything any more, except her need of Rupert, and thankfulness for his protection and devotion — the one haven where she could find temporary and perhaps enduring peace.

18

Months passed. The first wild sweet days of early spring drifted into summer, and Caroline gradually relaxed, as Rupert's deepening affection and passion for her helped to erase the painful memories of her life with Joel. The Captain arranged with his own solicitors to contact Joel to start divorce proceedings. At the beginning she was uncertain; the finality was frightening — mostly because of the children. Supposing Joel was given the right to have a hand in their futures? Even custody of Holly, who seemed by no means resigned to being parted from her blood brother? Rupert was convinced there would be no possibility of this. 'Your reputation's never been questioned,' he told her. 'Joel's in the wrong; a mother should have precedence in such cases—'

'Oh, Rupert! you sound so — so objective, and clinical almost—' she smiled. 'I'm afraid I'm more mixed-up. Human emotions are confusing.'

'Don't be confused. The legality will be a simple business. The only snag is that we shall have to wait so long before we can be married.'

Caroline didn't answer. More than anything, she told herself, she wanted to be Rupert's wife — to feel safe and cared for, and spoiled a little, which she certainly did already. But at moments she couldn't believe it could really happen. Joel's shadow still lingered at the back of her mind — haunting her. When she walked about the pleasant countryside around Greenvale, a cloud passing the sun would revive sudden impressions of another place — another land almost — of wild moors dotted with ancient standing stones and relics — of high seas pounding the rugged Cornish cliffs, and bitter memories of a man's arms round her, not the comforting strong arms of Rupert Reeves, but demanding and arrogant — Joel's arms. Passion would briefly stir in her — passion changing to anger when she recalled his faithlessness, the cruel threats and callous indifference that had eventually ruined her life with him. Oh! she didn't love him any more. Love held compassion, and he had killed this in her — simply because he didn't need it, or her. How she had belittled herself in responding so easily and with such abandon to his physical demands. And how ridiculous to look back. At such a point she always tore her mind back to the present, thankful at heart that Joel was no longer pestering her. In the Reeves' household his name was no more mentioned unless it was absolutely necessary.

'We don't want him calling again,' Joanna told her nephew more than once. 'If you've really made up your mind about Caroline there should be a clean break. Emotional scenes can be so upsetting for everyone.'

And so it had been.

Joel had made no reply to any communication concerning the divorce, which meant, presumably, that he intended to ignore them.

Actually the truth was very different. As he recovered from the shock of losing an arm and his health improved, bitterness and a desire for revenge rose in him. He had no intention of allowing Caroline to be free in order to marry Reeves. If she was so besotted by the meddlesome Revenue official that she had to live with him — let her, for a time; tongues would soon get wagging. The Captain would lose his job; he, Joel, would see to that, and Caroline wouldn't have a decent friend in the world left. She'd be sniffed at and ignored by her own set, whereas he couldn't care a damn what tales were spread about. For a man things were different. A woman scorned was a different matter. He, Joel, held all the important cards, too. Caroline's escapade on the moor was becoming common knowledge. He meant details to intensify unless she returned when he felt like it. In the meantime he had to recover his health, make the best of being a one-armed man, and plan ahead for his newly formed shipping

company. One day he'd have everything again — including his
wife, daughter, and the puny boy, Luke, who bore his name but
probably was not of his begetting. Already he'd legally adopted
Marcus. Marcus these days was becoming a focal point of his
existence — a worthy heir to what would be a magnificent
inheritance.

In his fanatical ambition for power, lack of judgement unfortunately for him, superseded wisdom. His investors and partners gradually began to withdraw from his various business
ventures. To erase the knowledge, Joel began to drink — moder-
ately at first, then as problems mounted, more heavily. There
were days when he shut himself in his study and nothing more
was heard of him until he was discovered lying on the floor the
next morning still sleeping off the effects of alcohol.

The popularity of Lionswykka started to decline. Word got
round that Mrs Blake, who after all was a Carnforth by birth,
had left her husband because of his infidelity, and affairs with
other women — Lady Perryn, her own half-sister included — and
that owing to drink and wild ways he was said to be in debt.
There were suggestions, later stated to be fact, that he was
concerned with illegal practices — smuggling in particular, and
mixed with individuals of ill-repute. Once the whispering
started there was no stopping it. Wasn't the disappearance of
Ariadne Perryn, for instance, extremely odd, considering Joel
had been in conversation with her the same night? Obviously
there had been an affair between them. And then that work-
man, the miner with the funny name, Swales — gone without a
trace; and according to servants' gossip there had been bad
blood between the two men.

'Not really—' one matron suggested to another '—the place
any longer *quite* suitable for respectable folk to visit.'

Merely drawing-room chit-chat at the start, but its escal-
lation had an inevitable effect. Quite bluntly by late autumn of
that year Lionswykka had a bad name. Some — artists chiefly,
and those with a liking for mystery — booked rooms at the hotel,
but they were in the minority. The staff began to fear for their
jobs and one or two left, followed by others.

Joel, fortified by whisky and the brandy bottle, put on a brave front, telling himself that in the spring things would revive. In cooler, saner moments, he doubted it. At periods he left for Falmouth or Plymouth making feverish attempts to settle financial problems and have the line working in an orderly, remunerative fashion, as planned.

It was simply no use. Each time he would return to Treescarne depressed by mounting debts and his inability to regain the confidence of former friends and partners.

Life at Treescarne became dark and embittered, as dark as the wind-blown trees which in the fading cold light of evening seemed to encroach upon the house with the menacing quality of ghosts from the past, and dreams gone sour.

Once, when Mrs Magor found him seated alone in the study with the heavy odour of spirits and cigar permeating the atmosphere, she said in her harsh Cornish voice, 'You should stir y'rself surr, an' get down t' brass tacks. Theer's work to be done here, an' that other place you built, Lionswykka. The baby, too. You shud think about 'en — *an'* me. Since the nurse left an' that village gel took over, things edn' done properly for 'im. I can't f'r ever be traipsin' up an' down between 'ere an' theer. If I was you I'd get my brain workin' properly. Leave the drink alone, an' see if that wife o' yours can't be got back. You must pardon an old wumman f'r speakin' out, but et's a matter o' duty.'

Joel looked at her from tired red-rimmed yes. The old face was truculent, a little fearful too, and she was shaking. 'Don't worry, woman,' he said in thickened tones. 'Everything will be all right in the end.'

'Not unless you do sumthen about it,' she muttered. 'Another thing — folks rely on 'ee, more fool them. An' you can't just shove off human beings like sacks of old potaters.'

She went out, leaving him to brood on what she'd said.

A little later he had his horse saddled and set off for a canter over the moors. Something of the old woman's tirade had penetrated his senses. It was true he'd neglected all he'd striven so hard for during the past weeks and months. Dammit, he had to get going again somehow. The trouble was he had no stimulus, no aim any more. With Caroline by him he'd felt a king, a ruler of his domaine, her life and his. Without her — but why the devil should a woman — *any* woman have such influence? She'd betrayed him, taken a legal son and daughter of his away, to join the aunt of the upstart swaggering Reeves. They might not be the Captain's children — he'd no way of proving it. The darker suspicion that Swales had fathered them was still an overpowering obsession, the one he believed. Reeves was far too fussy, too cunning and 'honourable' — what a farce the word was when he'd contrived so slily to break his marriage — to jump his fences. But in the end Joel hadn't a doubt he'd have Caroline all sweet and willing in his bed where she belonged.

And by God, he thought, as he kicked his mount to a gallop, he'd get her there — somehow, even though he might send her packing after.

Without really quite knowing which direction he was taking he crossed the western rim of the hills, and found himself in the vicinity of the Swales' cottage.

The widow, a gaunt, haggard-faced woman, was taking a bedraggled apron from a clothes line when horse and rider approached.

Joel jumped from the saddle, and leading the horse by the bridle approached the gate.

She stood for a moment quite silently watching, with no expression, or acknowledgement of his presence.

'Good day,' he managed to say politely, while thinking what a slattern she looked. She was turning to go away without replying when she changed her mind, and asked sullenly, 'What do you want?'

'Your help,' Joel answered shortly, 'if you can give it. I'll pay you well.'

She gave a derisive grunt.

'*Help? You?*'

'You know me, of course. Joel Blake. Your husband once worked at the mine.'

'Oh yes, *I* know ye.'

'He'd have been there still if he'd not taken to the bottle.'

'Bottle? How polite y'are, Mr high-an'-mighty Blake. A filthy drunk he was; among other things—' Her voice faded meaningfully.

'Women,' he interrupted. 'Yes, I'm quite aware of it.'

She studied him with a slow look of bewilderment and curiosity dawning in her small eyes. She wiped a work-worn hand on her apron and going nearer to him asked harshly, 'Women, you said and payment − how much?' He slipped a hand into his pocket and drew out a number of coins including a sovereign. The expression on her face turned to avarice.

'All that?'

He nodded. 'Maybe more, if I'm satisfied you're not lying.'

'Why should I lie about him? The brute. Go on mister, tell me what's in your mind and I'll do my best. Not that I can think of anythin' good about him to tell.'

Joel came to the point quickly.

'It's about my wife. They were acquainted—'

'Oh yes?'

'Did you know that?'

She shrugged. 'He was that kind o'f man − always lustin' after what he culdn' have. That's Barney all over.'

'I see.'

'Look 'ere − you edn' suggestin' they lay together, are you?' She almost spat the words out, like a greedy spiteful old she-cat, Joel thought contemptuously. His quick reaction to the question was to mount his horse and ride away. Discussion concerning Caroline with this unsavoury hag was not only disgusting but humiliating. However, there was something he *had* to know, and she was the only one who could give it.

'I'm not suggesting it,' he told her shortly. 'I'm *asking*.'

She laughed outright then. 'Been playin' about has she? One o' that sort? Well, if that's how she likes it, good luck to 'er.' She spat contemptuously at the ground. 'Men! they're all the same − mostly. *Muck!* But then there's different kinds o' muck, an' Barney was the other sort. Understand, mister?'

'No.'

'Afraid are ye? 'Fraid he fathered your brats?'

He had an impulse to take her scraggy neck between his hands and wring it as he'd wring a scrawny old hen's, but he forced himself to reply comparatively calmly, 'If you want any of this, woman—' showing her the gold in his palm, 'you'll hold your tongue about my affairs and give a straight answer. Otherwise there's nothing. *I'm* the one demanding information. Not you.'

She quietened then.

'Mebbe he did have a roll an' tumble now an' then,' she said, 'Barney was that sort; *had* to be a man. Oh, he was a real show-off. Fooled me all right he did, when he was young. But the truth is he couldn've fathered *any*thing, not Barney Swales. Lust? Yes. He could lust all right — but he hadn' anythin' t' give that a woman wanted. A fine strong hulk of a tree wi' no sap in him. That's what Barney was. I could tek my oath — ef I b'lieved in such things — which I doan't — that Barney never had a wumman in his life. If ee'd been able to, we should of 'ad a family an' all'd bin different wi' us. *Now* do you see what I mean. 'Ee could drink like a fish, swear until the lust'd died in 'im, then turn on me. Ef you saw my back you'd believe it. Every time 'ee took a boot or stick to me it kind o' got 'im goin'; a real man 'ee felt then, the swine. So you forget y'r fancies, surr; if that young wumman o' yours looked somewhere for 'er pleasure, et weren't Barney. An' if you want my opinion—' she paused before adding, '—she's not the sort to go astray. Not 'er. Real nice she's bin to me, more than once; 'elped me carry a sack of vegetables in one day when I was sick. Ridin' she'd bin, just like you. Now then, is that enough? Earned the gold 'ave I? What I've said's the truth, an' no more.'

Joel believed her. In a kind of daze he handed her the coins, and the next minute was riding up towards the ridge.

So he'd been wrong about Swales all the time. He was merely a sadistic pervert. But where did that get *him*, Joel? There was still Rupert to reckon with. On the other hand, Reeves certainly was not the type to have molested Caroline or any other woman on the moor; *that* had been Barney Swales all right, and Joel had no proof at all of any intimacy either in the past or present between the Captain and Caroline.

Moodily, still bemused from the drink he'd taken earlier that day, he urged his mount on wildly, careless of the pain that nagged him, and the fact that he had only one arm to curb the animal in case of a fright or stumble. The slap of wind and air stimulatd him with the renewed challenge of obstacles and danger ahead. Damn it! — his senses cried — he could do it yet! defy and beat circumstances whatever the odds against him. Curse Ariadne! — curse Caroline and all women for the way they managed to ensnare and trap a man, forcing him off course, so his real aims were thwarted and diverted into confusion. He wasn't confused though, not any more. From now on he'd ride the world as he rode the moor — free of passions and the shackles of sensual desire. All his untamed inner self rose to his defence — his armour against defeat. The fury of sea — storm, wind and air, raged through his blood, sending him blindly ahead, by twisted gorse, furze, and clutching bramble, galloping down the twisting steep track, between boulders and bog. As horse and rider cut through a broken circle of standing stones, it seemed to Joel he was conqueror of the elements and time itself. Forgetful of his disability he raised his one arm for a second to a sky grown sullen with cloud, shouting defiance as claimant of earth and air. Once it seemed to him the granite symbols of an earlier age half toppled towards him, pledging obeisance. He laughed, crying aloud wildly, not realising that the effort of the ride on top of his already weakened state, was draining the blood from his head, diminishing reason to a blurred sense of unreality.

'That's right,' he shouted. 'Bow, serve me. I reign — your king. Down with you — down—' There was a shuddering feeling of the earth stirring and the stones toppling towards him as the horse with a shrill whinny, reared, plunged on, and catching a stone, fell.

Joel was thrown and only escaped the waiting blackness of a bog hole by a clutching barrier of thick thorn bushes. The horse, after a minute got to its feet and cantered away. A gull screamed as it rose into the sky alone. Then all was still except for the sad moaning of wind through undergrowth and round granite boulders.

When, twelve hours later, he recovered consciousness in hospital, all he said was, 'Now I suppose I'll lose my leg, too. That's what you want, isn't it?' He had a lop-sided cynical grin on his lips. His eyes were narrowed, bloodshot and full of scorn. When the nurse in attendance didn't reply, he shouted, 'Get me a drink can't you? God! woman! what the hell are you here for?'

'Now, now, Mr Blake, you must be still; be quiet!' she ordered him, with emotionless calm.

'*Quiet?*' He tried to get up but was overcome by pain and faintness.

Presently she handed him a glass containing clear liquid.

'Drink that up; you'll feel better,' she said still apparently unperturbed. 'Then you must sleep for a time.'

His antagonism slowly died. He was tired — so bloody tired.

After the potion he gradually relaxed, and five minutes later was sleeping.

The next day he learned that his leg, which was in splints, would eventually heal, but that the process would take a considerable time.

Time! the one thing he hadn't got to spare.

Gloom and resentment filled him. It had been bad enough before when he'd lost Caroline. Now it was far worse. She'd never want a wreck of a man like him around in her life. What was more to the point — neither did he wish ever to look on her again. She was at the root of all his troubles. It would have been better, far better, if he'd never met her.

When Rupert heard the news, he agreed heartily with Joel's unspoken comments. While Blake remained master of Treescarne and Lionswykka, whether invalid or not, he presented a danger to Caroline. Eventually the Captain meant to have the buccaneer under arrest, but he doubted anything tangible could be proved against him. It had already been said that on the night of the smuggling episode Joel had been in league with the Law, and had lost his arm in defence of it.

In court his lawyers could stress the point, and far from getting the man behind bars the authorities would quite likely give a commendation on behalf of his bravery.

Ironic? Yes.

But then so much of the Captain's work was.

The innocent frequently suffered, while the guilty got the glory.

He'd do his utmost to see it didn't happen this time.

19

Weeks after Joel's fall, he was still limping about the immediate vicinity of Treescarne. His leg was not so badly injured as had been feared, and the physician assured him he would make a complete recovery.

Joel gave a derisive laugh. 'Indeed! and how do you propose to make a one-armed man whole again?' he enquired. 'Replace a limb with a stump of wood? Or a hook?'

'Wonderful things are being achieved in remedial surgery these days,' the doctor told him. 'You're lucky the arm was severed at the elbow and not the shoulder.'

'Oh yes. No doubt I should be grateful,' Joel conceded sarcastically. 'But I'm not. I hate the sight of myself and have no need of your puerile remarks. I suppose you're only doing your job. But I don't require sympathy or cheering up. Just leave me to face the truth in my own way, if you don't mind.'

There was a grunt, followed by a stiff, 'Very well.' Before he left, the physician added meaningfully, 'Your wife, I believe, is away. Pardon my saying so – it might be a good idea for you to meet her.'

'What the devil do you mean? And what business is it of yours?'

'There are illnesses harder to cure than physical maladies, and I think you're suffering one,' came the reply. 'I happen to have heard things, and my advice is to get Mrs Blake home as soon as possible.'

The door snapped to. Joel glowered. The insolence of the fellow, he thought. Interfering in his private life – trying to force a reunion with Caroline when it was the last thing he wanted. Once he'd thought of dragging her back home and to the marriage bed by force if necessary. Now the very suggestion was somehow shameful and humiliating. A *cripple!* and Caroline Carnforth. If she came on her bended knees, he'd dismiss her without a qualm. He no longer wanted or wished to see her.

That part of his life was over.

'You shuldn' brood so much,' Mrs Magor said one day. 'Limpin' about the countryside with that wild look on 'ee — never givin' anyone a civil word, simply wrapped up in y'r own miseries an' cares agin' the world. What's the sense o' et? An' you with business worries too.'

'Mind your own business,' Joel said roughly. 'You're not suffering. You get your pay, then keep your mouth shut over my affairs.'

The old woman sniffed, threw him a belligerent glance, and left.

While not admitting it openly, Joel knew that part of her statement was true. Brooding was no use to anybody, and he *had* got worries. Not only personal, but financial.

On impulse one day he wrote to Sagor suggesting they meet.

Because of circumstances beyond my control, I'm no longer able to devote the time necessary to the Blake Line. It has occurred to me that with your wealth and initiative you could make it a far more profitable undertaking than in my hands at the moment. I'm willing to sell the greater part of my own shares for a minimum sum and forego my chairmanship of the company. If you're interested let me know. I could meet you either here, or at Lionswykka.

    Awaiting your reply.

    Yours sincerely,

      Joel Blake.

A week later Sagor arrived at the hotel, and following an excellent dinner complete with vintage brandy and cigars, the two men came to an agreement.

When Sagor left the following day, relief, combined with a sense of defeat and flatness churned in Joel's mind. Hardly realising what he was doing he went upstairs to where Marcus was crawling about the nursery floor. The little boy chuckled when he saw him, then suddenly, without warning, started to howl.

The girl attending him appeared from an adjoining room. 'It's just that he doesn't see so much of you these days,' she said. 'He's good generally, aren't you, love?'

The baby grinned again and unpredictably thrust out a toy bear to his father. Joel took it, feeling immediately embarrassed. Children weren't really his 'cup of tea', he thought wrily. So unpredictable. But maybe Mrs Magor had been right when she'd suggested the boy should be at Treescarne.

Once he'd arranged practical details, the business was settled, and the little boy and nursemaid left the hotel to be in close proximity with Joel.

*

Weeks passed. Divorce proceeding had been started, and were being conducted, under the guidance of Rupert and his solicitors. At first, when the primary details were assessed and legally documentated, Caroline had felt resentful, a little apprehensive. So much was at stake — her whole future and that of her children. She would have delayed matters if she could in order that any such sordid details could be forgotten for a time, leaving her a period of peace for complete emotional recuperation.

Rupert, however, had been insistent.

'Do you love me, or not?' he'd asked. 'You have to force things, my love, and make your own decision. I won't *push* you in the direction I want — I've already gone pretty far, but no regrets if you please. I'm not the kind of man to want any woman knowing that in her heart she's longing for another. Do you understand?'

As she looked at him, so handsome and direct, his eyes unswervingly upon her face, all doubt receded. 'I wouldn't do that to you, Rupert,' she answered. 'I'm not that kind of woman, you should know. Of *course* I love you—' she smiled, and he'd taken her in his arms, disregarding her fitful mood.

'Very well. You'll be sensible then, and sign what papers are necessary — give clear and concise statements without any hedging?'

How very official he'd sounded, she'd thought, no compromise or delay any more — just a straight route to freedom.

Well, that was as it should be. After all, she was to marry Rupert; Joel was no concern of hers. He was a part of her past — nothing else, a part she would be so grateful to forget. A whole new era of peace and understanding lay before her, like a gold tinted calm landscape following a great storm. Yet there were days, as autumn came, bringing yellowing skies and the dead sweet smell of forgotten things — woodsmoke, the wet earth smell of tumbled leaves and rotting bracken — when momentary visions and echoes of her days in Cornwall swept over her. She dispelled them quickly, knowing such aberrations were merely touches of nostalgia. She had everything she wanted now — security, the knowledge of a strong man's love and passion; a new beginning. Eventually, when she and Rupert were married, they would probably — most certainly, have children. This would be good for Holly, as well as cementing the new union. Holly at the moment, though still a baby, puzzled her. Sometimes she fancied an accusing look in the child's eyes, which made a barrier between them because she was becoming day by day so uncannily like Joel.

In some of her rare stabs of resentment Caroline would think bitterly, 'That's good. If your father saw you now he'd have no more doubts of the relationship.' Everywhere — in the nursery, pram, or lying in her cot, Holly made her presence felt. If a late butterfly fluttered nearby, she put out her tiny hand to catch it. Luke was different. Solemn-eyed and content. In his own quiet way a beautiful baby, reminding Caroline of her grandfather, a studious man, who had died when she was very young.

'Hm!' William Carnforth, her father, had remarked on one of his rare visits to Greenvale. 'He's still a bit small, ain't he? Still there's a clever look about him, and the girl's a beauty. Like her father.'

Caroline winced.

'They're both like themselves. Individuals.'

'Pity you had to break up though, you and Joel,' Carnforth continued tactlessly. 'Not that I doubt you'll be happy with this Reeves man. But with a little gentle handling I should have thought you'd have been able to keep Joel in tow. Had such a promising future. Not quite of our class maybe, but full of ambition and guts. Now they say he's gone all to seed. Losing an arm and then that other accident—'

'What other accident?' Caroline enquired sharply.

'Hadn't you heard? Went wild one night and nearly did in his leg this time – still limps, but carries on again in his old way.'

'I knew he'd had a fall,' Caroline replied, tight-lipped. 'That's not unusual when you ride. Horses are unpredictable.'

Her father shrugged. 'They say he's gone crazy.'

'What do you mean?'

Carnforth tapped his head significantly.

'A bit out of his mind. Either shuts himself away in that cut off place, Treescarne, or goes galloping like old Harry over the moor at night. Keeps bad company too – that's what I've heard, girl. May not be all gossip, but he's getting quite a reputation at one of the kiddleywink places where they go in for risky business.'

'I didn't know,' Caroline said reflectively.

'Maybe all for the best,' her father said cheerfully. 'We don't want another affair like your sister had. Poor Ariadne. I tell you, Caroline, I'm not satisfied. I'm not saying Joel had anything to do with it, and I'm not a man to judge when I don't know the facts. But it's hurt me. I'll never be the same man again. Where's she gone? Where is she? Dead, if you ask me. No doubt of it at all. If she wasn't, she'd've got in touch.' He took a pinch of snuff, continuing, 'But I didn't come here to talk about your sister just to give my good wishes and find out how things stand – my duty, as Mrs Poldew said—'

That woman! Caroline thought resentfully. She *would* poke her nose in.

The interim ended on a chilly, almost embarrassed, note,

leaving Caroline uneasy, with a rising anxiety to visit Treescarne and find out for herself how things were there.

That evening, when Rupert returned to Greenvale, she reported what her father had said. The Captain's face darkened. 'Yes, I knew Blake was acting irrationally,' he said. 'One day soon he'll make a mistake, go too far, and then I'll have him.'

Just for a second or two Caroline felt alienated, a little shocked by the cool statement.

'Is it necessary to have him? I suppose you mean get him under arrest?'

Noting her tone Rupert softened slightly. 'It will have to come sooner or later, darling — and the sooner the better, for his own sake, as well as everyone else's.'

There was a pause, then Caroline remarked very quietly, 'I must go over to Treescarne, Rupert. No—' she raised a hand when he attempted to interrupt her, '—don't say anything, don't forbid me. I know you won't approve and it will worry me having to go against your wishes. But this is something I must do for myself — *see* — so that I can be at peace with you and know I'm doing the right thing.'

He placed both hands on her shoulders. His voice was stern when he said, 'Do you realise it could stir things up again — might put an end to all our plans and spoil our future? Are you still so overburdened by your ridiculous sense of duty that you have to put your own happiness at risk by even coming into contact again with that blackguard? What's the sense of it? — it won't do any good. He'll only insult you. You'll be frightened and depressed, and the whole nightmare will start up in your mind again. That's not what I want — for either of us. What about me? Haven't I a place in your conscience?'

A swift sense of compunction smote her.

'Oh, Rupert, of *course*. I *love* you. You know that. We're going to be happy together. But — perhaps I *am* being stupid, I can't help it though. It may be that I want to prove to myself more than ever how perfectly beastly Joel can be—' she broke off breathlessly. Rupert released her, saying heavily. 'You'll do what you like, of course. I can't keep you under lock and key. I only wish I could. I'm sure Joanna would think the same.'

But Joanna saw things differently.

'Caroline's bound to meet Joel sometime,' she told her nephew rationally. 'There are matters certain to arise concerning the children, and the divorce surely can't be affected at this advanced stage by one visit to her old home? Of course it won't be pleasant for her, and in my opinion that's all to the good; if you take my advice, Rupert, you'll let things go their own course. Caroline may have a strong will. I admit there's a reckless streak in her, but she has a clear head, and any meeting with Joel will only enforce her affection for you. There's simply no sense in being afraid for her.'

Rupert did not reply.

The subject ended there.

Two days later Rupert had a meeting to attend in Plymouth, and it was then that Caroline set off for Treescarne.

20

Joel happened to be at the stables when Caroline arrived. His groom and the youth had gone to Penzance in connection with a young colt recently purchased for future breeding. The day was grey and still, redolent with the smell of distant smoke, manure, and the certain animal smell that was somehow so evocative to her of past days. Caroline, in her green caped coat, over a full skirt which showed only the tip of pointed boots and a mere glimpse of slender ankles, stood quite still as Joel appeared at a door. Although he still limped slightly his powerful build and height held the same magnetic strength she remembered. His forearm was pinned against his breast. He wore tall boots, breeches, and riding jacket; as a dying ray of sunlight caught his strong-featured face at a sideways angle, its carved bitter lines were emphasised. He looked haggard, yet not beaten. Just defiant and obviously displeased to see her.

'What do *you* want?' he asked, after a short pause.

'Joel—' she swallowed hard before continuing, 'I naturally wondered how you were. I didn't know about the leg at first, I hope—'

'Thank you so much for your concern,' he interrupted. 'Very gratifying. As you see I can still walk and talk, as many cripples can, I believe. Does that satisfy you?'

Irritation sharpened her voice. 'No, not entirely. I'd hardly call you a cripple either. In any case there are many things we have to discuss.'

'*Are* there indeed! Such as—'

'The children. When — when everything's settled and over I expect you'll want to see them. Holly anyway—'

'And you wish to give your permission in a perfectly civilised way, hoping so soon to be the wife of your lusting lover? Well, madam, I won't need it, or anything at all from you. With or without your consent, the children will return to Treescarne at my own convenience when or if I wish it. I have certain facts up my sleeve which will make your precious captain appear a fool and a common cheap seducer in any court dealing with the case. After that may you both go to hell. I neither care nor want you any more. To me you're just a whore. So do you mind now leaving?'

He was shaking, but she did not see it. Her own face was white. Whiter than the froth of lace at her throat. How hateful! — how wild and cruel he was. Sobs were rising in her throat, painfully, but she managed to check them.

'You're a brute, Joel Blake,' she managed to say. 'How I hate you! But I'm glad now I came. I wanted to show some sort of sympathy. I was sorry — *genuinely* sorry about your accidents. I thought maybe—'

He took a step towards her. His teeth shone white in a mocking smile that held no humour.

'You thought perhaps to have me grovelling at your pretty feet as I *could* have done — several times in the past — when you scorned me—' he continued ruthlessly, 'only you never noticed it. That's your aim, and always has been, isn't it? — to entrap men. Good luck to you then. And may Reeves suffer as *I've* suffered—'

Her hands went out. Rupert suddenly had become a shadow — blotted out by the wild irrational knowledge that only through this man, Joel, could her own wild spirit thrive again and live. He turned on his heel and went towards the loft. At the door he looked back, and gave her a long stare.

She was still standing on the cobbles, motionless as a statue, her figure outlined by a rim of light. Weariness engulfed him.

'Go away, Caroline. I'm sick of it all. You bore me. For *God*'s sake—' his voice rose, 'why must you pester me — as I am? Isn't there a shred of decent feeling in you?'

She ran towards him, and without knowing it her body was against his chest, one arm clutching his shoulder. He winced.

'Caroline—'

'Joel — Joel — I *love* you. *Please* don't send me away. It was all a mistake, about the children, I mean — the quarrels and doubts, they *are* yours. And there's never been anyone else. Rupert's a friend. Nothing else. I'm fond of him in a way — but love! — don't you understand? *Can't* you — it's only you — you—' She broke off breathlessly. For seconds, minutes it seemed, he stared into her eyes as though searching her very soul.

'Do you know what you're saying?' he asked at last. 'Think hard. I'm ruthless, selfish, a one-armed rake, and nothing in this damn world will change that. Life with me would be hell very often. You know it. You've had a taste already. Then why push your luck, love? There's no fairytale ending for us, or ever will be—'

'*I don't want* it,' she insisted. 'I don't, I *don't*. I want *you*, Joel — reality—'

The pressure of his arm deepened. His lips were hot on her mouth, then demanding.

'And by God,' he whispered,' I want you too.'

Presently they moved into the shadows of the grooms' kitchen. From above, in the loft, the smell of stored apples and home made wines, crept down and lingered about them, as he eased her on to a pile of straw. With his one arm, yet with expertise, he loosened the neck of her cape; very gently she located the button of his shirt, and as the grey light deepened they lay unified and at peace.

No illusions any more.

Together, at last.

A DISTINGUISHED AFFAIR . . .

OFFICERS'
ladies

MARION HARRIS

Confidence, beauty and privilege were advantages
Lieutenant Kate Russell took for granted. Her aristocratic
parents had great plans for her: when the war was over she
would marry a man with a pedigree as sound as her own.

Then she met Robert Campbell, a mere staff driver. And
her family would only accept their marriage if Robert
climbed the ranks of the army. But when peace is declared
and Robert achieves the rank of Major, Kate finds she has
her own bitter and personal war to contend with. Trapped
by her parents' possessive demands, tormented by Robert's
passionate but wayward love, she fights her own lonely
battle to save her marriage and her reputation . . .

Also by Marion Harris in Sphere Books:
SOLDIERS' WIVES

0 7221 4876 3   GENERAL FICTION   £2.99

An enthralling saga of life in Alaska's harsh and
magnificent wilderness . . .

~ The ~
Great Alone

JANET DAILEY

A tale of intrepid men and women whose
dreams and adventures are as grand and
uncompromising as the lonely splendour of the
land itself . . .

Winter Swan, a native Aleut whose culture has
been wiped out by the brutal Russian winters;
Tasha Tarakanov – who has to choose between
her beloved Russia and the safety of her tribe;
Wylie Cole, a restless man defending his
homeland from Japanese invaders; and Marisha
Blackwood, who finds success and riches as
Glory, the most famous whore in Alaska . . .

0 7221 28207 9   GENERAL FICTION   £3.99

A selection of bestsellers from Sphere

FICTION

THE PHYSICIAN	Noah Gordon	£3.99 ☐
INFIDELITIES	Freda Bright	£3.99 ☐
THE GREAT ALONE	Janet Dailey	£3.99 ☐
THE PANIC OF '89	Paul Erdman	£3.50 ☐
WHITE SUN, RED STAR	Robert Elegant	£3.50 ☐

FILM AND TV TIE-IN

BLACK FOREST CLINIC	Peter Heim	£2.99 ☐
INTIMATE CONTACT	Jacqueline Osborne	£2.50 ☐
BEST OF BRITISH	Maurice Sellar	£8.95 ☐
SEX WITH PAULA YATES	Paula Yates	£2.95 ☐
RAW DEAL	Walter Wager	£2.50 ☐

NON-FICTION

THE SACRED VIRGIN AND THE HOLY WHORE	Anthony Harris	£3.50 ☐
THE DARKNESS IS LIGHT ENOUGH	Chris Ferris	£4.50 ☐
TREVOR HOWARD: A GENTLEMAN AND A PLAYER	Vivienne Knight	£3.50 ☐
INVISIBLE ARMIES	Stephen Segaller	£4.99 ☐

All Sphere books are available at your local bookshop or newsagent, or can be ordered direct from the publisher. Just tick the titles you want and fill in the form below.

Name _____

Address _____

_____

Write to Sphere Books, Cash Sales Department, P.O. Box 11, Falmouth, Cornwall TR10 9EN

Please enclose a cheque or postal order to the value of the cover price plus:

UK: 60p for the first book, 25p for the second book and 15p for each additional book ordered to a maximum charge of £1.90.

OVERSEAS & EIRE: £1.25 for the first book, 75p for the second book and 28p for each subsequent title ordered.

BFPO: 60p for the first book, 25p for the second book plus 15p per copy for the next 7 books, thereafter 9p per book.

Sphere Books reserve the right to show new retail prices on covers which may differ from those previously advertised in the text elsewhere, and to increase postal rates in accordance with the P.O.